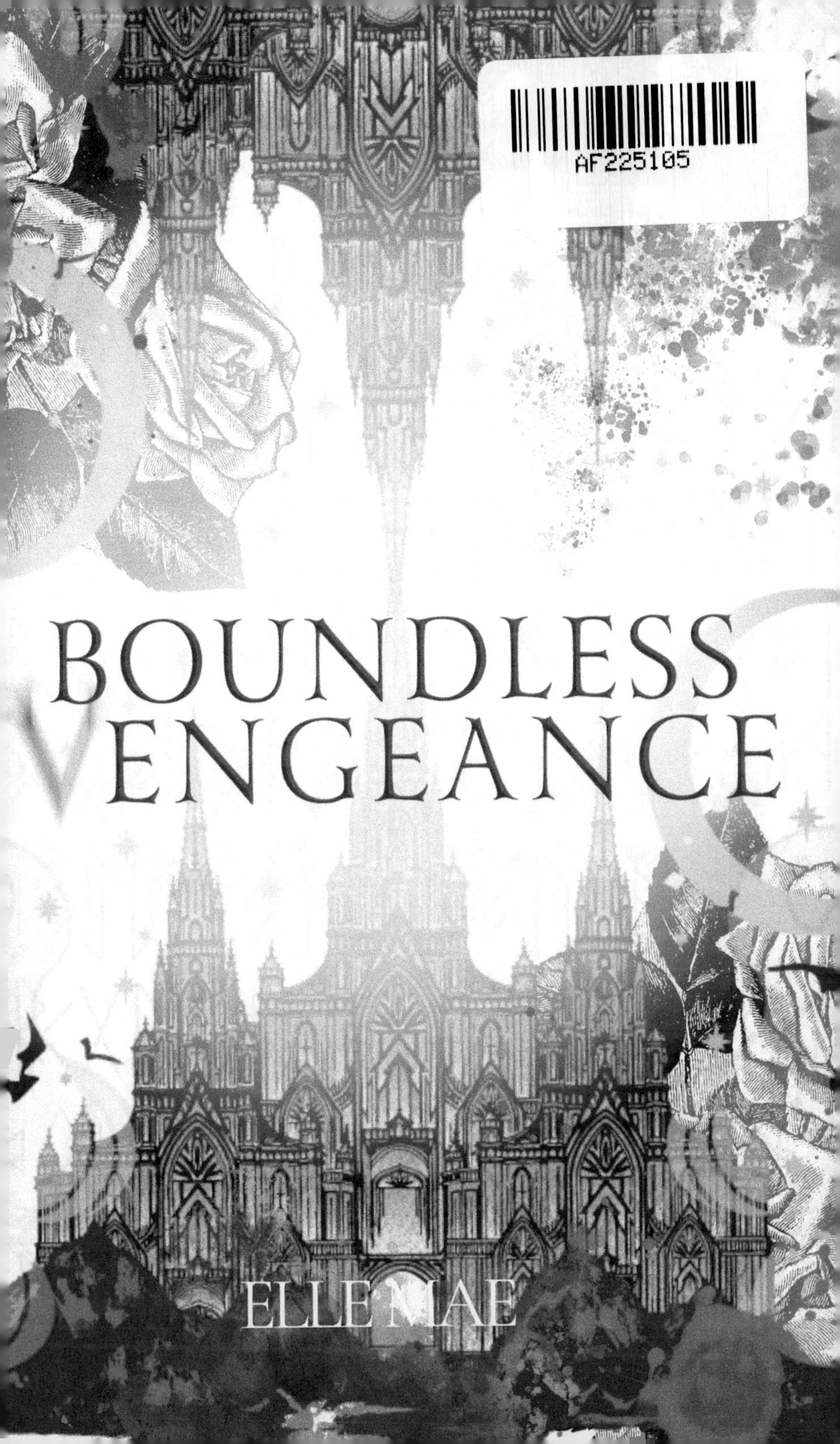

BOUNDLESS VENGEANCE
ELLE MAE
AF225105

For my angry girls who like to be dominated by a hot masc while making the other beg for your strap.

BOUNDLESS VENGEANCE

ELLE MAE

NOTE

This is a work of fiction. Names, characters, business, events and incidents are the products of the author's imagination. Any resemblance to actual persons, living or dead, or actual events is purely coincidental.

Before moving forward, please note that the themes in this book can be dark and trigger some people. The themes can include but are not limited to: torture (past), torture depictions, murder/attempted murder, beheading/decapitation, human sacrifice, people/child trafficking, death/death by fire, dead bodies/corpse abuse, parental death, abandonment, blood play, gore/violence/graphic violence, torture, family violence/abuse, voyeurism, stabbing, biting, physical altercations, verbal, mental, and physical abuse, ableist language, bullying, depression, first person POV death, scars/body issues, Dubcon role play, Forced orgasm/orgasm denial, Captivity/imprisonment, Cults

If you need help, please reach out to the resources below.

National Suicide Prevention Lifeline
1-800-273-8255
https://suicidepreventionlifeline.org/

National Domestic Violence Hotline
1-800-799-7233
https://www.thehotline.org/

ALSO BY ELLE MAE

ELLE MAE

Blood Bound Series:

Contract Bound: A Lesbian Vampire Romance

Lost Clause

Blood Royale:

Eternal Captive: A Dark Enemies-to-Lovers Sapphic Vampire Romance

Divine Deception

Boundless Vengeance

Winterfell Academy Series:

The Price of Silence: Winterfell Academy Book 1

The Price of Silence: Winterfell Academy Book 2

The Price of Silence: Winterfell Academy Book 3

The Price of Silence: Winterfell Academy Book 4

The Price Of Silence: Winterfell Academy Book 5

Winterfell Series Box Set

Short and Smutty:

The Sweetest Sacrifice: An Erotic Demon Romance

Nevermore: A Deal with a Demon

Stolen Demon Brides:

Taken to the Deadlands

Taken to the Shadow Realm

Taken to the Demon Court

EDEN EMORY

The Ties That Bind Us

Don't Stop me

Don't Leave Me

Don't Forget Me

Don't Hate Me

Two of a Kind

Hide n' Seek

Queer Meet Cute Anthology

Love Me Not

Hurt Me Not

PATREON ONLY

Wicked corruption: An FF Mafia Romance

Watch Me

Taste My Ruin

EC Comic

Runaway With Me

"A day will come when the singular Castle bloodline comes to maturity, and a child born with poison for blood will usher forth an end to their rule."

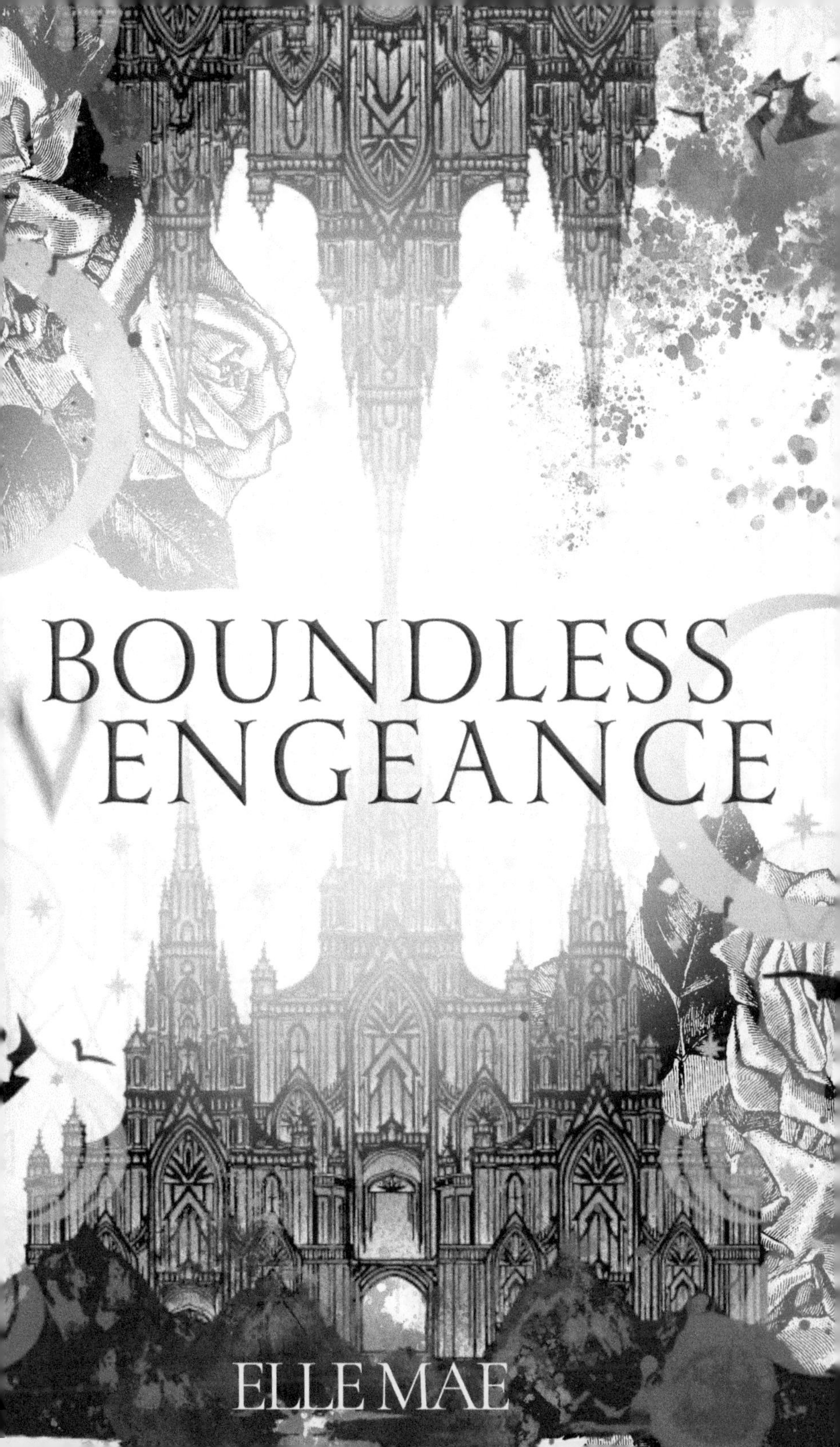

BOUNDLESS
VENGEANCE
ELLE MAE

PROLOGUE

They left me.

They truly left me in the dungeon without a second thought.

No food. No sunlight. Only blood.

I'm tired. All I can do is lie on the floor, clutching my middle.

It hurts. I can't tell what does anymore, though.

My stomach? No, my head. All of it. My whole body aches.

I'm hungry, but no matter how much I keep drinking, it doesn't do anything.

I'm still hungry. Hungrier every time, actually.

My energy is leaving me as the darkness crowds in.

Sometimes I see them. *My lovers.*

The princess stands there, looking at me with a sneer, saying cruel words she never said—and I don't think she ever would. They spin around in my mind.

My witch has her back turned to me. Like she truly left me behind.

I always try to reach out to them, but they never get any closer.

My mouth waters when the next batch of blood is delivered. Suddenly, it's not so bad anymore.

The pain slowly subsides.
My strength returns.
I feel myself... changing.

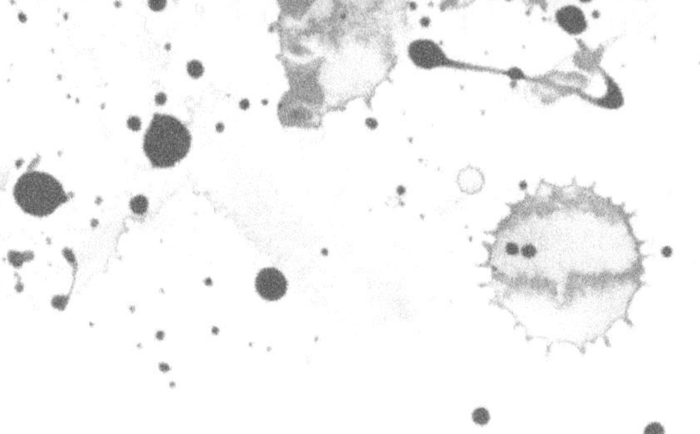

AURELIA

"Next!"

The line of vampires coming to greet the Castle family's new king was out the door. The room that my father loved so much had been torn down and remade to fit my brother's new aesthetic.

Adrian had a flair for the extravagant. Sparkling stained glass windows. Black ceilings covered in glittering gold that made it look like the night sky was shining above us. The chandelier that was hanging from the ceiling was made to look like sharp blood droplets were starting to fall on the people below. A red carpet was rolled out on the marble floor.

The vampires knew better than to stand on it as I waited for Adrian to call them, all of them standing to the side.

The air was tense as everyone waited for the first official appearance of the new Castle king. Eyes darted around as many tried to figure out what was coming.

It all happened so fast. My father's murder. The ousting of our stepfamily.

They were lucky he didn't kill them, but still they ran as fast as their legs could take them.

I'd always wanted to be rid of the step-bastards but never like this. It left a bitter taste in my mouth.

He then went on to destroy everything our palace once was.

He kept Father's throne, though. One of the only things that signified he had taken over from him, a cruel sign of power that only he could come up with. A reminder that, while my father's legacy was still alive through his children, he was no longer in charge. Just like Father, he pushed me out to the side, forcing me to stand during these occasions.

"My lord, this is Roman and his son Adam," said the vampire to the side of us.

My eyes shot to him, trying to keep the anger down. He was one of the men who killed the witches when they ambushed us.

Levana's shocked, dead face was forever frozen in my mind. I pushed it away just as someone else caught my eye.

General Lee. He stood tall, his hair cleanly brushed and his mustache well-kept, wearing the uniform provided by the council, making him look every bit the part of a general indeed.

Adrian had brought his army—his most loyal vampires. They were cruel attack dogs waiting for his every order. But General Lee had been a shock. Specifically sent from the vampire council to oversee the transfer of power.

They said it in a way that made it seem like he was here trying to keep the peace, when he was actually just another one of my brother's lapdogs.

And a huge fucking issue.

"Congratulations on your rise to power," Roman said, forcing his head low. I had seen him on occasion at my father's galas, but never really talked to him. "We brought you gold and jewels—"

My brother let out a bark of a laugh that had both Roman and his son jerking back as if they'd been slapped.

Here we go.

Adrian had been relatively well-behaved today. But with him, it only took something small, like offering him something as common as gold when he had an entire kingdom filled with it.

"You really think I have any use for gold?" he said as he waved his hand around. "There hasn't been a new king in a millennium, let alone one born to a powerful family such as mine, and you thought it would be smart to offer me *gold*? Don't insult me."

I held in my scoff.

A powerful family such as mine.

Even though he was an unverified bastard, he sure as hell seemed to belong here. It irked me to no end.

I had suffered for my role. I *continued* to suffer for my role. But somehow he had gained enough power—and rabid followers—that he had been able to kill our father with his bare hands.

The outsiders didn't know just how crazy he truly was, though. Not until a moment like this.

It would have been better if they had shown up with nothing, simply bowing in front of him and pledging their loyalty.

It was all for show anyway. The real Blood Rites wouldn't happen for a few more weeks at the earliest. That was when everyone in the family and his followers would blood-bond themselves to him. *That* was where the true power lay.

This was just a show of wealth. Royals peacocking in front of a madman in hope to gain his favor.

The rumors about him had spread far and wide, and it would be impossible for any vampire out there not to know he had taken over, so families and clan heads from all over decided to make the trip on short notice. The vampire world ran on connections. On the checking of each other's power and shared resources of blood, wealth, and land. It would be especially insulting for them not to show up for the new king since my brother would undoubtedly put them on his shit list.

I once thought he was crazy enough without power. Tearing witches' heads off. Stalking the lands in search of easy vampire prey to kill. But knowing him now, that was nothing but a preview of the real him.

"I'm sorry, My Lord—"

"Kill them."

Roman jerked back, fear twisting his face. The lackey to my side took one step forward, ready to end it all, but Brother Dearest raised his hand.

His head snapped to stare right at me, looking so much like Father in that moment. But his piercing blue eyes, somehow crueler than my father's ever were, glittered with excitement.

"Aurelia, you do the honors."

This time I didn't fight my sigh. He was constantly putting me through it, testing how far I would go before I broke.

He thought I was nothing more than a spoiled princess. That I had lived my life just waiting for a chance to get married off to be pampered until my death.

I played the part well. It had been my role since birth, so I fell right into it.

But what he didn't know was how I had been forced to be the beautiful princess on the outside and the cruel attack dog on the inside.

What he was asking was child's play.

"You just love getting my dresses dirty, don't you?" I asked and took a step forward.

He let out a chuckle.

"No one asked you to get decked out today."

I hadn't. This was my normal princess uniform. My hair was curled, up and out of my face, so it fell around my shoulders. My dress was mostly black with hints of deep red, with a corset and skirt that hugged my body. The sleeves fell off the shoulder, and I wore a large jewel necklace that sat heavy on my chest.

Underneath it was my own little secret. The only thing that mattered.

My heels clacked as I lunged forward to grip Roman's hair, studying him with one hand on his shoulder. He looked at me with fear in his eyes. With betrayal. Like I should be saving him.

"Please don't," his son forced out.

It was useless. There was no negotiating with my brother. And I had the image of a cruel princess to uphold.

In a blink, I ripped his head from his shoulders. The lack of hesitation caught him off guard and made it easy for me to end his life without much of a fuss.

His son, on the other hand, was already running down the bright red carpet. I followed, bolting down the steps of the platform the throne was on, and yanked him to the ground.

He thrashed and pushed me, and if I hadn't had the experience of fighting the rogue with Cedar and Vesper, I might not have been able to pull this off.

My chest ached every time I thought of them. But even doing that was dangerous. I forced images of their green and golden eyes away from my mind. Tried to forget the way their heated touch felt against my skin. How their lips tasted. How their moans—

I forced my heel onto his chest, digging the sharp point in as he let out a pained yelp. I leaned down and grabbed his head between my hands.

"Please, princess, I never meant any harm. I'm loyal to you—"

It took a good part of my strength to pull his head off. Dark vampire blood sprayed all across the carpet and, of course, my dress and face.

As I looked up at the throne, my brother was already staring down at me with a smile. I held up the head for him.

The vampires lined up to my right knew better than to gasp, but I could feel their eyes on me as I dropped the head to the floor and motioned for one of our vampire staff to clean it up.

My eyes lingered on General Lee. If he was who he said he was, this would be cause enough to report me to the council.

But his face just twisted into a smile.

"Next!" I yelled, my voice echoing through the room.

The next pair went up, but instead of looking at them, my brother's eyes were on me the entire time, that same playful smirk on his lips.

I could smell who it was long before he spoke.

"Quite a show, princess," General Lee said, meeting me in the long, covered hallway that showcased the now all-black roses surrounding all sides of our palace.

They had once been a brilliant red that made the castle itself stand out like it was floating in a sea of blood. But just like with everything here, my brother had brought it into ruin.

His whole slogan was that he was going to *bring it back*, but all I could see was the careful, systematic way in which he was destroying it.

"I'm sure Kyan would love to hear about it," I said, not looking at him as he joined me by the window.

The sun had fallen, the stars bright above us. The moon was full and shone a light directly on us, putting us in the spotlight. *Is this Krae's way of watching us?*

"You and I both know the council doesn't care about these things," he replied, inching closer "But I did hear something interesting about your *pet*. Do you want to know?"

I couldn't stop my body from reacting. The bond in my chest might be dulling, but it was still there. *She* was still there.

She will always be there.

Vesper or Cedar crossed my mind at any given moment. The urge to run to them was almost more than I could handle. Especially as the gross-smelling general's skin brushed up against mine.

I looked up at him, trying not to show just how much I was yearning for any news of her. I had been lingering in the halls among the staff and guards, trying to eavesdrop on anything at all, but there was not even so much as a whisper about the silver-haired hunter.

"She's been given to the Leclair family," he whispered. "Weird how they didn't show up here today, isn't it?"

"Many vampires didn't show up today," I noted. "The Leclair family already sent in their gifts."

Feeders. Elegant ones, reserved for royal feedings and decked out in jewels and fabrics that oozed wealth.

I filed the information away. I would need to figure out a way to call upon their daughter. Maybe I could send her a letter and convince her to come in person—

"Aren't you worried your pet will find a new master?"

My gaze snapped to him, a growl forcing itself from my chest. I got it under control the moment I saw the triumph of getting to me flash across his face.

"What is your game here?" I asked. "The council sent you here to *oversee*, but I'm starting to think that's complete bullshit."

He raised a brow at me.

"Do tell me, princess. Why do you think I'm here?"

I turned to face him fully, letting a smile of my own spread across my face.

"I think Kyan doesn't care about you anymore," I whispered, running my hand down the shiny bits of his uniform. "I think you wormed your way here and are trying to align yourself with the strongest. Almost like... *you're* the *pet* looking for a new *master*."

His hand grabbed mine harshly just as it got to the center of his chest. A sort of power radiated from him, one that caused me to panic and try and pull my hand away.

I tried to play it off.

"You're not the only one," I added. "In fact, there is a line out the door of vampires willing to bend for him. What makes you stand out, especially if Kyan has turned her back on you?"

Anger flared.

"Kyan hasn't turned her back on me," he hissed. "I rose to this position myself. I protect and oversee entire armies. You have no idea just how important I am to the council."

With a forced smile, I snatched my hand back and made a show of wiping it off on my dress.

"People of real importance don't have to prove it to anyone," I said and started walking away. "Let's just hope my brother hasn't gotten close enough to smell the *rot* on you."

He didn't reply. I took one last glance at him as I walked on, only to see him clenching his fist and shaking.

There's something about him. Something wrong.

It wasn't until I was safely up on the fifth floor of the castle that I let out a breath and sank against the cool window that looked out over the palace grounds.

I was a rat stuck in a den of snakes, each one looking more venomous than the last.

Vesper, Cedar, hold on. Don't give up on me.

CEDAR

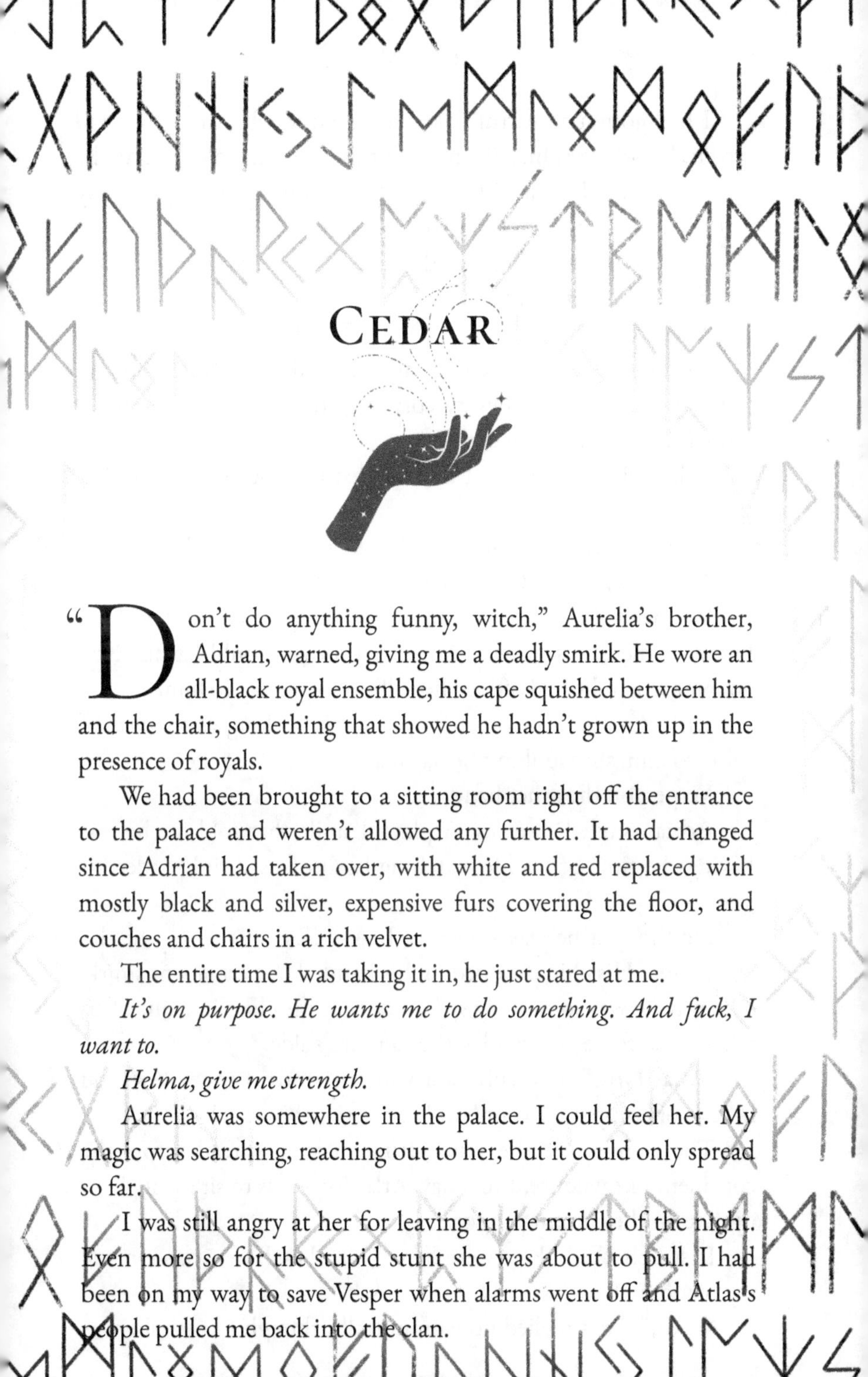

"Don't do anything funny, witch," Aurelia's brother, Adrian, warned, giving me a deadly smirk. He wore an all-black royal ensemble, his cape squished between him and the chair, something that showed he hadn't grown up in the presence of royals.

We had been brought to a sitting room right off the entrance to the palace and weren't allowed any further. It had changed since Adrian had taken over, with white and red replaced with mostly black and silver, expensive furs covering the floor, and couches and chairs in a rich velvet.

The entire time I was taking it in, he just stared at me.

It's on purpose. He wants me to do something. And fuck, I want to.

Helma, give me strength.

Aurelia was somewhere in the palace. I could feel her. My magic was searching, reaching out to her, but it could only spread so far.

I was still angry at her for leaving in the middle of the night. Even more so for the stupid stunt she was about to pull. I had been on my way to save Vesper when alarms went off and Atlas's people pulled me back into the clan.

I had gotten an earful from the vampire who thought I had stolen the princess. Imagine my surprise when she told me Aurelia was *not* back in bed like I thought she was but already on her way to the Castle palace to meet with her brother.

The entire time all I could think was... *how could she? How could she just up and leave us?*

Leave me?

And now I was stuck with an egomaniac vampire who was dragging me around to every corner of the earth to try and get Aurelia back and feeling useless.

Atlas shifted in her seat and swirled the cup of blood in her hand.

"Don't worry," she murmured. "She's well trained."

Fuck, I'm going to kill this vampire.

We needed Vesper for this. I wanted to go to her first, knowing there was no way Aurelia's brother would let his sister go. Not when she had offered herself up so prettily to him.

Unfortunately, or fortunately enough, as long as she was of value to him, she wouldn't be harmed.

Vesper, on the other hand...

Adrian smiled at Atlas. A playful smile that told me he was having the time of his life watching both of us shrink under his gaze.

He thought he was above us. It was clear in the way he did everything. His chin propped on his hand. The permanent smirk. The way he was so casually spread out on the chair in front of us when I was forced to stand at the vampire's side.

"Atlas Nox," he finally said with an amused tone. "Are you here to offer my sister your hand in marriage?"

The rumor that she was getting married spread across the continent like wildfire. Every day, Atlas forced us to sit through an update on the current proposals.

Last I checked, there were fifty-six, and each new name made my blood boil.

"I am," Atlas replied noncommittally, though I knew she was

freaking out inside. I had come to know the vampire more and more over the last few weeks, and she cared about Aurelia more than I originally thought.

Something I was none too happy about.

Though I should have known it from the moment she showed up to "help," it was more than obvious now that said help extended to Aurelia and Aurelia only.

"Well, that's a waste," Adrian said as he stood from his chair, running his hand down his long fur cape. "She already said no. Maybe I would have considered forcing her if you'd come the other day to declare your loyalty, but sadly, you were absent."

I had urged Atlas to come, but she wouldn't, saying it could be a trap. Though I couldn't see how sitting across from him right now in his own palace while his guards watched us was safer.

My eyes went to the door. There was a vampire standing there, watching us.

The one that killed Levana.

He gave me a smile and waved his fingers at me.

Bastard.

Atlas raised a brow. "No? Vampires all over have been vying for my hand in marriage for decades. Marrying me would give her all the power in the—"

"She said no." Adrian cut her off and motioned her away. "End of story."

"She may be misguided, but you must know—"

"About your family?" he asked with a raised brow. "How your bloodline spans almost as far back as Aurelia's? How your mother and father were from two of the most famous royal families in existence and you simply... left?"

My eyes shot to Atlas. Her long black hair fell around her hardened face. Her everyday attire suggested royalty, usually with gold embroidery or even jewels sewn into the fabric. But what I thought was just a show of wealth and status had just taken on a whole new meaning.

Who is she, really?

I didn't know anything other than her enormous clan spread out far and wide. I never questioned why people would want to be under her in the first place. If I were still in the clan, I could sneak into the archives and try to pull something about her. But I hadn't had the foresight.

"It seems like this marriage would be mostly for your benefit," he continued pointedly. "I heard the families were getting antsy with someone of your bloodline still unmarried. And with such a large clan? You should know best what happens when vampires get scared."

Even without vampire hearing, I could make out the unmistakable sound of Atlas's teeth grinding.

"And if I convince her to marry me?"

He let out a scoff.

"Good luck with that. While she may have the choice, you forget I am the Castle family head now. And like I said, which you so rudely *ignored*, you weren't here to show your loyalty to me."

His dismissal was obvious, and Atlas let out a growl. I could feel the tension rising in her. A darkness spread out from her, and she was practically vibrating with fury.

The sensible part of me knew I should probably do or say something to calm her down before she went ahead and ruined this for us. I wouldn't be surprised if she just lunged forward and went after the so-called king.

The other part of me wanted her to. Wanted her to show the fury that I wouldn't allow myself to. I wanted to tear the whole place down. *Burn it.* The palace, the crown, and everything it stood for.

The only thing stopping me was that Aurelia left to come here. I trusted her. I wanted to, at least. But I truly didn't understand what she was doing.

"I apologize on behalf of Atlas for not being able to make it," I said, bowing my head. I hated submitting to him, but unlike Atlas, I was willing to for Aurelia. "She got tangled up in clan affairs. As she mentioned, many clans have been vying for her hand. It takes days sometimes to quell them."

He gave me a long look, then let out a huff.

"You let the witch speak for you?"

I hated how dismissively he sounded. Like, just because I was a witch, I was beneath him. But there was a reason why vampires and witches had always fought. Why both parties were desperately trying to stop a war between us.

We were just as powerful as them, if not more, since there were more of us.

"She is right," Atlas offered, her tone obviously annoyed.

"We will do anything to prove our loyalty to you," I continued. "Name your price."

I could feel Atlas's disapproval. I was taking this too far, but I couldn't just stand by and do nothing.

"And if I ask for your life?" Adrian asked. "Better yet, what about your magic? I could drain it all and put it in a bottle for me to use whenever I please."

Fear gripped my heart. I wouldn't be surprised if he had truly thought of it before. While it wasn't that common anymore, there had been cases of vampires trying to steal our magic and use it for themselves.

I met his eyes.

"If that is what you require. But I am sure you do not want a war with the witches. You know just how *touchy* they are when it comes to stealing another's magic."

"Is it stealing if you give it to me willingly?" he countered.

"The council wouldn't—"

"The council doesn't have power here," Adrian said, interrupting Atlas again. "Tell me, witch. How far would you go for my sister?"

I let my magic out, feeling the area around him, and unexpectedly, I could feel something. A sort of power surrounding him that hadn't been there before.

One that felt like the late king's.

"As far as I need to," I answered.

"Then say it," he ordered. "Say you would give me your magic. That you would drain yourself until you lay dead at my feet, your pitiful life wasting away, all for my sister." When I remained silent, his anger rose. He leaned forward. "*Say it!*"

Atlas's hands were suddenly grabbing me and forcing me into a fully standing position.

"I apologize for the disrespect she's shown you," she said quickly. "I will see to it that she is punished. Do not worry about my loyalty, it belongs to you."

Just as I thought he was going to burst, the vampire that had been standing at the door walked in with another. They were wearing the very same outfit Vesper and I did when we were in the palace—all black, weapons strapped to their hips. It seemed to be one of the only things that had remained unchanged.

It was jarring to see what we would have been like if we'd never left the palace. Like fragments of some weird parallel universe.

"Feeding time," the one who wouldn't stop looking at me said.

Adrian gave me one last lingering look before he turned and left the room. The vampires lingered, letting us know our time was up and ready to escort us out if needed.

"Let's go,' I said and nudged Atlas to the door.

"You just had to open your goddamn mouth, didn't you?"

She stormed out of the room, with me following closely behind her.

Guilt and anger filled me. *I would do anything for Aurelia, so why... Why was it so hard to offer my life for her?*

"You know what we have to do now," I told Atlas, who still wouldn't look at me. "Vesper has been waiting. We have no idea what is going on in—"

"I'm not done trying," she hissed, walking faster, and my fist shot forward and grabbed her arm, turning her to look at me.

Her eyes widened. Her nostrils flared. She bared her teeth at me as she pushed me off her with her vampire strength.

"Watch yourself, *witch*. I have been more than accommodating."

I couldn't hold back anymore. I let my magic seep out of me and conjured red vines to slither up her body so fast she didn't know it was happening until one of them was brushing against her cheek.

She froze but still let a warning growl rumble deep in her chest.

"Atlas, what a *surprise*."

We both turned to see a new person in the hallway, a tall vampire with slicked-back hair and a mustache. He was wearing a uniform I hadn't seen before, and there was... something about him that made my skin crawl.

Instinctively, I stepped back and pulled my magic back to me. I couldn't tell if he was worse than Adrian or not, but my mind was telling me to run.

Atlas stepped closer, obviously not sensing the same thing.

"*General* Lee, is it now?" she asked, a bit of apprehension sinking into her voice.

"It is," he replied with a proud smile. "The council sent me here to oversee the transfer of power. Funny seeing you here. Especially when you didn't show up the other day."

The stare down between them told me something was wrong here.

"Funny thing." Atlas narrowed her eyes at him. "If I remember correctly, even in your prime, you couldn't even fight off a single witch, let alone another vampire. But someone made you a *general*?"

He puffed up dangerously, the aura that made me want to run getting stronger.

"I trained. Evolved. Took some time, but all things come to those who deserve them, am I right?"

Atlas made a noise in her throat but didn't look convinced.

"We were just leaving," I said and pulled Atlas by her wrist, which she allowed me to do as the general stared at us.

It wasn't until we were in the car and back on our way to the clan that she spoke.

"Him being here creates a problem," she whispered. "He has more support than I thought."

"The vampire council, right?"

She nodded but continued looking out the window, deep in thought.

"It's odd. I've never seen the council get involved in something like this."

"Even more reason why we need to get Vesper," I said. "We tried your plan. It's not going to be as easy as waltzing in there."

She let out a hum. I called my magic to me again, forcing the vines around her, and that finally got her attention.

"We stick to *my* plan now."

My vines gave her a warning squeeze. There was no room for negotiation.

Vesper, we're coming for you.

VESPER

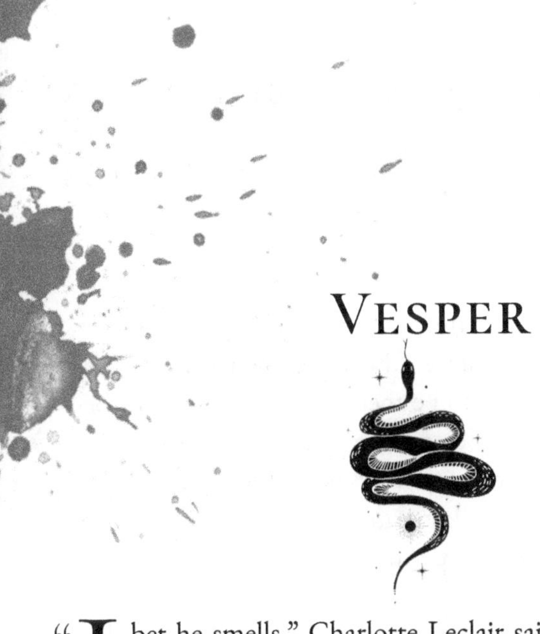

"I bet he smells," Charlotte Leclair said as she leaned against the wall, bloodred ruby-like candies in her hands.

A child at heart who still likes to pop blood candies whenever she gets the chance.

She looked over at the man her parents were talking to with a pout. We had been stuck in this corner for most of the event as she sulked. Great for me because I didn't have to move, sucked for her because she—well, both of us—would be hearing about it later.

Her curly bright blonde hair bounced as her gaze kept darting around the room. She was done up as any princess would be in this situation, but she hated these gatherings, opting to look unapproachable and bored instead of greeting her suitors with a warm smile.

"He's a vampire, he can probably hear you," I warned and shifted her empty glass in my hands. "Plus, your parents won't stop until you're married. At least he looks like he has money. You'd be well off."

Charlotte let out a scoff.

"As if they'd marry me off to someone who *wasn't* rich. It would be an insult and unthinkable to myself and the family to marry for anything other than the expansion of the family's wealth or heirs."

She said it like she had once dreamed otherwise. I gave her a long look, noticing her childlike nature. She was probably being forced into this role without so much as a say.

Much like Aurelia.

With a sigh, I stared off at the party, letting my mind wander.

It had been three weeks since I'd been stuck with the Leclair family. Three weeks assigned to be their youngest daughter's best friend, servant, bodyguard, and anything else they wanted.

Charlotte was a lonely vampire who, just like Aurelia, had grown up in the confines of her parents' palace. But Charlotte wasn't as cruel, spoiled, or temper-tantrum prone. She wouldn't hurt a fly.

And that line of thought only served to remind me of all of Aurelia's so-called flaws and how much I loved all of them.

"Oh god, can she just not show up to these things?"

Well, there was one fly she absolutely detested and might actually harm.

There was a reason Charlotte wasn't cruel. Why she was able to grow up as a pampered vampire princess with no duties in the world other than to be married off to someone she thought worthy.

It was because the Leclair family had a dirty little secret.

Right at the side of the ballroom, near the back exit, a small hybrid vampire came slinking in. Her stark white hair hid most of her face, but the deep scars still showed through. They were impossible to hide.

Jewel-like eyes, one green and one blue, shone from across the room. She spotted us immediately before fixing her gaze back to the floor.

In the world of vampires, witches, and humans, Rose Leclair was as black a sheep as they came. She was the product of an affair her father had with a human feeder who had kept her pregnancy hidden until her birth.

At her mother's insistence, the feeder had been killed and the baby given to her mother to raise. And, like Aurelia, she received the wrath of her family for it.

"She'll leave soon," I murmured, noting she was heading to the long table filled with blood, blood candies, and even some human food for the half-humans, herself included.

I felt bad for her, but honestly I didn't care to intervene. Not when my mind was always on Aurelia and Cedar. I didn't have the time or headspace to attempt a rescue mission.

Especially when it felt like I needed rescuing myself.

These three weeks had been worse than the time in the Castle palace when I was trying to kill Aurelia. At least then I could escape if needed. Here there was a vampire at every corner just waiting for me to step out of line.

"Fine," Charlotte huffed, pulling me back from the darkness. I was awarded a few more moments of silence before she added, "She still hasn't picked a suitor, if you're wondering."

My eyes met her blue ones. She had a small, pitying look on her face. These were the moments when she truly seemed to care.

My heart threatened to break in two. I didn't want to hear about it. While I was here, forced to serve another vampire family, Aurelia was out there getting married off.

Again. How could she?

I had waited while they locked me in the dungeons. Starved me. Humiliated me. Forced me into this station and to act like I was *theirs.*

My eyes burned. My throat ached. My teeth pulsed with a need I didn't want to name.

Did they forget about me?

Maybe they were secretly happy they would never have to deal with me and the vampire hunters ever again. If I could even be called that anymore. They'd forsaken me, just like everyone else.

Charlotte handed me a candy. "For your eyes."

I hesitated to take it from her. I knew I wasn't supposed to, but just like the poorly hidden bastard child of the Leclair family,

I was starving. It was a constant thing. Ever since the dungeons, I just could never get enough to fully satiate me.

I popped it in my mouth. Sweet blood burst across my tongue, and the stinging went away immediately.

Something happened during my time in the dungeons. I tried to stay away from the blood, but I was starving. It felt like I was dying. I drank it, and in turn... I *changed.* Changed into the one thing I spent my entire life trying to kill.

I hadn't even realized it until I wasn't passing out on the cold floor. Instead of my stomach cramping, my throat ached for blood. The darkness became clearer, my anger stronger than ever.

Will they accept me after this? Knowing how I changed?

The hints had all been there.

Everyone but me knew that half-vampire children were like a plague in the hunter organization. Vampire blood never hurt me like it did humans. And then there was my strength and my ability to smell magic, not to mention the feeling of it burning as it entered me.

More and more came to me the longer I was stuck in the small broom closet they deemed my bedroom. I couldn't sleep anymore. The ability was taken from me when they forced my vampire self out, killing the human part of me through starvation and beatings.

I couldn't reply to Charlotte, much to her dismay. She kept mumbling to herself while I watched Rose slink back out of the room.

My breath caught when I saw a flash of red.

Is that...

My body moved on its own, taking a step forward and trying to follow the flash. But as soon as I got there, it was gone, and I was left with a burst of disappointment.

I'm seeing things.

That had been common in the dungeons as I went from sleepless nights to the last bits of slumber I ever got as a human. But even if I were, it didn't stop me from feeling things.

Hope.

All this time, I kept hoping someone would come save me. That I would be freed from that cold, lonely place. That maybe I would wake up and this would all be some type of nightmare.

But this was my cold, cruel reality, and I was stuck here. Never to leave again—

"Vesper?"

That isn't Charlotte's voice calling my name.

My heart leapt into my chest. *This is real... right? Please, please be real.* Too many times I prayed to the gods in my mind. Krae, the witch gods, the human gods. Any who would listen.

But they never answered me, let alone in a way that sounded this real.

I was scared to turn around. Scared to hope and be disappointed. But I couldn't stop myself. Because hope, the annoying addictive emotion that it was, seized my body. It made me wish, long for things that could never happen, and no matter how many times reality crushed me, hope was still there, pulling me up through the tiniest of cracks.

I turned toward the voice. There, before me, standing tall, was the witch who had changed my life.

Cedar looked at me with a pained expression that slowly morphed into a small smile. She looked so different as I watched her with my new eyes. Her gaze was brighter, her skin more freckled. I wanted to memorize it all and was upset that I hadn't thought to do it from the beginning.

I was so taken by her that I almost didn't notice the long-haired vampire by her side.

"You've gotten taller," Cedar said, swallowing thickly as if she had some sort of knot in her throat.

I tried not to flinch at her words. And then I tried to stop my mind from going back to the cold, dark place they locked me in. But it did anyway.

I couldn't breathe. My stomach was so hollow, it hurt to even exhale. The blood, once metallic tasting, was getting sweeter as the days went on.

Day? Weeks? I couldn't tell.

Pain. All I felt was pain. My teeth ached. My mind was going crazy. Hallucinating. Hunger. Always so hungry. And the blood poured over my lips—

She said I'm taller. Does that mean she knows? Is it that hard to look at my changed form? Does she hate it? Hate me? Does she still want me like this? Will she ever want me again?

I needed to know. It pained me to think that I was going to lose her because of this.

I moved to step toward her, but Charlotte was there, pulling me back by linking her arm with mine.

"Let's not get my Vesper in trouble, hm?" Charlotte commented, a reminder of my status here. *Right.* Hope began to dissipate, and I deflated. "Atlas, it took you long enough. Have you thought about my proposal?"

The vampire looked at her with an expression I could only describe as disgust. She looked the same, the only difference was the power that emanated from her. Atlas seemed to be a lot more powerful than I ever thought. Or maybe I just couldn't tell until now.

"One dinner, one chance, no promises, and then—"

"You give *my* Vesper back to me," Cedar said, her voice full of the kind of strength that had me wanting to fall to my knees in front of her.

She came. For me. This is happening. It's not all in my head.

But regardless of how happy I was, there was still one overarching worry.

Where is our vampire princess?

AURELIA

There were a few places that I avoided in the palace since coming back. They brought back memories I'd rather keep dead and buried for more reasons than one.

But on the day before the eve of my wedding announcement, I found myself wandering the garden that my mother loved so much.

I thought my brother would have destroyed all of it, but I was pleasantly surprised to see the flora and trees coming to life here once again.

The sweet smell of the roses hit my senses, even if they were dying, and I was called to the fountain in the middle. The only thing that seemed to remain stuck in time.

I kneeled down, running my fingers across the cracked stone, and memories of the Vesper I knew back then flashed through my mind.

"Should we have a bachelorette party?" she had asked.

Of course, only she would have had the balls to show up drunk while I was sulking about being married off to an abusive prince. *Just like now.*

It wasn't uncommon for vampires to live long enough to see history repeat itself, but even this felt a little too soon.

I missed Vesper. There was a constant ache in my chest, and not just from the bond that was trying to force us back to each other. Everyone said it would only last a few months, but it was nestled so deep in my heart that it would take more than Vesper's dagger to claw it out of me.

And Cedar...

I wanted to run to her when I heard she had come to see me. I had to stop myself, locking myself in my room so much like my father used to do to me. I knew what they were trying to do, but it was no use.

The prophecy was bigger than the three of us. It didn't matter what we wanted. It didn't matter that it was forcing me into a life of torture. To be married off. To have my royalty and bloodline stripped from me just so I could integrate a new one.

I hated it.

This was my kingdom. My crown. My people.

But more than that, I wanted to save Vesper and Cedar. I had taken the seer's words to heart.

We wouldn't be happy. We couldn't survive if the prophecy wasn't fulfilled. And I was going to make sure that it was, no matter how painful it might be for us.

"Oh, how the mighty have fallen! What would the people think if they could see you now?"

I tried not to let out a sigh as the voice broke through my sulking.

Turning, I saw my brother standing there in his new uniform, which consisted of a fur cape and a tightly tailored all-black suit. All he was missing was a crown, but that was tucked away in the throne room for when he needed it.

He took his new role as king of the Castle family very seriously.

Anger boiled me alive from the inside. Everything was a joke to him. I was a joke. The vampires we murdered were a joke. All he cared about was coming into power because he was so goddamn strong, no one could stand up to him.

"Can't a girl have some privacy around here?" I stood, brushing the dirt off my skirt.

The sun had fallen, and the sky had started to darken around us. Wisps of blue, purple, and pink were brushed across the sky, like a beautiful painting.

But there was nothing beautiful left in the palace anymore. It was all a cover to hide the ugliness inside.

Just like him. The only thing giving away his horrid nature were the scars running down his face.

"You and I both know you're not entitled to privacy here."

I crossed my arms and raised a brow at him.

"How can I help you, my dear brother?"

His lips pulled into a dangerous smirk.

"If I didn't like you so much, I would punish you for your snark," he said and walked closer to me, reaching out to grab a lock of my hair. A deceivingly soft gesture that sent a burst of fear through me. His nostrils flared, letting me know he could smell it, and the flash in his eyes told me he enjoyed it. "Two more days and you'll make me the most powerful vampire king in existence."

"You don't even know who I'm marrying yet. You left the choice up to me, remember?"

His smile dropped at the reminder.

"I have final say, *remember*? If you choose someone unsatisfactory, I will step in for you."

Which is exactly why Atlas is not on the list. It would have been easy to sign myself away to her, and I wasn't ignorant of her feelings on the matter. But the risk of him stepping in at the last moment and ripping away any hope that I had at freedom was too high.

I needed to be smart about this. Cunning. Just like my father raised me to be.

"I remember," I all but spat at him and jerked my head to pull my hair from his grip, but he held on tight, sending a searing pain across my skull.

"You never did thank me for that," he commented as he leaned close.

I didn't want to thank that bastard for anything. I gritted my teeth. The urge to attack him ravaged through me. If I were the old Aurelia, I would have snapped at him and tried to pull his head from his neck with my bare hands.

But I'm not.

That Aurelia wasn't here anymore. Inside, there was still that vampire that would rage at anyone who tried to harm her regardless of what the consequences were.

But this time it wasn't just about me. Because right then, as I was looking at my brother's eyes, something flashed in them.

He thinks this is a game.

The playfulness told me he knew exactly what was going through my mind, and he was just waiting for me to lose it.

But he also knew about *them.*

"Thank me, *princess,* or I'll send word to the vampires watching your lovers that you're *uncooperative.*"

Ice-cold fear struck me right through the heart. I had been naïve to think that he wouldn't ensure that I was being a good little vampire. I thought offering myself up on a silver platter would be enough for him. That showing that I was willing to kneel in front of him and expose my neck—*degrade myself*—would prove my loyalty.

He was smarter than that. And crueler.

I guess it runs in the family.

"Thank you," I spat at him.

He held my gaze for a long moment before pushing me away, and I only barely caught myself before I stumbled into the dry fountain.

"Remember your place, Aurelia," he warned, all the joking gone from his tone for the first time.

With that, he turned away, his cape swishing behind him as he disappeared back into the castle.

My anger was boiling up. Violent thoughts raged inside me.

Images of me pulling back his cape and sinking my fangs into his neck, tearing it out violently, and painting the dying flowers red flashed through my mind.

But so did the memory of how easily he had taken out the witches. *And on how he had set his eyes on Cedar next.*

My vision blurred. My breathing quickened. His shape was nothing more than a black blob now.

Not really caring what anyone else would think if they heard, I let out a shriek that came from the deepest, most anguished parts of my soul. I turned around and started pulling out the weeds at the bottom of the fountain, throwing them across the garden at the wall that separated me from my freedom.

When that wasn't enough, I started pulling my hair, gripping at the roots until I crumbled into a screaming mess. Anything to let out the anger that was eating me alive inside.

I'd been able to hold it in front of him, but as soon as I was alone, it all came rushing out. All the fury. All the fear. All the hopelessness.

I did this to myself. I did it for them. *For us.* I couldn't let them die. Couldn't let them get taken away from me. This was the only way.

But that didn't make it any more enjoyable.

I was Aurelia Castle to my core, for better or for worse. Soon to be the broodmare everyone thought me to be.

I took a deep breath and turned up to look at the now dark sky.

I had one last thing to do before my marriage. One final chance to make it all worth it.

Pull yourself together, Aurelia.

My mother had once told me to hold onto my fierceness, but now was the time to push it back. The time to act like the perfect submissive princess and let the rest fester until it was time to unleash it all.

"Princess?" another voice spoke.

I looked to see my driver for the night waiting for me at the edge of the garden, who had obviously been standing there longer than necessary, based on his pitying look.

"Coming!" I said with a sigh and stood.

One last night. One last party. One last chance.

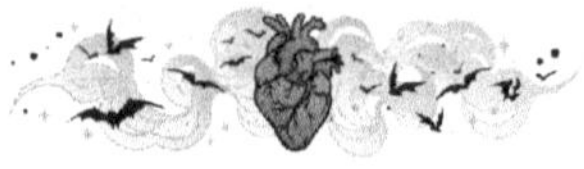

It was a strange feeling to be back at the club. It had once been the only outlet from the chains of my father's rule.

I had almost expected my brother to shut it down, but since it was on the outside of the boundaries of our family's rule, it was supposed to stand on its own. A place for all the powerful vampires in the area to gather.

I pushed open the door, the loud music swirled around me, and for a second I wondered... If I closed my eyes, maybe I could pretend to be the Aurelia I had been back then. The one who would use these parties as an escape.

But then came the stares. The whispers. We all knew there wasn't much you could hide from vampire ears unless you were behind one of the reinforced walls of the upstairs bedrooms, so they whispered things under their breaths, knowing I could hear all of it.

I walked in and slipped my coat off, giving it to a random person off to the side. I didn't even care if they were the actual hostess.

Slowly, the party started to try to go back to normal, but most of the stares lingered. Still, I held my head high and walked through the middle of the foyer. The small stage at the end of it had four vampires, one of them sliding down a pole with hardly any clothes on, and the other three covered in blood, teasing the vampires around them.

"Want to play?" one of them asked as I got close.

"So sweet," I replied, reaching into the pocket of my dress to hold out four jewels for them. "But no, thanks."

The woman took them faster than I could blink and divided them between her fellow colleagues.

This had other vampires whispering even more. Annoyed, I turned around to look at them, all but littering the hallways. Some of them I recognized, some of them I didn't. But all of them stared at me like I was some freak. A circus show for them to watch.

They didn't look at me in fear. They only showed a gross interest that made my skin crawl.

"Keep looking, and I'll have your eyes gouged out. Anyone got anything to say?" One of them actually had the audacity to open their mouth. "Rhetorical. If anyone utters a single word, I will have your tongue cut out. Now get back to it."

There was a moment of silence before I heard, "Aurelia!" and Dalia wrapped her arms around me. "I missed you! I can't believe they tried to tell me you were dead. I knew you weren't, but I never expected you to be bumming it with some witche—"

"Okay, okay," I interrupted with a sigh and let her pull me to the side. "Just because I like you, it doesn't mean you're exempt from the tongue-cutting rule."

She gave me a wicked smile and continued to pull me further into the house. The party had continued behind us, with Dalia breaking the ice far better than my threats could.

Fredrick was sitting in his seat, waiting for his lover to bring me back to him. But he didn't meet me with a smile this time. His face was filled with... concern? I couldn't tell if it was for me or the state of the world, given what my brother's rule meant for him.

Every time there was a bloodthirsty uprising in the vampire world, it never stopped at one kingdom. Once the vampire got a taste of power, they would try to expand, usually by starting a war with the ones closest to them.

"We're glad you showed up," he said as Dalia went to sit on

his lap and he pulled her to him with ease. "We thought maybe that brother of yours wouldn't let you come to this."

I looked around, my eyes scanning the room to see if I could make out a familiar face.

"He knows image is important," I murmured, then turned to look at them. "I have some important things to take care of tonight. Dalia, I will be reaching out to you soon. For something I think both of you will be interested in. For now—"

"Whose side are you on?" Fredrick asked just as I was turned to leave them.

The dark hardness of his tone told me to tread carefully.

"What sides are you talking about?" I countered, raising a brow at him.

"The other royal families are wondering. Your father's or your brother's? Will you uphold the Castle dignity or let it go to ruin?"

Voices in the room silenced.

"Be careful, Fredrick, or you may catch the wrong type of attention."

Dalia's face twisted, her eyes shooting to Fredrick as he looked me up and down.

"Simple answer," he said. "If you can't answer, we will have to assume..."

"Mine," I replied and turned away. "My side. Back then, and now."

He didn't stop me this time. I would need them, but not now. I needed to find the person that was going to change all this for me first.

I found him in the corner of the furthest room on the second floor. He was slouching in a chair, a cloak covering his face and casting a shadow over him. If he were human, I might think he was sleeping.

No one else was in here, knowing to leave him alone, so he growled when I grabbed a chair and pulled it up to sit right in front of him.

"I don't give a shit who you are, if you don't get away from me—"

"Caspian Hart, parents died months after you were exiled. Your sister, set to take the throne, was killed by a rogue vampire. You were the last living heir, meaning that, regardless of your exile, you became the new leader of the Hart royal family. A family that was once one of the most powerful in the region is now just sitting there with unused resources and power."

Slowly, he started to look up, glaring at me.

"You spend all your time in this house, but you've never been seen with anyone. All your meetings take place in this small room, and you leave in the morning to go back to your kingdom, only to come back at night. You're trying to ruin your family's image and spend the entirety of your fortune until there's nothing left."

His head was raised now so I could make out his features. Growing up, I had seen him with a clean-cut face. His aristocratic air ran in his family. He was one of the more powerful ones, one my father hadn't dared touch because of how extensive their resources were.

All it meant was that they had money and people. But they kept to themselves for the most part.

"I could live a millennium and never spend all our money," he growled.

I sent him a smile.

"But that doesn't mean you won't try, hm?"

He pushed his hood back and leaned forward.

"What does the disgraced Castle princess want with me? Shouldn't you be busy shining your brother's shoes or something? How does it feel that he so cruelly pulled the rug from under you? Doesn't it make you angry?"

My smile wavered.

"I never wanted to kill anyone more than I want to kill my brother," I replied, truthfully. I caught him off guard, his eyes widening, but then he slowly sat up straight in the chair.

"Well, at least we have a few things in common," he said.

"The rogue..." I said, letting my voice trail off.

His jaw ticked.

"A coincidence that the rogue attacks stopped when your brother took over, isn't it?"

Unease settled in my chest.

"But you're here, sulking in a dark room all alone, every single night. It can't simply be that you're running away from the responsibilities of your family... Aren't you ashamed?"

He lunged forward, his hands on the armrest of my chair. His face was now close to mine, his fangs bared, and a growl rumbled from his chest.

"Don't talk about shit you don't understand."

I got him right where I want him.

"I understand more than you think." My voice didn't waver, and I didn't flinch. "My mother. My friends. My lovers. All of it has been taken by the Castle family. Which is why I need to do this."

"I don't care," he said, pulling away and setting himself back on the chair. "Now get out or I will—"

"Caspian Hart, I want you to marry me."

Silence spread out then. Until he threw his head back and let out a booming laugh. It was so loud that I jerked back, surprised by the suddenness of it.

When he finally calmed down, he looked at me, wiping away fake tears.

"I haven't laughed that good in a long time." Remnants of his laugh still played at the edge of his voice. "Are you insane or just stupid?"

"I have been forced to marry someone one too many times," I said with a sweet smile. "I don't give a fuck about marriage. The real people I want to marry are not an option. My brother is going to make my life miserable, so the only way I can do this is if I pick my husband."

"And you chose me?" he asked disbelievingly.

"Don't you have a fortune you want to get rid of? And I can promise you that we will make my brother pay."

For the first time that night, it felt like he was truly seeing me.

"Why did you come back?" he whispered. "You could've stayed hidden."

"I..." A knot gathered in my throat. There were so many reasons. It was complicated since I was trying to protect myself and my lovers while fulfilling the prophecy. But all of it would end only one way. "I'm going to kill my brother. But first I need to be married off."

He looked me straight in the eyes. There was another long silence before a smile spread across his face.

"Sure, why not? I think I could like you."

He sounded so nonchalant about it, it had my jaw dropping.

"That's it?"

He nodded and stood.

"There is a lot that goes into this, but let's just say that, for the most part, you're right. I want to get back at him for my sister. But there is another person who dropped me as soon as the news came out. Someone who's just as ashamed to be with me as I am ashamed of myself."

He held out his hand to me.

"What do you say, Aurelia Hart?"

I cringed at the name but slipped my hand into his and let him pull me up.

"We have a lot to discuss," I said, but the weight of the universe felt just the slightest bit lighter.

"We have time. First, let me show you your new kingdom."

I let him walk me out of the room, taking the first step into a life that I could finally control.

Cedar

I stood next to Vesper, the need to reach out and touch her too much to handle.

I had been waiting, every single night plagued by dreams of the day when she was taken from us. All I could remember was the way she looked at us for help... but we couldn't.

It took far too long to get to her, and now that she was *finally* here, instead of wrapping my arms around her, I was forced to watch as two spoiled vampires had the blandest conversation I'd ever seen in my life.

Atlas and Charlotte were at a large dining table, but instead of sitting at both ends, they chose to sit on either side of the middle, a more intimate position, since they were forced to stare at each other.

They had called this "dinner," but for these vampires, that consisted of various cups of blood, ruby-red blood candies, and human blood bags offering a bit of their wrist to them every few minutes.

The dining room itself was dark with chandeliers hanging above. All the lights had been dimmed for a more romantic vibe, I guessed. Windows spanned behind Atlas, all of them covered with vines, dark enough to block out the setting sun.

It was quiet. No conversation except for theirs.

We were cast off to the side, our backs against the wall as we watched, neither of them really paying attention to us.

"Is the council still restricting your clan intake?" Charlotte asked, turning to the human waiting at her side. She grabbed his wrist, already open and bleeding, and she placed her lips on it to suck a few mouthfuls.

Vesper shifted at my side, her arm just barely brushing across mine. It caused a jolt to go through my heart, something that didn't go unnoticed by the vampires. Atlas gave me a look as if asking me to control my reactions.

I tried not to look at Vesper. At least not until I was able to get us out of this room. I was barely holding on, and I feared that if I gave her even a single glance, I would lose my composure.

But that didn't stop me from leaning into her.

"They will probably do that until the day I die," she muttered and lifted her cup for the human on her side to pour her blood in. "The curse of attracting Kyan's attention."

Charlotte dabbed at her mouth with a napkin in a mock show of table manners.

Vesper's hand reached out just slightly, the tips of her fingers brushing against the back of my hand. Electricity jolted through me again.

"Addressing the council head so casually? Aren't you afraid of how she may react when it gets back to her?"

Atlas scoffed. "She can't kill me. That's why she's punishing me like this."

Charlotte hummed, though Atlas's importance in the vampire community didn't seem to be as much of a shock to her as it had been to me.

Fuck her.

Atlas was the one who got us into the room we were in now. The only chance we had to take Vesper back. But she was also the reason she was here in the first place. Atlas was apparently from some special background, and even the council wouldn't kill her, but she couldn't stand up for Vesper?

I grew a little bit bolder. My hand reached out to Vesper's, but I was much too fast. She stiffened and jerked away, almost as if on reflex, and I finally took the moment to look at her, unable to stop myself anymore.

The vampire conversation drifted to the background as I got a good look at her for the first time in weeks.

She had changed since she was last dragged from the sanctuary of Atlas's home. She had grown taller, her hair was whiter, her scars were still embedded in her skin, but they looked deeper, more prominent.

And, of course, the biggest change, the eyes that were slowly reddening the longer we stared at each other. The tension between us was undeniable. The electricity from where our skin touched still singed.

I couldn't handle it anymore.

I looked around, noticing an exit not far behind us. I took one look at Atlas, but her eyes were already on me as she gave me a subtle nod.

Finally. I wasn't going to take this opening for granted.

Charlotte twisted her head, like she was listening in, but did nothing to stop me as I grabbed Vesper's wrist and pulled her along with me out the door.

As soon as we were out, I looked for a quick place to hide. The hallway itself had even more windows alongside it, causing me to feel exposed. The sun was setting and the hallway was darkening, but I needed to get us out of sight. Even just for a moment.

"Cedar, I can't be running—"

Found it.

Almost unnoticeable, but there was a small alcove covered by a tapestry. We would barely fit, but it would give us the illusion of privacy, and that was enough for me.

I pushed us into it, forcing Vesper against the wall. Her eyes glowed in the darkness. I inhaled deeply, taking in her scent, and even that had changed slightly. But I could tell this was still her. Beyond any doubt, the person in front of me was the Vesper I fell in love with.

"Cedar, I'm not... This is..."

She was afraid. Her eyes darted around, unable to keep them on me for long. The once powerful and feared hunter was now averting her gaze and looking like she wanted to run away from me.

"What are you so afraid of?" I asked, my hand running down her face. At first, she was unmoving, but slowly she leaned into it. "I'm here to take you back."

Her pained expression had my heart breaking.

"I'm not... I'm not *me* anymore, Cedar." Her voice caught. "Before they gave me to the family, I was in a dungeon. They... They only fed me blood. It... changed me."

It hit me then that she was afraid I wouldn't want the new her. Wouldn't accept her. I looked at her then in a new light. The feared hunter who had once taken down vampire after vampire becoming one herself, and not by choice. It was forced upon her, and now she was scared that I, out of all people, would push her away for it.

How dare they? How dare they lock her up? How dare they treat her like nothing more than an afterthought?

She deserved better than this. The world had already proven to be cruel with her upbringing and the prophecy forced upon her. How could it continue to do this? *How can I even begin to help her? What could I possibly do?*

I felt useless. I wanted to help my lover, but there was nothing I felt like I could do that would be enough to make up for the level of depravity of what had happened to her.

I wanted to curse the gods. Demand that they give me an answer. But I knew it would get me nowhere. The real enemies were the ones in the council.

Pushing down the anger, I did the only thing I could think of. I lunged forward, gripping her shoulders, and forced her lips to mine.

She let out a pained groan, her hands coming to my hips, pulling me to her. I tried to tangle my hand in her hair, but she was stronger, faster. She turned us, pushing me against the wall, her mouth opening to push her tongue inside mine.

I let out a noise of protest that quickly dissolved into a moan as she kissed me. I wanted to talk to her. It was supposed to just be a kiss to show her how much I wanted her. How nothing had changed for me. I never meant for it to go this far, but I couldn't fight what was happening between us.

If we couldn't say it in words, then we sure as hell would be able to say it with our bodies.

It was hard, rushed, all the time we spent away building up to this moment. But it felt like coming home.

The part of me that was missing was right in front of me. *Kissing* me. We were melding together, forcing our bodies against one another, but in the back of my mind, no matter how relieved I was... there was still something missing.

Someone.

Our perfect princess.

She moved down, her lips trailing down my face and neck, and I leaned my head to the side. When I felt the brush of sharp fangs, I realized what was happening.

"Wait! Vesper, we need to—"

Her hand covered my mouth, and in a flash, her teeth were buried in my neck.

My magic flared, reacting to the threat. Red magical vines swarmed around us, circling Vesper, but instead of fighting her, they pulled her closer.

My magic accepts her. Even when she's burying her fangs in my neck.

I let my body sink into her.

My mouth opened in a silent scream, but all too quickly I started to feel the heat of her venom work its way through my system. It was different from Aurelia's. Back then, when she pumped me full of her venom, I turned into a horny mess, but this...

There was something stronger about Vesper's venom. Something that made the burn so intense that my stomach began cramping almost immediately.

"Oh god." My groan was muffled by her hand.

She pulled away, blood dripping down her mouth and onto our clothes. She'd never looked more dangerous than in that moment. Her eyes red, a hunger in them that sent a jolt of electricity straight through my entire body. She was ravenous for me, and it made me fall apart.

Just like that, an orgasm was building up in me. I couldn't stop it. And all it took was just the tiniest bit of her venom.

"You taste good, my witch." Her voice was deep, sultry. Not at all like the human Vesper I once knew.

"You sure have changed," I whispered as she pulled her hand away. I wanted her. My body was desperate for her. My cunt was already aching. Wetness pooled in my underwear.

She leaned forward, her lips barely touching mine as her hand trailed down my front, dipping into my pants. I hissed as her fingers met my clit. I needed more. I needed her to fuck me hard, to pull the orgasm she was teasing me with out of me.

"You tempted the monster in me, and now I can't stop it," she murmured. "I'm not the desperate little vampire hunter you once knew."

I spread my legs and tilted my head to the side, baring my neck to her.

"And I want it all. Take what you need from me, Vesper. And after this, we go get our princess."

She let out a growl. It went straight to my core.

In another second, her teeth were buried in the other side of my neck, and I let out a strangled moan. The venom was a shock to my system and had my body writhing against her.

More. More. I wanted to say it out loud, but my body wasn't cooperating.

She slipped her fingers inside me, and for the first time, I felt totally conquered. There was nothing I could do to shake her off. She was pushing me against the wall, her hand gripping my arm so I'd stay in place, the other one between my legs, fingers pumping into my wet cunt without mercy. I didn't realize how much she overpowered me now with her new height until her body was covering mine.

"Give it to me," Vesper growled as she pulled away. "I need it."

I couldn't stop my orgasm even if I tried. I plunged headfirst into it, my sight blackening at the edges at the intensity of it. Even though we had dipped into the alcove, there was no hiding the sounds coming from my mouth.

Whispered begging turned into loud whimpers.

She forced her teeth out of me, no easy feat given how red her eyes were. Her teeth were bared, my blood all over them and her mouth.

It was one of the hottest things I'd ever seen.

Vesper was breathing heavily, her eyes slowly starting to turn back to their normal golden hue as she took in the mess she turned me into. I was still riding the high, pleasure still coursing through my being. There was no room for me to feel any embarrassment.

At least not yet.

"We have to be careful," she said as she moved away from me, but that wasn't what made me panic. Her words did. "I'm not... myself anymore. I'm sorry I hurt you."

She's retreating.

My hand shot forward to stop her.

"I liked it. I liked it. Please..." I forced myself to take a breath. "We will work on it." Her eyes widened, letting me know she expected me to push her away. I could see the guilt and shame written all over her face. "I'm not letting you go, Vesper. Never again."

I pulled her closer, my hands running down her body, caressing her, but she stopped me by gripping my wrist.

"Let me show you," I whispered.

Her eye flashed red again, but then it was gone.

"Not until our princess is back."

My throat constricted, but I knew where she was coming from. The days I spent in Atlas's castle, in the bed I had shared with them, were the loneliest I ever had. They were in my dreams, only for me to wake up every day disappointed to realize the bed was cold and I was alone.

Now that it was only Vesper and me, we still weren't complete. But at least we had each other.

Vesper's head snapped to the side, her jaw tensing. Just as I was about to ask what was happening, she moved the tapestry covering us and peeked out of the alcove.

"Do you have no decorum?" Atlas's voice came from down the hallway with a scoff.

"I think it's cute," Charlotte said with a small giggle, her hand trying to hide her smile but obviously failing. When I glanced at them, I saw them waiting in the middle of the hallway. Charlotte gave me a wink. "A deal is a deal. One dinner and you guys get Vesper. It sucks because I really liked having her around, but I know you're better off searching for that princess of yours."

She said it with a pout, but as annoying as the vampire seemed, it sounded like she had a good heart.

As we walked out, the shame of it all finally heated my skin.

"Speaking of..." Charlotte's eyes flashed to Atlas and then to Vesper. "We got news."

My heart stopped. Vesper took a step forward.

"She made her choice?" Vesper asked, hope and despair threaded in her tone.

Charlotte gave her a pitiful look.

"Yes," Atlas growled. "And we have to hurry. We have an engagement dinner to catch."

INVITES YOU TO
THEIR SURPRISE ENGAGEMENT
CEREMONY

CASTLE FAMILY GROUNDS

TONIGHT

AT SUNDOWN

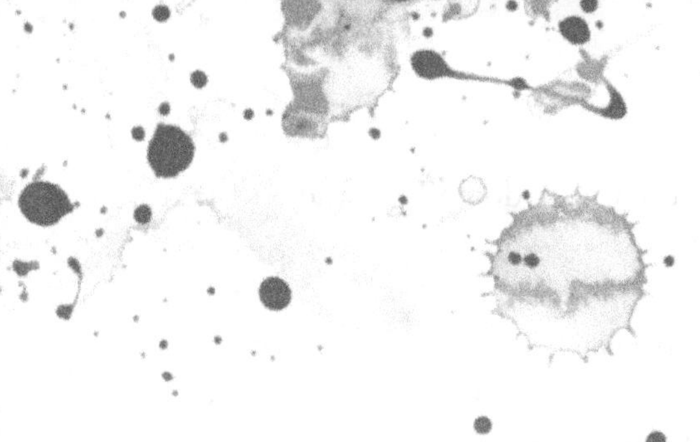

AURELIA

I was screaming inside as I smiled at every single vampire that offered me a congratulatory smile.

I imagined severing their heads from their necks every time they let out that little laugh. I might be smiling and dancing, but inside my mind I was stabbing a sword through their torsos and watching as the blood sprayed over everyone here, ruining their extravagant dresses and suits.

It didn't help that Adrian had changed the colors of the room. Blacks and golds with red rubies and crystals scattered throughout in a way that made it look like blood had already been spilled. It only made my fantasies that much more realistic.

Vampires were packed into one of our ballrooms, though it didn't look like one since Adrian had renovated it to make it look like another throne room. He even had a new throne made just for this occasion with a platform just tall enough for him to peer over the crowd and watch everyone.

"Congratulations!" a pair of vampires said as they passed me. I forced myself to give them a proper smile, even as their deaths played out in my mind.

They were all so gross. So fake.

They were there to see the obedient vampire princess marry to help her brother secure a new kingdom. They thought that they had escaped my wrath.

They're wrong.

And this time, I wasn't waiting for anyone to save me. This time I was the one who was going to take fate into my own hands and force it to its knees in front of me.

My husband-to-be was waiting patiently in the crowd for his debut, the announcement a surprise even to my brother, who was watching over the entire party with a soft smirk.

He thinks I'm under his control.

As if reading my mind, his eyes drifted over to me. He held up a glass of blood to me, so I stopped a waiter as he passed, grabbing one to make a show of toasting him back.

Good little princess, his eyes whispered.

Stupid fucking dickhead, mine hissed.

He thought he was going to be the one announcing my marriage tonight. As if I didn't know he had already picked my fiancé. As if I didn't have ears in the hallways willing to spill everything they heard my brother discuss in exchange for the littlest bribery.

We had one deal—I could choose my husband—but I was no idiot.

He used it as a way to control me, lulling me into a false sense of security while he schemed in the background. Everyone in the palace put on a show for him. Just like me, they were acting like the perfect subjects, excited to have a new and strangely powerful king.

But behind closed doors and in the dark corners, people were scared. They were furious. And that made everyone all the more willing to spill everything they saw.

Well... almost everyone.

I made my way to the side of the room, where my first target awaited me. In his freshly washed council uniform, holding his own glass of blood, General Lee stuck out like a sore thumb, but he seemed to enjoy the way other vampires were giving him space.

He smirked when he saw me.

I returned it with a polite smile.

"You seem happy to finally be getting this behind you," he said.

"Very," I replied. "But I have something for you."

He raised a brow at me, and I took a step closer and dropped my voice to a whisper.

"I left our conversation so rudely the other day." I looked up at him through my lashes. "I want what you were offering, but I want to prove my sincerity."

His eyes shifted to the party behind us, almost as if he was afraid we were going to get caught.

He cleared his throat.

"And what can you offer me that I cannot get myself, Princess?"

I forced myself to keep smiling.

"Not much. Except..." I turned to look at the hallway to our right, where my present was waiting. There stood a young male feeder, probably in his early twenties. Normally, it wouldn't mean anything, we had feeders galore, but this one... "I hear virgin blood tastes sweeter. And he's willing for you to be his first."

That got his attention. I had to swallow my disgust. Vampires like him loved the idea of innocence, or rather, the idea of taking it for themselves.

General Lee let out a huff of a laugh and shook his head, almost in disbelief.

"It does sweeten the deal," he whispered as he turned to move toward the human. "Tell me what you want. Information on your pet?"

"More. I want her transferred to me."

The only sign that he was offended was the twitch of his eye. To the outside world, it would look like we were just having a pleasant conversation, but I saw the way his hands balled into fists.

"That would be going directly against the council," he murmured. "You think a virgin will get you that?"

"Most definitely," I answered with an even bigger smile, showing my fangs. "Because I know what my brother plans to do, and you know the thing he needs most is a pliant, submissive sister who will make him look good." I took a step closer, lowering my voice. "You want me to behave? You want this reign to go without issue? Go fuck your little virgin, and then, before you come back, I want you to arrange her transport."

I looked up at him, his sharp gaze sending a jolt through me. Time froze, and for a moment, I felt like I had poked the wrong bear. The hair raised on the back of my neck, my body jerked back as if anticipating an attack... but it never came.

He smiled at my move.

"What makes you think I care if you behave? You're the one going to reap those consequences."

I shrugged, trying to play off just how tense he was starting to make me.

"Just me? Sure, if that's true, go tell him right now."

I stepped to the side, acting like I was giving him the space to go, but he didn't move from his spot. I knew he was as shady as they came, and I don't know what my brother had on him or why he was chained to him, but part of his job had to be ensuring that my brother kept power.

And he did not need a bratty princess trying to ruin it all.

Though that didn't stop me from panicking inside as he took his time figuring out if he wanted to take my bribe or not. I was bluffing, and I didn't know him well enough to tell if he could figure me out just yet.

"Just because I'm taking this doesn't mean you have the power here," he finally said in a low, threatening tone. "Don't forget your role."

This time, my bitter smile came unbidden.

"Yes, I will bend over for my husband to unite the families so we can prosper. I get it. Now go get fucked and give me my silver-haired toy, or I will make a scene the moment the announcement leaves my brother's mouth."

His smile told me he accepted, but his eyes told me he was killing me in his head right now.

"Fine," he spat. "I will have news for you when I get back."

I nodded and sent him a cheeky wave, watching as he went off with the feeder, who, at the last second, sent me a smile of his own.

When they disappeared, I finally allowed myself to take the tiniest breath.

One down, one to go.

I turned around, looking at the sea of vampires, particularly the one who was now leaning down and talking in a hushed tone to my brother. The head of the Solei family.

The way he looked so much like his son was jarring, but it wasn't my experience with his son that ran through my mind. It was the fact that he and my father had fought over my mother. That all they had wanted to do was breed us so that we could give them the Krae blood. *Disgusting.*

Vesper and Cedar passed through my mind, unwarranted. I couldn't keep them at bay. At least not for long.

I miss them. I missed Vesper and Cedar more than my soul could handle. The bond ached constantly, reminding me we were so far apart.

I knew only I could save us. And I had a plan. As painful as it was, I held onto my violent daydreams and used them to fuel me as I threw myself back into the crowd, flitting from vampire to vampire, conversing about everything and anything.

Adrian's heavy, lingering gaze was always on me and hard to ignore. I could tell that he was enjoying this little game of ours. He loved that I was flattering his ego. Showing the world what a good sibling I was.

Taking it up a notch, I decided it was time to start showing off. When the music changed to a waltz, I joined in without hesitation. It took only a few partner changes for me to get to

Caspian Hart. His familiar face provided me with the comfort I needed.

"Just a little longer now," he whispered.

As our dance came to an end, I was passed to another partner. But right in the middle of being tossed, bright red flashed across my gaze. Panic and hope rose in me, but I didn't let myself get excited.

She can't be here. If she is, I may just ruin—

The male vampire dancing with me now tried to say something, but it all sounded like underwater gibberish. My eyes darted around, trying to catch another glimpse of the impossible.

And then I saw the flash of white behind him.

My breath caught in my throat. The sore spot between my breasts where the unfulfilled bond ached made itself known.

Vesper?

No. I couldn't let myself get distracted. There were only a few more minutes until I changed the course of my fate. This was my mind playing tricks on me.

I was twirled again and sent off to the next partner, only to come face-to-face with...

"Vesper?"

The world floated around me. All the panic and hope swirled together and threatened to burst out of my chest at the sight of her golden eyes.

The bond thrummed to life between us, begging me to bite her. But there was something different about her. She was Vesper, there was no doubt about that, but she was... taller. Her eyes were sharper and... *red?*

"My princess, don't you look beautiful tonight."

Even her voice held a husky quality that wasn't there before.

She was wearing an all-black ensemble embroidered with swirls of silver. Something vampire royalty would wear, not a vampire hunter. It fit her well, hugging her shoulders and arms, showing off her muscled figure.

Her skin was smooth, save for the scars that seemed carved

even deeper than before. I wanted to run my fingers down them, trace away the bad memories they left. I almost did, until I was snapped back to reality with one thought.

The Vesper in front of me was no longer mostly human with a small percentage of vampire.

She was changed.

My heart ached for her. The selfish part of me was happy that she would live as long as I would, then I was hit with the pain of the realization.

What happened to her?

I wanted to ask. Wanted to pull her to me. Wanted to run away.

But I was done running.

"You need to go," I said through gritted teeth. Forcing the words out was harder than I imagined. It felt like barbed wire was tied around my throat.

My eyes pricked with blood as she gave me a small smirk.

"What? Are you getting tired of me saving you?"

Before I could respond to the obvious jab, I was twirled and sent straight to the arms of another. One inhale told me it was a witch. *My witch.*

Cedar met me with a smirk of her own. My stomach twisted as I was hit by a bitter thought.

Is she mad at me?

As her eyes flicked from mine down to my body, my next thought was, *I hope she is.*

"So, *Brat...*" She dropped her voice to a whisper. "You really thought you could get away from us?"

Shivers ran down my spine. Her hands were on me, burning their way through my dress.

"I'm doing this for us," I hissed and looked over my shoulder to my brother, who was currently being entertained by a feeder.

Thank god. But it wouldn't last long, and I needed to make sure that the two of them were out of here before he caught on. *And before they ruined the plan.*

I was turned around, but instead of going to the next awaiting vampire, I was taken back into Vesper's arms. This time, she got close enough for her lips to brush against my ear.

It was too much. I couldn't pull myself from her even if I wanted to.

"If you think I'm letting you get married, think again," she said and twirled me so hard, I lost sight of the crowd. The only eyes I was able to make out were hers and Cedar's. I couldn't feel their lips by my ears, but I could hear their voices as if they were being whispered right next to me.

"You're ours, Princess."

"And we're here to claim you."

It wasn't a promise. It was a threat. They were angry. They'd come here to make sure I knew where I belonged.

Their hands were on me, burning and claiming, just like their whispers.

But that was part of the problem.

Everyone was trying to put me back in my place. To quell the cruel side of me. Lock me in a cage, only to be let out to do their bidding.

They loved me. I loved them.

But it was time I let that side out.

I pulled them to me, forcing the three of us together. Our waltz jerked to a halt, just like everyone around us, who slowly started to realize that these people were not supposed to be here.

"Aurelia," Vesper growled.

I let my hand brush across her cheek.

"Vampirism looks good on you," I told her. Her eyes widened before her mask was back on. Almost like she was shocked that I would accept it, let alone like it. I then turned to Cedar, one finger brushing across her lips. "But this is not the time. Whatever you're about to see, I want you to remember what you both mean to me. *Trust me.*"

I lingered for a moment, taking them in. I didn't know if I would be able to see them again after my marriage, and them being here was like a slap in the face. Not because they were trying to mess everything up, but because I was going to betray them.

My guilt attacked my body like a hailstorm. It hurt to do this without them here. But now that they were standing right in front of me, it felt even worse.

Stoning my expression, I pushed them back, the tension between us changing.

Shock crossed their faces. Vesper let out a low growl, and Cedar's hands came to her arm as if to stop her from pouncing on me.

"Who let them in?" I asked, raising my voice.

The music stopped. Vampires spoke in hushed tones. The sound of Adrian's amused chuckle reached my ears. Using his vampire speed, he came to my side, his hand grabbing mine.

"Naughty things! They weren't on the guest list. I could forgive that, but touching you in such a manner? Maybe I should teach them a lesson."

I looked around, making sure General Lee wasn't here. Luckily, my plan worked well enough to keep him away, but if I didn't move quickly and make the announcement, it might as well be for naught.

Fear clawed at my throat, but I merely turned and looked at him with an amused smirk.

"And let them ruin our fun? Don't forget I still have a surprise."

I could see the slight annoyance in the way his eye twitched, but he didn't let it show. Not when so many people were watching.

Atlas stepped forward then, her midnight black hair shining under the lights of the chandelier. I'd never seen her gaze this cold, and guilt tugged at my heart again.

In another life, she would have been the perfect person to tie myself to for eternity, but that was the issue. She was too perfect, and my brother wanted power, not my comfort. I needed someone he couldn't refuse, someone even better than a Solei.

"Atlas, you're a powerful ally. A strong and revered clan head," I said, raising my voice so there would be no doubt about what I was saying. "So you know what your actions mean. You bringing them here is unacceptable."

"I meant no disrespect." Atlas lowered her head ever so slightly. "I came, excited for your announcement. They are merely part of my guard."

I scoffed, but my brother, on the other hand, couldn't contain his laughter.

"Take them outside," he ordered. "As a show of *mercy*," If I weren't so scared for Cedar and Vesper, I might have let out a laugh at that. "I will let you off with a warning, but hear me when I say that there won't be another. If you can't keep your *pets* on a leash, I will have to lead by example."

When he said the last part, he wasn't looking at them. He was looking at me.

I didn't cower from his stare, making a point to look right at him as they dragged my lovers out.

"Well," I said with a clap, calling all eyes back to me. "Now, since I have everyone's attention, I'd like to inform you that you are not here for an engagement."

Seeing Cedar and Vesper's gaze as they were being pulled from the room almost had me faltering. My brother was silent, but I could feel the murderous intent radiating off him.

I was stealing his show. *Good.*

"You're here for..." I held out my hand as Caspian detached himself from the crowd. Tall, midnight hair with a blue tint, playful red eyes, and dressed in a deep red that matched my dress. "Our wedding."

He kneeled before me and made a show of grabbing my hand and placing a kiss right on my wrist, a promise to myself and the crowd of what was ahead of us.

"Is that... *Caspian Hart?*"

"The Hart family hasn't been heard of in decades!"

I didn't care about their murmuring because all I could hear was the pained sounds my loved ones were making as they were forced out.

Adrian looked at me with an unreadable expression. I had one-upped him. In front of everyone. His lapdog wasn't here to intervene, leaving just him and an angry Solei king right behind him.

"Alright," he finally said, his smile turning vicious. "A wedding it is."

VESPER

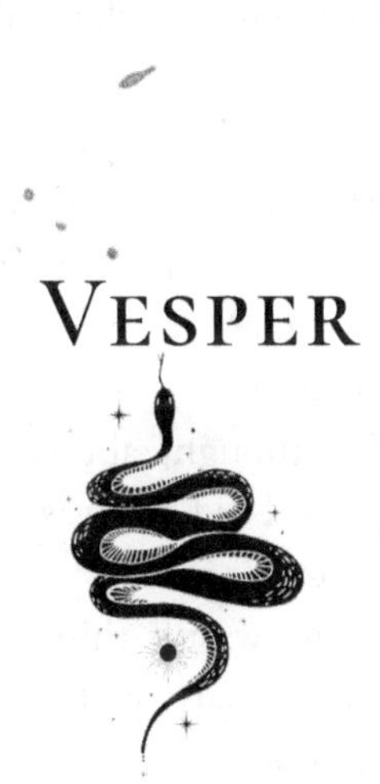

I fought against the guard. It was almost too easy to push them back now.

But then there were two, then three guards. When I started trying to snap at them, Cedar intervened.

"Vesper! Pull back! Vesper!"

She wrapped her red vine-like magic around me, forcing me away from the guards, who stood there stunned.

"Vesper? Isn't that the one assigned to the princess before she—"

"That's her alright. She looks—"

I growled in the guards' direction, my mind vaguely recognizing them from my days at the princess's side. I didn't care for them or the fear they were showing as they took in my changed form. They were just that bastard's lackeys with no brain of their own.

All I wanted was her. *Aurelia.* How dare she say those things? How dare she make us look like the bad guys? How dare she let us leave without her?

And willingly. She stood back and watched as the guards took us. She was the one that called them on us. It was a betrayal as hot as the sword I shoved through her chest all those months ago.

Was this payback? Did she do it to get back at me for that night? I thought I had shown her why I did it. I thought I had apologized enough.

I thought I was enough.

Why did she do this? Who was that man? Was she with him now? Was she with him while they kept me in the dungeons? While I was in forced servitude?

She didn't even try to save me.

The entire time, all I thought about was her and Cedar. I cuddled up to the vampires. I did as I was told. Played the perfect pet. All for a chance to meet her again.

But the entire time she wasn't thinking about us. She was there, orchestrating her own marriage like she hadn't begged for me to save her from her last one.

It didn't even register that the magic was burning me until the scent of my flesh hit my overly sensitive nose and Atlas appeared in front of me. Her angered expression only added to my annoyance.

She brought her hand up and delivered a stinging slap to my face, the vine wrapped too tightly around my body for me to stop it.

"*Hey*! Watch yourself with her," Cedar spat.

"Snap out of it!" Atlas growled. "Act like a blood-crazed newborn, and we're never going to get invited back in."

The magic was starting to really hurt now, but I was far too angry to care about it. If anything, I wanted more of it so that the physical pain would match the emotional one inside me.

"Don't you get it?" I bared my teeth at her. "We won't be getting invited back because she's getting *married*! We were supposed to stop this! This was supposed to be an engagement dinner, not her wedding, and I am missing it—"

The vines let me go, and I lurched at her. We fell to the ground in a heap.

"It was supposed to be me! I don't know how you did it, but

you messed it all up! If you hadn't come and ruined it all, I would be getting married to her!"

My hands shot to her throat. My gaze was covered in a red haze, my fangs aching to tear out her throat as Atlas's hands clawed at my wrists. But her attempts to force me off her were futile.

"She's *mine*," I spat. "You thought you were going to take her from me?"

Atlas's eyes were red, her growls mixing with mine.

Suddenly, Cedar's hands were on me, caressing my arms, my neck, my back. So gentle. So soft. More than the monster I'd become deserved.

My mind stuttered. The rage lifted just for a moment so I could turn, and Cedar's face entered my mind.

There she was.

She had always been there. Even when I knew nothing about her, on the sidelines, watching and guiding me. Whether that was to fulfill the prophecy or now, when I was losing my mind, she had been a constant force trying to push me in the right direction.

Guilt shot through me. She was here, yet I had been ignoring her, too blinded by rage.

"Ours," she corrected with a soft smile. "And no one will take her from us, marriage be damned. Now... We need to get out of here."

Her eyes shifted, and as I followed her gaze, I saw that the guards were slowly backing away, seemingly not wanting to get caught in my grasp.

Good. At least someone could see the true monster I had been made into.

"My poor hunter, eyes on me."

Even if Cedar couldn't.

When I didn't move, her hand gently cupped my face, forcing me to look at her.

"So lost, so angry. Let me help you."

Maybe it wasn't that she couldn't see it. Her eyes told me she did. She saw my bloodthirst. She saw my craving for violence and destruction.

She simply wasn't scared. She accepted it with a grace I refused to give myself.

Atlas squirmed under me.

"Make her let me go."

Cedar didn't even look her way.

"I think we should probably let her go," she murmured. "No matter how badly I love seeing you overtake her with your new strength."

But I couldn't. No matter how good her honey-coated words and soft caresses felt. The anger was too much, and I needed to let it out. I needed to sink my fangs into something.

I needed to storm back into the castle and take Aurelia away from her soon-to-be husband. And I wouldn't stop until everyone's heads were rolling at my feet. Especially his for daring to touch what was mine.

Cedar's gaze softened.

"Sorry about this, love."

Magic burst and sank deep into my skin. I tried to fight it, but when I removed my hands from Atlas to pull at my skin, my body felt lethargic. Panic rose in me so sharply, it made my head spin.

My now slow, almost nonexistent, heartbeat flipped in my chest.

"What are you doing?" My mouth struggled to force the words out, making them sound garbled, but she only shushed me and ran her hand down my hair.

"Just let go. I got you."

I had no choice but to fall into her awaiting arms.

"I know where she'll be..."

Cedar shushed me again.

"Just close your eyes. We will talk when you wake."

The world started to fall away. I panicked, desperately trying to grasp at the edges of my consciousness and force it back to me.

The last time I felt this way, I was dying. But this time I wasn't alone, so I tried to hold on to her gaze. It was warm, unmoving. It relaxed me.

"Since when can your magic knock us out?" Atlas asked with a hoarse voice.

Cedar gave me a smile, her hand running down my face as my eyes closed.

"What? You think I spend all my time in that hideous castle of yours twiddling my thumbs?"

The shocked gasp threatened to pull a smile from me, but I was already too far gone.

For the first time since my change, I fell into a deep sleep.

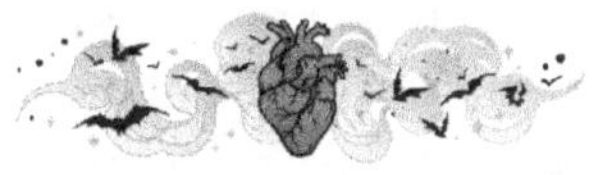

"Hm, this is unexpected. But you look good, I guess."

My head twisted to the side to meet Max. He looked older, but not much. Like a preteen more than a child.

We were back in his cage, and he was still chained to the wall.

How did I get back here?

My head swiveled around to find the door, but there was none.

"I'm dreaming," I exhaled. "You've done this before."

There was something nagging me at the back of my mind, telling me I was forgetting something important. *What is it?*

"You never cease to amaze me, Vesper."

His sarcasm had me frowning. I was angry. I could feel it deep in my chest, burning away everything in its path. But my confusion stopped me from attacking him right away.

"Are you here to warn me?" I asked, my voice rising in a panic. "Do I need to get Cedar and Aurelia out of—"

Of where? When I tried to bring up the memories of where we were, I couldn't.

"Warn you? I guess, but not in the way you think. You're messing it up. Or at least close to."

"Messing what up?" I tried to rise, but only then did I realize I was shackled by the same chains he was, biting into my arms and legs. I pulled at them again, and a searing shot of pain ran up my arm.

I glared at him.

"This isn't fucking fun—"

"Time's ticking. Do you want to hear me or what?"

Snapping my mouth shut, I gritted my teeth. My instinct was to snap back at him, but I toned it down and gave him a jerky nod.

"Vampires have always been a bit old-fashioned," he explained, lying down on the ground and waving his hand to the wall behind him. Light splashed on it, and the shadows started moving, making shapes. Like hand puppets he never raised his hand to make. "The women were married off, men ruled. The clans had a way to shift the balance away from the royal bloodlines, but, well... You know what happened."

The shadows showed various clan heads and their followers fighting each other until nothing was left but dust.

"The royal families prey on the fear of war. They force vampires to their side and make alliances through blood sharing, feeders, and, of course, marriage."

The shadows changed to a girl looking suspiciously like Aurelia, waiting near a throne, a man wearing a crown kneeling at her feet.

"Aurelia figured it out. Can you?"

The shadows showed the man slitting his wrist and the woman kneeling to take gulpfuls of his blood. More than I'd ever seen a vampire take from another.

The memories hit me like a truck. Aurelia standing there. Kicking us out. Announcing she was getting married right then and there.

I tried to stand up but was stopped by the chains.

"Let me out! I need to stop her!"

Max sighed. He waved his hand in the air, and everything on the wall disappeared. "That newborn rage. Better get that under control, or you really will mess it up."

"She can't marry him!" I growled, but desperation and hurt were showing through. My heart felt like it was breaking into a million pieces. *Mine. She's mine!*

"She *has* to."

Max was now in front of me, his glowing eyes stopping my struggles. Stifling power washed over me as everything except his face was wiped from my sight.

"There are two ways to end a bloodline. She would have to die or..."

The pieces were starting to come together, but I still said nothing.

"If she gets married..." His hands were on my face, forcing our contact. "She's no longer a Castle. None of her children will be, if she has them. Then, it's only her brother, so..."

"She was always going to get married..." I breathed. "Her father, he would have forced her."

Max smiled. "If not for you, Aurelia would be stuck in a family that abused her and impregnated her without her consent, all for some made-up power play that would have meant nothing in a few decades." The venom in his voice didn't match his innocent look. "*You* played the perfect pawn to the prophecy. Killing him opened a way for the Castle family to fade into history like they should have long ago. Because now, Aurelia has something to fight for."

Darkness took over my vision, and I was sent plummeting back into my consciousness, but not before I was hit with images.

Images that didn't make sense. Not at first.

I saw her in the garden.

Roaming the halls.

In the middle of the throne room, her body covered in blood.

The images changed. I saw her in the middle of an auditorium-like room. Chains bound her arms and legs. She looked awful, hanging there with no energy, her body weaker than I'd ever seen it.

"Remember what's at stake before you go messing with everything again."

Jerking awake, I was met with a shocked Cedar, her eyes wide. Atlas was behind her, her arms crossed and a frown on her face.

The last image I saw just before my eyes opened lingered. A place I knew all too well.

"No time," I gasped and got up from my position on the hard ground.

"You weren't supposed to wake up yet—"

I grabbed her and walked us both in the direction my bonded was calling me.

"I know where she is."

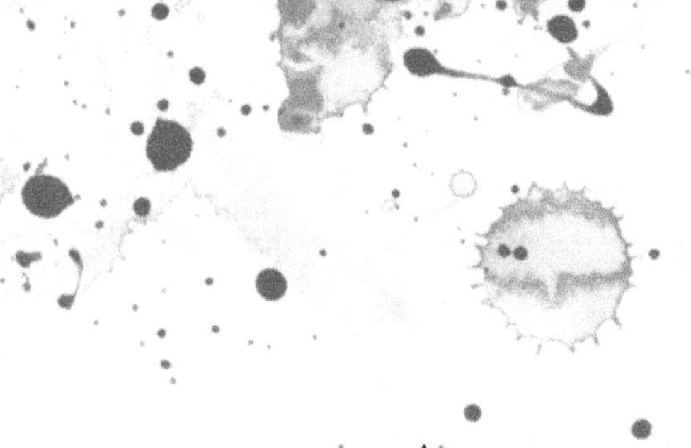

AURELIA

I downed another glass of blood, hating the feeling of *his* blood still in my mouth, knowing all the blood in the world wouldn't get rid of the pull in my chest to the man sitting right next to me.

I leaned into him and laughed at something random he said. My brother was eyeing us from across the table, looking for a flaw. But there wouldn't be one.

Caspian wrapped an arm around me and left a kiss on my forehead. It was enough for my brother to look away.

The wedding party was small, with only a few of his most loyal allies and a few hours of laughing and kissing their asses. We would be done soon, though, because there was one thing we were required to do to keep our standing in the vampire community, and my brother knew it.

There was only one thing royal vampires loved more than a messy wedding.

A messy after-party, perfect for blackmail.

General Lee was at the end of the table, his eyes lingering on me for far longer than they ever had before. He was pissed, it didn't take a genius to understand it.

I pulled one over on him to get this done, and his gaze told me

I would pay for it, but he would have to go through my brother first. And, by the looks of it, he wasn't going to escape punishment from Adrian that easily.

I pulled away from Caspian with a sigh.

"Well, this has been fun, but Caspian and I have to go…"

I trailed off and gave him a meaningful look.

"Break in this new bond," he finished for me with a devilish smile that I'm sure any other vampire might have swooned over.

Inside, I was holding back my gag.

"Congratulations to the happy couple," my brother said, raising his glass. His face held a smile, but his eyes were sharp and watching my every move. "I will see you in the morning."

For punishment and a debrief.

As per our custom, we should be taken back to the family estate, but my brother wasn't going to let me out of his sight so easily.

"How could we miss our first transfer?" Caspian said with a knowing smile. "Three hundred vampires, ready to take their bond, fifty feeders, and the deed to a very profitable gold mine. Just like we agreed on."

On the outside, my brother's face didn't change, but the glint in his eyes was back. The other vampires around the table could barely conceal their gasps and whispers.

"Off with you now," he said, his smile dropping as he turned to the rest. "Where were we?"

We turned, arm in arm, keeping close until we left the castle and were loaded into the awaiting car. As soon as the soundproof divider was up and we were away from hearing distance, I pushed him away with a scoff.

"Did you have to get so touchy-feely? Krae, the bond feels so *gross*." I let out a noise of disgust and rolled my eyes.

"You think your blood was any better? I can't get the disgusting taste out of my mouth," Caspian replied, shooting me a glare as he continued to rub off the invisible dirt I somehow left on him.

"The blood you gave me was far more than I gave you. *I* should be the one complaining about the feeling of the bond," I said with a hiss.

I could still feel it settling deep inside me, trying to push Vesper's bond out. I hated how invasive it felt.

Back when I had been accidentally bonded with Vesper, I had been pissed. It hurt. Like I had been forced into a position I didn't want. But then I realized it was just because I had been scared of what it meant to be bonded. Scared to lose her. Lose myself. Not because I didn't want it. *Her.*

Now that I was bonded for the purpose of marriage to someone I barely knew, I started to understand what it truly meant for the choice of who I loved to be taken from me.

This was supposed to be the most important moment of my life. But the person was all wrong, and it was tainted with anger and the hope of revenge.

I shifted, trying to get as far away from him as possible. He signed on to this to help me. He was barely getting anything out of it. But I couldn't help but hate every moment as the bond settled in my chest.

We were lucky Adrian accepted us without a public fight, though I was concerned about what it meant when I finally made my way back home. He hadn't hurt me yet, mostly only threatened, his power enough to control me.

But I had a sinking suspicion my luck was running out.

Images of Vesper and Cedar as they fought against my brother's guards came to my mind. I was happy she had been released. At least I hoped that's what happened, given what Atlas said about them being her guard.

I yearned to go to them. To let them take me away like they promised. It was a dream. One my mind had wondered to more than once.

My bond with Caspian pulsed as I thought of my lost lovers. It felt like an intruder.

"Thanks," I muttered after a few long moments. "For helping me."

I turned to look at him, but instead of looking disgusted, he seemed only slightly uncomfortable. Both of us were coming to terms with the fact that, while this might not be what we wanted, it was working.

"It's not like I have any use for my family's fortune," he said, then his gaze turned dark. "Plus, I would do just about anything to see that bastard pay for what he did to my little sister."

The pain in his eyes pulled my own from deep inside me. The memories I tried to bury from my time in the witch coven were pushing their way to the forefront.

"Still, I'm sure there's someone out there wanting to marry you for real." I gave him a small, but forced, smile.

His eyes shifted to his hands, then the window.

"No, he made that very clear. This marriage, while not fully what I imagined for myself, will send a good message."

I nodded and looked outside again.

I didn't think it was my place to ask anything else, so I let us sit in silence the rest of the way to our destination.

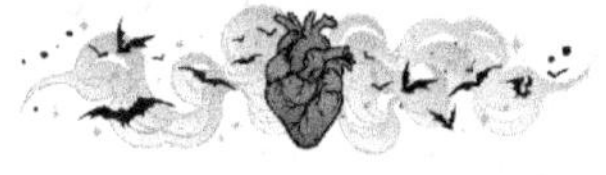

After the wedding, the small club seemed like another world.

It was the same place. The same vampires. The same purpose. But it just felt... different.

Maybe it was because *I* was different. And now I had my husband at my side.

Well, not really. I looked over to see my new husband at the far corner of the room, two vampires leaning over him and a human in his lap, his fangs sunk deep into his neck.

He was enjoying himself while I was stuck watching Dalia and

Fredrick suck face, drinking a glass of blood laced with some magical drugs.

I may as well live a little while I still have the chance.

I didn't normally dabble in it, preferring to keep my wits about me, but this very well could be the last time I could have this freedom. After this, we were putting our plan into action, and for better or worse... I was going to end it.

Just as I was running through my plans in my head, my chest started aching. An annoying feeling that only got more persistent as the seconds went on.

I looked at Caspian to see if it had anything to do with our bond, but he was still fangs-deep in the human.

When it got more intense, I sat up. A prickle at the back of my neck told me something was off. Like the calm before the storm. My internal warning system was telling me to prepare for a fight.

Is something happening?

Then I heard it. The light murmurs of vampires in the house as new guests were welcomed.

Intruder.

But instead of evacuating, which was protocol, there was the sound of shuffling, like whoever it was was being let through.

Next, I smelled them.

The comforting smell of sage and a slightly newer—sharper—amber smell.

Vesper and Cedar. Atlas had to be with them, or they would have been turned around at the door.

Shit.

I had only a few seconds before meeting them and risking ruining this whole thing.

Caspian met my eyes, and with one look, I told him to stay put. I left the small room I was in and headed to the one upstairs, the same one I found Caspian in when I proposed.

It would promise us the tiniest bit of privacy, and it had to be enough.

"Come find me, Little Mouse."

I knew she'd hear me, but her small growl was a good confirmation.

Excitement zapped up my spine as I hurried up the stairs. I looked back over my shoulder, taking in the debauchery happening in the main foyer. Vampires with their fangs sunk into necks, most of them wearing next to nothing, many with their faces twisted in pleasure even as a vampire hunter and a witch stood at the door.

Cedar and Vesper stood side by side, both looking up at me. Vesper's eyes were narrowed and red. Cedar's jaw was clenched.

In their gazes were promises of a punishment.

And I want to take it.

Everyone watched as they came in. Atlas was somewhere near the entrance. I couldn't see her, but I could feel the heaviness of her gaze. Turning, I finished climbing the stairs and ducked into the room, which had nothing but a few chairs around the edges and a chaise lounge.

I sat right in the middle of it, trying to look nonchalant, even though the bond was stirring to life in my chest. Mere moments later, they burst through the door, their eyes finding me immediately.

"Can't stay away now, can you?" I said, trying my best to sound like the spoiled princess they once knew. I even leaned slightly, letting my dress fall to the side.

My body was aching for them, and I knew with one look they were yearning for it too.

They were breathing heavily. Vesper was puffed up, looking like she was ready to attack.

But I didn't expect her to actually do it.

CEDAR

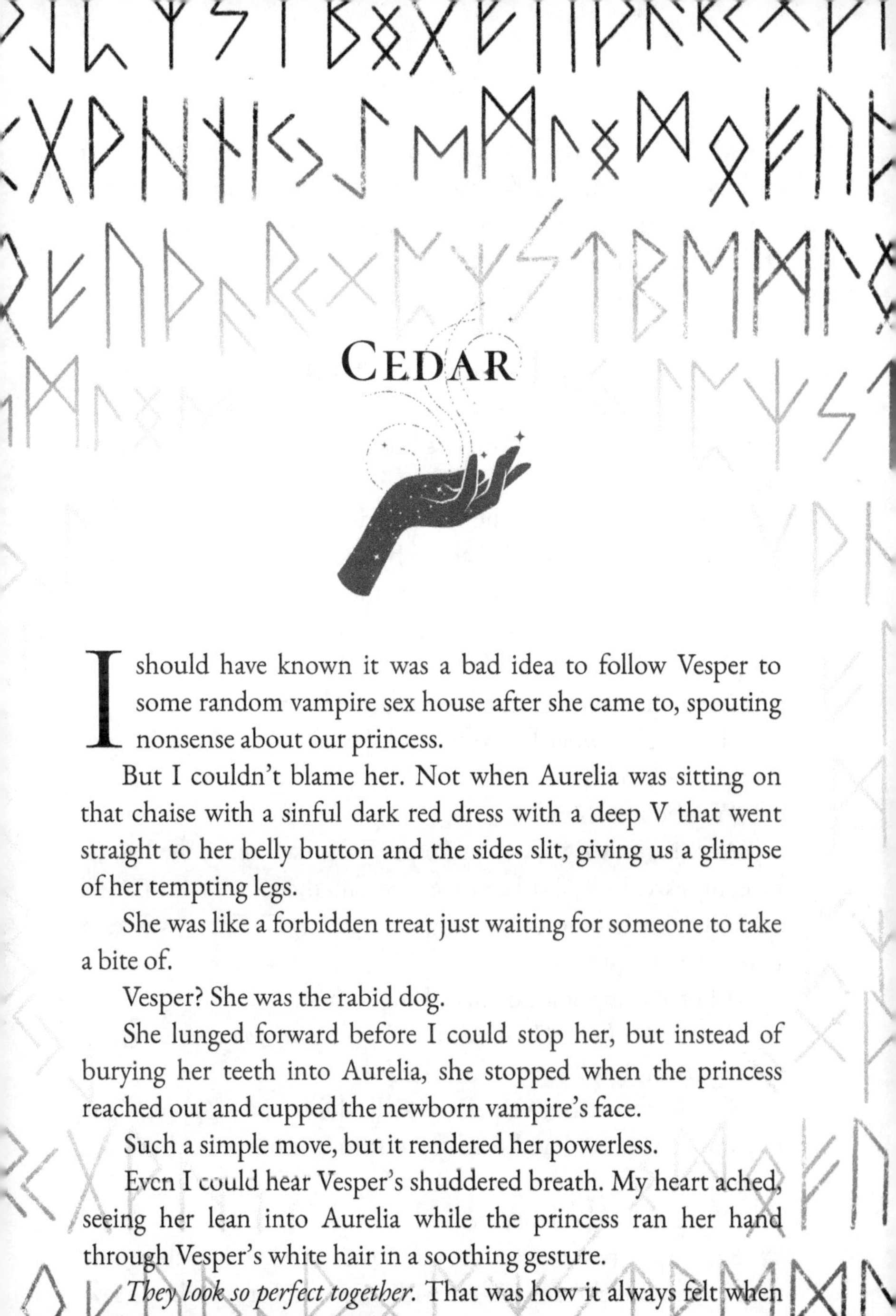

I should have known it was a bad idea to follow Vesper to some random vampire sex house after she came to, spouting nonsense about our princess.

But I couldn't blame her. Not when Aurelia was sitting on that chaise with a sinful dark red dress with a deep V that went straight to her belly button and the sides slit, giving us a glimpse of her tempting legs.

She was like a forbidden treat just waiting for someone to take a bite of.

Vesper? She was the rabid dog.

She lunged forward before I could stop her, but instead of burying her teeth into Aurelia, she stopped when the princess reached out and cupped the newborn vampire's face.

Such a simple move, but it rendered her powerless.

Even I could hear Vesper's shuddered breath. My heart ached, seeing her lean into Aurelia while the princess ran her hand through Vesper's white hair in a soothing gesture.

They look so perfect together. That was how it always felt when I was looking in, watching them.

It was torture having them away from me for so long, but for them? Their bond must have made it excruciating.

My heart twinged. I felt more like an outsider than ever before. They seemed to fall back into their roles so easily, but me? There was still something gnawing at my chest, a violent emotion that had me banging at the cage around my heart.

"Poor Little Mouse," Aurelia murmured, her voice full of mock pity.

Anger rose inside me, and my body moved of its own accord. I marched forward, ready to grab her by the hair and show her what it meant to leave us, but Vesper's broken voice stopped me in my tracks.

"You abandoned us," she whispered.

I could tell how hard that hit by the look in her eyes. For a minute, the mask dropped, and I saw the princess I knew.

"Without a word," I added. "I only figured it out when Atlas's people came to drag me back, saying you had left."

When she looked at me, I saw a flash of... *shame*?

"I am doing what I need to do," she said. As she slowly rose, Vesper grabbed her.

"You bonded him."

Aurelia refused to look at Vesper, but that meant she had to meet my gaze. I was shocked to see the pain there.

"That's what we do at vampire weddings." There was zero remorse in her tone.

A hot, cutting emotion licked at my chest.

She bonded him. The random vampire. And now she was going to go off and do gods know what with him.

She got away from Vesper and stalked forward, stopping right in front of me, her hand reaching out to brush mine. Electricity zapped.

"You'll see soon. Trust me."

She walked past me. I turned in a panic, my hand reaching out to grab her, but she dodged me with ease, and I froze when I saw who was waiting for her in the doorframe.

Her new husband.

Caspian stood there, looking at us with an unamused expression. My gaze lingered on his bloodied mouth and clothes.

"Are they bothering you?" he asked. As soon as the words were out of his mouth, the anger was back. I stepped forward, but Vesper's hand took mine, stopping me.

"You know they aren't," Aurelia hissed. "Let's go before we really cause a scene."

She left us without another glance, and just like that, I was cast aside again. *We*. But somehow it felt more targeted at me. She let Vesper touch her. She soothed her.

But me?

She barely had anything to say to me, and when I tried to reach out, she sidestepped me.

I don't understand.

Before Vesper was taken, I thought we were together. The three of us. But maybe I was wrong.

"Why'd you stop me?" I asked as Vesper came to stand at my side.

"The seer came to me in my dream," she replied.

"What?"

She nodded, her face strained.

"But first, I need blood, or I might actually kill someone."

Her arms wrapped around me, and I tilted my head to the side.

"Good witch." Her deep timbre had shivers going up my spine.

In a flash, her fangs were buried deep inside me. Intense fire ran through my neck and shoulders before being quelled by the venom.

I didn't fight the reaction it pulled from me.

I wanted to lose myself in it. Wanted to lose myself in her if it meant forgetting the betrayal for just a moment longer.

I let her back me up to the chaise Aurelia had been sitting on. With her fangs still in my neck, she hastily laid me down, moving on top of me. I held on to her, pulling her closer as the pleasure coursed through me and pulled me under a wave of warmth.

But all I could think of was Aurelia and the painful expression she left me with.

I couldn't take it anymore. I started trying to unbutton Vesper's clothes. I needed her closer.

She pulled her fangs from me, and I had to stop myself from begging her to put them back in. The hit from her venom was too much. My core was clenching, and I was unbelievably wet for her.

"I need you," I whispered. But the moment she met my eyes, it was like cold water splashed through me. "But..."

I swallowed the knot in my throat. I was aching for her to touch me. My cunt was begging for her to fuck me hard enough to seal away these unwanted feelings.

But Vesper, even in her bloodlust haze, saw something in me and paused, waiting.

"But I want her here too," I admitted, my voice wavering.

Shit. Pull it together.

I couldn't. I could feel the tears breaking in my eyes. I blinked rapidly and looked up at the ceiling.

And then Vesper wrapped her arms around me and laid her head on my chest.

"Soon," she vowed. "We will get her back."

I pushed my palms into my eyes, trying to stop the tears that were coming. I couldn't fully understand why it hurt so bad. Couldn't understand the reaction I was having.

How had this vampire princess gone from being the biggest annoyance I'd ever met to one of the two most important people in my life?

It was in that moment that, for the second time in my life, I prayed to my gods for someone other than myself.

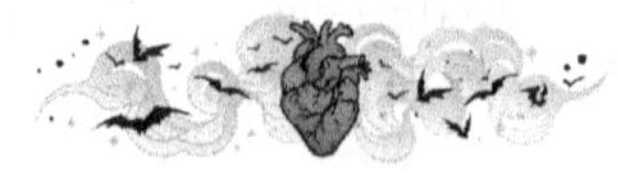

The dreams always started the same.

I was back in the coven. A young child watching as two people were burned alive with magic in front of her.

The same dream over and over again. It happened almost every single night. When I closed my eyes, the first thing I would see was the pain on my parents' faces.

I learned that if I concentrated hard enough, I could close my eyes. I could try to drown out the screams. I could pretend like they weren't dying right before my eyes.

I had blocked it out for so long and I wanted to keep it that way. But there was something—or should I say *someone*—forcing me to come to terms with it.

"You have to face it," the seer, Max, said from somewhere in the room, his voice louder than the screams.

"Stop showing me this," I asked, my voice hoarse from the effort it took to keep my screams inside me.

"The answers to your future are in your past. If you push this away—"

"I don't care!"

But it was a mistake because the moment I yelled, my eyes popped open, and I was met with the bodies of my parents engulfed by flames. It hit me like a ton of bricks. My chest twisted, my gut turned, and I felt like I was going to vomit.

My coven leader was right by my side, his hand on my shoulder.

For the first time, Max showed himself in front of me, blocking most of the bodies. Seeing him in his child form brought me back to myself, making me realize that this was a dream. That it couldn't hurt me.

No matter how much I didn't want to look at it, at least it wasn't happening right now.

And that's when I noticed something I hadn't before.

The runes.

I couldn't make them out, but I could tell that they were different from the ones we originally had on the cathedral floor.

And they weren't just near my parents—they were everywhere, their magic shining just as bright as the flames.

"The coven will burn."

Max met me with a smile, but it looked twisted, and suddenly his face started morphing. It changed into the face of my coven leader. Then Aurelia's father. Then her brother, who lunged at me, and—

I sat up with a gasp, my breathing coming heavy. Sweat dripped down my face, and my heart raced in my chest. There were hands on me, and I quickly tried to push them off.

Fear ate at me as I scrambled to get away from the hands. It felt like they were chasing me, forcing me down.

"Cedar!"

Vesper's voice brought me back. I blinked once, twice, three times. The room started to come into view. It was the same room she and I, and once, Aurelia, had occupied in Atlas's clan. Familiar territory that calmed my heart.

Vesper's eyes were turning red as they looked at me, but her expression was pained.

"It was just a dream," she said in a soothing voice. "I tried to wake you, but I couldn't."

I let out a sigh and let my head hang while she rubbed soothing circles over my back.

I tried to push away the images of my parents. But I couldn't. So I kept my mouth shut, unable to tell if the dream I had was the seer trying to get in touch with me or just my fucked-up trauma.

"Sorry," I muttered.

There was silence and then the shifting of the bedsheets as she got closer.

"They happen almost every night."

I looked up at her, shocked.

"You can tell?"

I thought I had been handling them well, waking up and turning away from her. As a vampire, she didn't need to sleep, but she still kept me company at night. Being able to wake up and have someone there helped with the nightmares.

They were worse when she wasn't there.

Vesper gave me a small smile.

"Your heart rate increases. You know, vampire hearing and all that."

I swallowed thickly and nodded.

"Ever since Max showed me the vision of my parents, that's all I can see. But I'm tired. Let me just—"

She pushed me back down onto the bed and wrapped her arms around me.

"Sleep, witch. I'll protect you from those bad dreams."

I managed a small laugh, but inside a feeling of dread came over me because I wasn't sure if she could save me from them.

"I'm sticky and sweaty," I said and pushed myself away from her. "I'll shower quickly and come back."

I sweetened my words with a kiss to her lips, and she smiled.

"You have ten minutes, then I'm coming after you."

Wishing I could tell her I'd be waiting for that, that I could be that carefree because I was just taking a random shower, I nodded before practically running to the bathroom.

I turned on every faucet to the max, hoping to drown out the sound in my head, then the shower to as hot as it would go.

I stripped, and only as the steam started to coat the mirror did I allow myself to turn and look at the scars that ran across my back.

Angry. Red. Pulsing.

My stomach twisted at seeing them. I could still feel a part of his magic running through me. Normally, the scars were barely there, but it was like my dreams called forth his magic, allowing it to show through my skin.

Jumping into the scalding hot water, I grabbed the nearest rag and started scrubbing my back as hard as I could in an attempt to rid myself of the dirty feeling.

Wishing Vesper would barge in here like she promised while knowing there was nothing she could do to help me.

VESPER

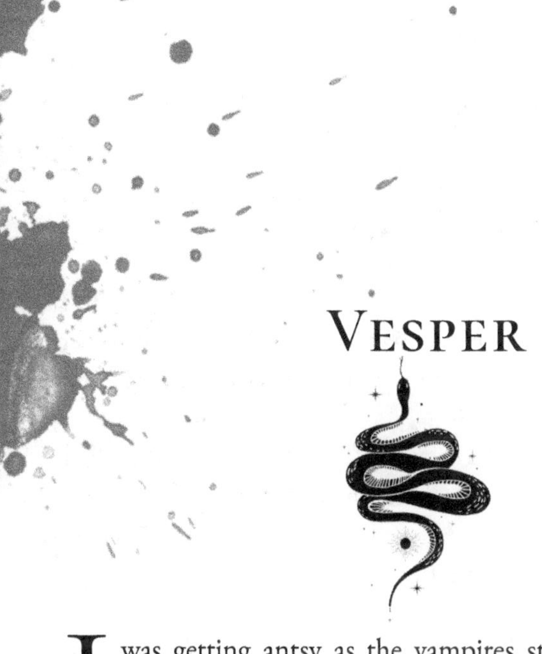

I was getting antsy as the vampires started to fill the small space.

Our meeting place of the day was a random, seemingly abandoned bar on the edge of a desolate town on the outskirts of Atlas's clan borders. It was run by a human, looked like it had had no customers for decades, and there was a special backroom that we used for this illicit meeting.

It smelled of stale beer and dust. My nose itched, and I fought to stop myself from sniffling. The tension rose as vampire after vampire ducked through the small doorway, their eyes always landing on me first, then Cedar, then Atlas.

Even though I was a vampire now, my training had me on edge and watching all of them on the off chance they'd attack.

My mind supplied me with some of the names and lineage, but mostly I had no idea who they were and how Atlas found them. The boarding school the hunter organization put us through had extensive backstories on the most prominent families, but we skipped over any they thought unnecessary.

My eyes shifted to Atlas, trying to use her as a gauge, but I couldn't tell whether she actually liked any of them. They were all met with the same deadpan stare.

She was wound extra tight after the wedding. If I was being honest, we all were.

Aurelia had offered no explanation. She simply told us to trust her. Given that she had left in the middle of the night to pledge her allegiance to her brother, it was hard to.

But no matter how mad I was, my heart told me she wouldn't tie herself to him. If anything, she may have been taken against her will and was trying to make sure we wouldn't cause a scene and make it worse for her.

Maybe she's protecting us. Anything made more sense than her *wanting* to go off and marry that random vampire.

Caspian Hart.

I tried to search my memory for him, but I was drawing a blank.

That's what I get for focusing more on combat than history.

When the last vampire stood around the table, silence fell around us. The dim lighting hanging overhead flickered. Everyone looked to Atlas to speak, but she made no move to. It was too tense to sit. Too tense to talk.

Cedar was by my side, her arms crossed, staring down at the vampires across from us. I didn't realize until that moment that she must be feeling very out of place. When one of them looked at her a little too long, I shifted so I was in front of her.

She caught my eye, and my mind went right back to the moment she woke up from her nightmare. That had been days ago, but she had one every night, and I hadn't been able to wake her since.

It hurt to see her in pain, clinging to the pillow and calling out for her parents.

I tried to hold her. Shake her. Call her name. Nothing worked. I was even considering biting her if it would pull her from her nightmare.

It would go on for a while. Hours sometimes, constantly stuck in the dream. Sometimes, when I thought it was over, she'd just start breathing heavily again, her heartbeat would pick up, and it would resume.

She woke up exhausted the following day, and even when I probed, she didn't want to talk about it. I knew it was about her parents, but I couldn't help but think that the stress from everything that was happening only made it worse.

My eyes shot back to Atlas. Things were getting uncomfortable.

"What are we waiting for?" I hissed at her under my breath. Her arms were crossed, and she kept her eyes trained on the door.

She dressed surprisingly casually today. Her coat lacked the jewels she normally wore, and there wasn't a strand of gold or silver in sight, but there was no mistaking the regal power she held over everyone in the room.

"One more," she grumbled, not looking at me.

"While we wait, I believe there are other matters we need to discuss," one of the older vampires said, his eyes traveling around the room. "The *princess* and her marriage."

My invisible hackles raised when she mentioned Aurelia, my hand coming to my side only for me to realize that I didn't have my sword or daggers with me. The council had taken them all away.

"I thought she would hold out," another said with a huff. "But she kneeled to her brother's whims, just like she did to her father's. It complicates things."

"Did you hear they already transferred three hundred vampires?" someone else asked. My fists balled, the urge to tear their throats out for even mentioning her threatening to overtake me.

"She's actively making this harder for us. We should include what to do about her as a topic in this meetin—"

I opened my mouth to shut him up, but the door slammed open, and all words dried on my mouth.

"I didn't know that I was such a *hot topic* in these parts."

Aurelia stood there in an all-black dress that hugged her

figure. Her dark brown hair was in waves around her, framing her face. Her eyes were turning red, the threat of her anger clear as day, lips a matching blood red, looking ready for us to ruin.

Notably, her husband was missing from her side.

An audible gasp filled the room.

She looked over every single vampire, almost as if she was forcing them to recognize her. The power she held over them was greater than Atlas's. As soon as she stepped inside, all eyes were on her, and people turned their bodies so they were facing her. She had this magnetic pull, and *fuck,* did it make me angry.

I held back after what the seer told me, though. I didn't want to ruin this. I wanted to trust her.

But why the fuck did she have to go and get married like that?

No matter what anyone said about fixing fate and the prophecy, I just couldn't get behind the fact that a random *man* was calling my bonded his *wife.*

"Great! Now, if we're all done complaining, we can get down to the actual work."

I shot Atlas a look, but she ignored me once again. She obviously knew Aurelia was coming but chose to keep it from Cedar and me.

"He's getting stronger," Aurelia said, addressing the room. "I don't know how, but I'm working on it. I have people in the castle reporting his moves, but he rarely leaves. Even so, it's a notable difference from when he first took over, and even then he was able to kill my father without blinking an eye. If we want to act, it needs to be soon."

"What can we even do?" one of them asked.

"Right. We're outnumbered. He has more guards at his disposal now that your *husband* gave him some," someone spat. "Even if we gathered everyone we have, it still wouldn't work."

She let out a low growl. A zap of excitement went up my spine.

I had always loved the feisty version of her, but now that I was a vampire, it was even stronger. Like my feral side was reacting to hers.

"Even half of the original Castle guards would demolish all your clans combined," she hissed. "We need people, but that's only one aspect. We are missing power. A power that *they* don't have. We need..."

Her eyes shot to Cedar. *Oh no.* I couldn't help the growl that came from my chest.

"We need witches at our side."

My eyes shot to our witch. She met Aurelia's gaze head-on, not flinching. The tension skyrocketed, the two of them locked in an intense battle, neither wanting to be the first to give in.

I tried not to shift as heat curled in my belly. Seeing the two of them go against each other did something to me that I never expected. This was really not the time and place to get turned on, but here we were.

I missed them. I missed us. I wanted to push them both inside a room and f—

"So you're here to order us around now?"

Aurelia's lips quirked.

"Is that how this is reading to you, *witch*?"

The last word was spoken in a low, deadly tone.

My brat is coming out to play.

Judging from the electricity bouncing between them, I could tell they were both thinking of our time together at Atlas's castle.

"She's here to help," Atlas hissed at Cedar.

I straightened up to my full height and turned to Atlas, giving her a warning glare. One she returned with even more venom.

"I think she's asking for it instead," Cedar said and crossed her arms over her chest, a cruel smirk spreading across her face. "Say it again, *Princess.*"

That smirk looked so unnatural. The witch I'd grown to love had never been cruel.

Is she mad?

My hand found hers, and she faltered just slightly.

"I am," Aurelia said, not breaking character. "In order to bring him down. We all need to pitch in to do that. The prophecy warned us of this, or did you forget?"

At the mention of the prophecy, Cedar stiffened.

"I remember," she spat. "But this won't be easy, and I won't be putting my—*our*—lives on the line without something in return. And I have a condition."

Aurelia smiled. "Name it."

"Out. Everyone."

The vampires looked at each other at Cedar's command. Then there was a small chuckle, no one even bothering to move a muscle.

I growled, not liking how they were belittling her.

"Surely it can be said in front of the whole group," Aurelia offered.

But Cedar was the one smiling now.

"I'm calling in my favor, *Princess*."

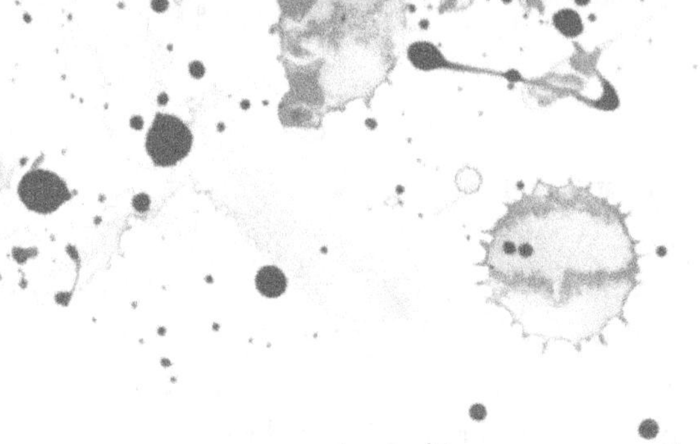

AURELIA

I cursed internally but fought for it not to show on my face.

How does she even remember that?

I kept that part of us far back in the past, not even thinking about it after Vesper stabbed me in the fucking chest.

It was the price of her helping me bring Vesper back.

This is a punishment.

The look in her eyes told me she had been holding on to it for a moment exactly like this. A time when she could force me to do whatever she wanted. My body vibrated with anticipation at what it could be.

The salacious part of my mind wanted me on my knees for her.

The other part just wanted to feel her skin against mine.

I deserved whatever it was she was about to unleash on me. Maybe if it was extra painful, it'd help me get over this grief I was feeling. Though my back ached at the idea of physical punishment, still sore from the one my brother bestowed upon me.

But what choice did I even have at this point? If I didn't get them back on my side, there would be no winning against Adrian.

Something told me her *favor* was one I wouldn't want the others seeing. Especially since I was newly married and didn't need anyone outside those stupid fucking parties knowing just how fake our marriage was.

"And you will get it," I said before turning to the rest of the vampires. "As for all of you, we need to start gathering more clan heads, royal families, anyone with even an ounce of power that is able to keep their mouth shut. I don't care if you have to cross borders to get it done."

Some vampires looked around, unsure if they should listen to my command, but in the end, they all bowed their heads to me. *As they should.* I might not be the head of the Castle family, but the power still ran through my veins. They would be idiots not to recognize that I was one of the only people that could get an in with my brother.

Each vampire in the room had been affected by Adrian one way or another. He had been indiscriminate in his killings before ascending the throne, which meant most of the people here had probably lost someone, even if it was just a clan member.

Atlas cleared her throat. "It is decided then. Everyone here is to go out and start recruiting. And don't think I don't have eyes in each of your ranks. I will know if one of you has so much as a thought of betraying us."

"And I won't hesitate to come collecting heads," Vesper added, her deep growl sending a shiver up my spine.

The tattoo on her skin shone under the dim light like a bright warning light. Her eyes turned red, daring anyone to try and fight her.

"Now, if there are no questions, everyone except the hunter and witch—*leave.*"

The vampires started filing out, but Atlas stopped at my side, waiting until the others left.

"Are you safe?"

I tried not to flinch at the softness of her tone. It was so disarming that I almost spilled everything to her. *Almost.*

"Thank you for your concern, but Caspian isn't—"

"I mean General Lee," she cut me off, causing me to rear back in shock.

He wasn't my favorite choice of guard, but he hadn't hurt me. Not even after my obvious ploy to get him out of the engagement ceremony.

"No," I said in a whisper. "What do you know about him?"

Atlas looked back at Cedar and Vesper, who were watching us with narrowed eyes and matching cross-armed stances.

"I knew of him in another life, and he was never this strong. Not enough to get rank in the council. Whatever he's done, I would guarantee it's the same thing your brother's doing."

My mind swirled with possibilities.

"It would make sense since he tied himself to Adrian," I murmured. "Though he acts more like a lapdog than a council overseer."

"Be wary of him," she advised. "I'll try to see if I can get eyes on him. In the meantime, I'll let you—"

"Can we get on with it?" Cedar asked with a sinister smirk.

Atlas let out a growl and turned, leaving the room and shutting the door behind her.

Well, looks like those two aren't on the best of terms.

I let out a sigh, both relieved and stressed to be stuck in a room alone with them.

"Look, Cedar, I get that you're mad, but this is bigger than us—"

"Shut up, *Brat*."

Anger, desire, and shock burst to life in my veins as Cedar commanded my attention not just with her voice, but with the magic that burst out around us.

"Cedar—"

"This is my favor, Vesper," she hissed at the hunter. "You weren't the only one she abandoned."

Her words were like a thorn digging into my heart, but I took them in stride.

"Say it," I growled and puffed up my chest. I couldn't deny

how hot her anger made me. I had been fantasizing about this day since the moment we'd been separated.

"Why are you doing this? Marrying him? Leaving us in the middle of the night? *Abandoning* Vesper and forcing her to live out her punishment without so much as a second thought?"

Guilt shot through me so potently it turned into a knot in my throat, making me go from hot and horny to ashamed far too quickly.

"I'm doing what I need to do. Have you even considered that?"

With each passing moment, she took another step forward, stalking me like she was a big bad wolf and I was small, quivering prey. I couldn't help the steps I took back, but I was cornered when my back hit the wall.

"I've been filled in," she spat. "You're being naïve if you think *this* will fulfill the prophecy."

I stood firm as she came to stand in front of me.

"I made a calculated choice. I am positive it will fulfill the prophecy requirements," I said, my voice wavering. The way she spoke had such sureness, I was scared that I truly made the wrong decision for a moment.

My life, and theirs, hinged on this. If I made one wrong move, I would doom all three of us.

"Do you feel him right now? The blood bond?" she asked, her hand moving to rest on my chest.

The contact burned. My breath hitched.

"Yes." It seemed to stir whenever he was mentioned. There was a bit of confusion and annoyance, which meant he could likely feel what I was going through.

Cedar let out a long breath, her eyes trailing down my body. I became acutely aware of every single curve shown through my tight dress.

I dressed to show the crowd I was in charge, but her undressing me with her eyes made it obvious who was truly in charge here.

"First Vesper, now this random fucker." Her eyes shot to mine. "I have to admit I'm a bit jealous."

The air felt like it was knocked from my chest.

"You *want* to bond me?" I asked, unable to come to terms with what she was asking.

A witch, bonded to a vampire... Would it work? Would a witch even want to be connected to a vampire like that? We'd never been on good terms as a species.

More importantly... Would she?

I had been so angry when Vesper bonded me, taking the choice away from me, but I never thought any other being would actually *want* to be bonded to me.

I felt... *needed.* Desired in a way I never felt before.

The look in her eyes told me she knew what she was asking. The weight of it.

"I want to do so many things to you, Princess," she whispered. "But a bond sounds like the perfect way to start."

She lifted her wrist to my mouth. My fangs ached to sink into her skin. I could smell the blood just below the surface, calling to me. Vesper's venom was mixed in with it, making it that much sweeter.

"I'm calling in my favor. It's up to you if you want to be a woman of your word."

I smiled and grasped her wrist.

"Vesper, come hold our witch."

Cedar raised a brow at me, but Vesper obediently obeyed, like the little sub she still was. But there was something more than that. It was the way her eyebrows were pulled together. Her pupils dilated.

And *her scent.* Maybe it wasn't that she was being subby, but that she couldn't hold herself back any longer.

"Precautions," I murmured and brought her wrist closer, licking her pulse point. "I would have bonded you even without the favor. All you had to do was ask."

And with that, I sank my teeth into her wrist.

She'd taken my venom well before, but how would her magic react when the bond was settling?

I guess we're about to find out.

She leaned back into Vesper, a sigh falling from her lips, but I kept my gaze on her as my venom pushed through her veins. Only when that delicious redness rose on her cheeks did I start to take down gulps of her blood.

Her flavor exploded in my mouth. Earthy, a bit tangy, and a whole bunch of sweetness. Different from before, or maybe I had just forgotten how mouthwateringly she tasted after being gone for so long.

Heat started gathering low in my belly, the need to touch her becoming unbearable, especially as she let out the smallest moan. Vesper was there, her hands rubbing up her sides. I tried not to gasp when red eyes met mine.

I forced myself to pull away.

Bringing my wrist to my mouth, I sank my teeth into my flesh. Pain flashed through me, but then Cedar was there, grabbing my wrist and forcing it to her lips. She took gulp after gulp, her eyes closing as if she was... *enjoying it.*

The voracity of her drinking had my breath catching.

She moaned into me, acting like my blood was the most delicious thing, just before her eyes snapped open.

It was the only warning we got before her magic started expanding around us.

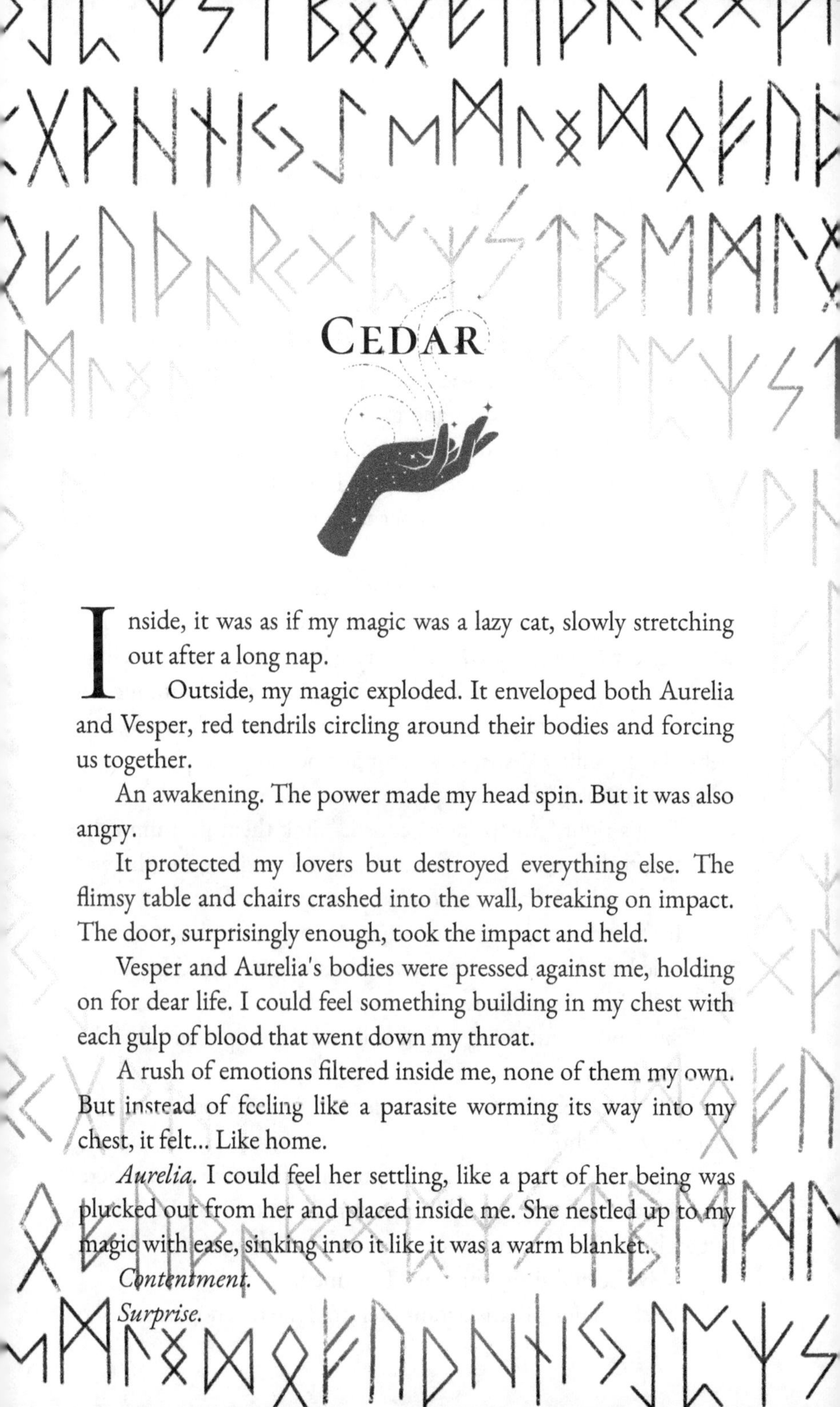

CEDAR

Inside, it was as if my magic was a lazy cat, slowly stretching out after a long nap.

Outside, my magic exploded. It enveloped both Aurelia and Vesper, red tendrils circling around their bodies and forcing us together.

An awakening. The power made my head spin. But it was also angry.

It protected my lovers but destroyed everything else. The flimsy table and chairs crashed into the wall, breaking on impact. The door, surprisingly enough, took the impact and held.

Vesper and Aurelia's bodies were pressed against me, holding on for dear life. I could feel something building in my chest with each gulp of blood that went down my throat.

A rush of emotions filtered inside me, none of them my own. But instead of feeling like a parasite worming its way into my chest, it felt... Like home.

Aurelia. I could feel her settling, like a part of her being was plucked out from her and placed inside me. She nestled up to my magic with ease, sinking into it like it was a warm blanket.

Contentment.

Surprise.

Satisfaction.

"Cedar," Vesper groaned behind me. "Reel it in or—"

"Bite me," I breathed, my gaze on Aurelia, and I felt it in my chest before I saw it flash in her eyes.

She wants us.

She had been hiding behind that cruel mask of hers, but I saw right through it. Now, with the bond, I had a direct link to her true feelings. Her blood was sweet and a bit spicy, just like her personality. It coated my tongue and throat and warmed my belly.

Vesper's teeth grazed my throat, and the world slowed, the three of us moving together as the bond solidified in my chest.

When Vesper finally buried her teeth in my neck, our princess let out the most sinful gasp.

Pain played at my senses. I knew ingesting vampire blood was painful for mortals, and even as a witch, I could still feel a bit of it. My magic was working overtime, trying to burn off the feeling, only to be overwhelmed as Vesper pumped her venom into me.

I lowered Aurelia's wrist, and she immediately moved it behind me, pulling Vesper closer, forcing her fangs deeper.

I was unable to hold in my gasp.

"That's right," the princess cooed. "Sink them in, pump the venom into her veins." Her voice was husky, telling me she was just as affected as I was. "Are you happy now?"

Her face came close enough that our lips were almost touching. I tried to close the space between us, but she pulled back ever so slightly, just out of my reach.

The most humiliating whine fell from my lips, and Aurelia tilted her head.

"Oh, my poor witch. So neglected. Has Vesper not been treating you right?"

Vesper growled, the vibration spreading from the place where my back and her chest met. In my wanton state, I couldn't help but arch into her, wanting more than just her fangs in me.

"We've been waiting for you," I moaned.

The sharp tick of satisfaction I felt told me just how much she liked to hear that, just as she placed her other hand on my chest, right where the bond was, and slipped it inside my shirt.

I groaned as her fingers brushed over my nipple. She started teasing me, rolling the sensitive bud between her fingers, but when she moved her hand down, it got caught on the buttons.

Without thinking, I ripped my shirt open for her.

"So desperate," she said with a little chuckle that had my toes curling.

Vesper pulled her fangs from me with a roar, and I felt hot blood drip down my neck.

"Put me out of my misery, Princess."

Her lips twitched.

"Who's begging now?"

Vesper's hands moved to explore my chest while Aurelia's fingers slowly made their way into my pants.

My breathing deepened. The pleasure, even from such light touches, was setting me on fire. My head was spinning, my body yearning for more.

There was only one thing that would take away this pain.

Being filled.

By both of them.

"I need you," I gasped. "Both of you."

My cunt was so swollen and needy that the first time Aurelia's fingers brushed against my clit had me crying out. Vesper's hand followed, guiding her fingers to my entrance.

"Lean back into me. Spread your legs," Vesper commanded with a growl.

"Princess, on your knees," I ordered and let them undo my pants.

"Anything for my bonded."

Aurelia fell to the ground with a thud. Her dress was so tight that it rode up, showing me her legs as she knelt for me.

It was intoxicating to watch her below me, her breasts spilling out of her top and her thighs bared to me.

Once my pants were off, she positioned herself between my legs.

"This seems like a lot more than only one favor," she teased.

My hand tangled in her hair, and I pushed her mouth to my pussy.

"Lick, Brat. I want to send you back to your husband with my cum smeared on your lips. When he kisses you, I want him to taste me."

I swear I felt her smirk against my cunt. But when her lips circled my clit and began the slow, sucking motion, I lost myself.

Vesper kept her end of the deal, holding me with her vampire strength. Placing one leg between mine, she pulled me back, opening me even further for our princess.

Then her fingers came into play, spreading my folds so Aurelia had complete access to me. At that point, she was the only thing holding me up. My knees would have given out if not for her.

My first orgasm hit me without warning. I was so focused on feeling both of them and the bond igniting inside me that I didn't notice it creeping up on me.

I cursed as I came, losing my balance entirely when Vesper shifted, and my hand shot forward to catch myself on the wall.

"What the fuck—"

Vesper's hands pulled the rest of my shirt off so she could leave hot kisses on my back.

"Perfect," Aurelia purred, her lips right at my clit. Her fingers teased my entrance. "Cedar, tell our hunter what you want."

I was going to, but I lost my train of thought when she resumed sucking. I was annoyed that she was trying to control the situation, so I tangled my hand in her hair and guided her where I wanted her.

"Tell me what you want," Vesper whispered against my skin.

"Fill me, together."

Her hum of approval had me lighting up inside, and then her fingers trailed my back, lower and lower, until they were able to slip between my legs and—

"Oh gods," I forced out, and I could feel their laughter against my skin where their mouths were touching me.

"No gods are coming to save you now," Vesper whispered in my ear.

Both had two fingers inside me, letting me get used to the feeling before they started moving them in tandem.

The bond was roaring to life between Aurelia and me, and I was loving every single moment. It strengthened the longer we were connected. My magic had calmed down, becoming a constant low hum that surrounded us.

Complete. For the first time since the three of us got together, I felt complete.

"Is our princess a woman of her word?" Vesper asked from behind me, her fangs teasing my back.

"She has a long way to go," I said breathlessly, earning a glare from her as she continued to suck on my clit like a good brat. "But this is a good start."

I wasn't going to last much longer. My second orgasm was rising as my cunt squeezed their fingers.

Together, they plunged deeper, deeper than ever before, and when Aurelia curled her fingers, I threw my head back.

It overtook me.

This time, my magic didn't hold back. It expanded, throwing the already destroyed room into further disarray.

I held onto the feeling of the three of us for a long moment, forgetting everything that brought us here. If I closed my eyes, maybe I could imagine we were back in Atlas's place together.

But that wasn't real.

Aurelia stood, and I leaned back, my eyes falling to her lips, waiting for... something? She hadn't touched Vesper, and she was her bonded too. But she just shook her head, almost as if she knew what I was thinking.

"Your favor is paid in full, witch," she said, and just as she was about to turn away, she paused. "And I'm not a *princess* anymore. I'm—"

But the word wouldn't come.

"You'll always be our bratty princess," I offered.

With a huff, she took off, slamming the door behind her, leaving only Vesper and me, both of us unmoving for a while. I knew Vesper had to be hurting, dying for her too, so I didn't say anything.

Until her hands wrapped around me, her lips at my ear.

"She's still ours."

I swallowed down the hurt of her leaving and nodded.

"Ours."

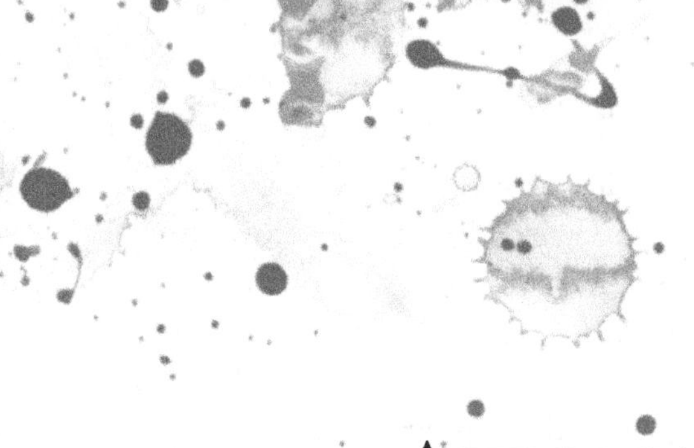

Aurelia

I fought the urge to cover my mouth as thick vampire blood sprayed in the air.

The sun had just started peeking over the mountains, and the first thing Adrian decided he wanted to do was spar, which meant lining up the strongest guards in the palace and decimating them. Today, that included most of his inner circle. He had long since taken out most of the other vampires' guards and was now forced to go after his own men.

Less work for me, I guess.

Adrian was shirtless, blood drying on him from previous battles. I didn't even know how many—I lost count at eight. We were in the outer courtyard, luckily away from the gardens and anything else that was left of my mother.

It was the same place where my father had put the hunters on display. It wasn't that long ago but felt like centuries.

I wished the hunters gave a shit about this new development. Maybe sending more to help take him down.

What a thought. Vampire hunters actually doing good for once.

In any case, if Adrian kept doing this, he might end up cannibalizing his inner circle himself. No intervention needed.

A woman can dream.

His inner circle of vampires, which he had brought with him and was now down to three, General Lee, and I were standing in the front row. Behind us, family members started to line up to watch, knowing how annoyed he got when they missed one of these.

My brother laughed when the vampire that once protected him fell to his knees, blood gushing from the wound on his neck. But it wasn't enough. Adrian grabbed his head and tore it off with the ease of plucking a petal from a flower.

He showed it off like a trophy, stopping when I met his gaze, and I made a show of giving him a polite clap.

"Where's your *husband*?" General Lee asked, coming to stand by me.

"In his palace, where I should be, and yet here I am. Watching a bloodbath."

General Lee let out a huff.

"Where you should be is with Solei," he said, a low growl lacing his words. "But somehow you managed to get out of that."

"And now I am stuck in the Castle palace until I'm deemed trustworthy enough to go out on my own." I turned to him with a saccharine smile. "But who knows if that will take a month or an eternity?"

General Lee gave me a venomous smile back.

"That didn't stop you. One of my men told me you were supposed to meet your husband yesterday, but you showed up an hour past the agreed time. Care to share where you went?"

I tried not to let the panic show on my face as images of Cedar's pleasure-filled face flashed across my mind.

"Should I warn my husband that you have spies in his ranks, or is this just some type of far-away-with-binoculars, creepy-stalking shit? Either way, that's a little embarrassing for a *general*, no?"

"Deflecting doesn't look good on you," he hissed, keeping his voice low, but there was an obvious spike in tension between us. Something brushed across my skin. It felt dark and caused a chill to go up my spine. "You won't get away with this insolence."

I made a show of looking at my nails with a frown.

"On the other hand, failing your kind and being knocked down a peg looks *really* good on you."

Threading my hands behind my back, I gave him a mock bow, not bothering to say goodbye to Adrian as he was already claws-deep in another vampire. Leaving the courtyard, I entered the palace, only to catch the same feeder I bribed to fuck the general lingering in the shadows.

Taking my chance, I went after him, letting him lead me further into the house. It wasn't until we reached the covered outdoor corridor that looked over the garden that he turned around to speak to me.

"First off, that man fucks like he has *experience*, and I mean, like, *good* experience—"

"Get to the point. What did you find out?" I asked with an annoyed sigh.

He gave me a smile.

"If you must know, he has a nasty scar on his chest."

"A scar?" I scoffed. "If that's all, you can get out of my sight—"

"Not a random scar. Like a drawing. It was disgusting, if I'm being honest, but I could ignore it since I wasn't facing him most of the ti—"

"Can you draw it?"

I didn't want to get caught talking to him. I had given him specific instructions to stay out of sight, especially where the general was concerned. But something about the way that he was describing this scar made me instantly suspicious.

He nodded. "Well, most of it. It looked a little weird. I'd never seen anything like it, but I can try—"

He was cut off, a claw coming straight out of his chest. The vampire's eyes widened, and his mouth stayed open in a frozen scream. I jerked back as blood sprayed my face, a scream about to be unleashed from my own throat when I saw the general's face peeking from behind.

He looked more murderous than ever. His eyes red, his face twisted in a snarl. But that wasn't all. Black veins were coming from his eyes and going down his neck.

He pulled his hand from the vampire's chest and pushed his body to the floor, his life gone in seconds.

"I've been looking for him," the general said and walked forward to wipe his bloody hand on my dress. "Thanks for leading the way. It's not often that I leave them alive afterwards, but, you know, I was busy."

For the first time, there was a newfound fear in my heart.

He reminded me so much of Adrian when he went up against the witches, but there was something different about him. And the black lines told me magic was somehow involved.

"You're lucky your bloodline is important, or I would've torn out your guts and decorated the castle with them."

He said it with an actual smile. A real one that looked like he was excited about the idea.

"You and my brother have a flair for the violence and gore. Even killing innocent feeders and guards. I wonder why."

He looked at me for a moment, and then his hand was around my neck.

"I need you alive," he spat. "But that doesn't mean I can't make your life miserable. Think twice about speaking to me like this again. And don't try to manipulate your way into getting dirt on me. It won't work."

"I came pretty close. The scar I heard about—"

His nails dug into the side of my throat and stole my breath. I was rendered useless, something forbidding about the way his face was changing, turning him into something else, giving me pause.

"If you know what's good for you, you'll forget all about that. Trust me, whatever answers you think you'll get won't do you any good."

I gave him a sweet smile, but both of us knew there was no way I was letting this go.

"Sure thing, General. Now, unhand me."

For a moment, I didn't think he would, but then he slowly backed away from me. I tried not to look at the vampire on the ground, his death weighing on me.

He was nice.

"I came to find you because Atlas's men are here. She just can't seem to get enough of you, can she? Was she who you were visiting? Maybe the little toys she has in her possession?"

Too close for comfort.

I wanted to tear his throat out for referring to them as *toys*. But I needed to play my part. I couldn't let my excitement show.

"She said she has a wedding gift and that she was going to send someone to pick me up today. I totally forgot," I lied quickly, and I was ready to turn when his chuckle stopped me.

"Funny, they said something similar."

I turned back to look at him. The veins were slowly fading away.

"Do you need anything else from me?"

"Not yet, Princess. Soon. You'll see."

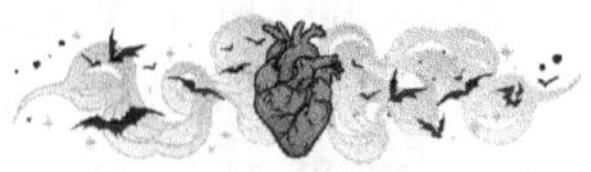

Coming back to Atlas's castle was like a shock to my system. It towered over me, the darkness cloaking it menacingly.

The last time I was here, Vesper was taken from me by force.

A lifetime had passed since then, and it felt different now. I had Cedar deep inside my chest, the bond between us tugging me closer to her. Vesper was there as well, albeit her bond was not as strong. The two of them twirled together inside me in a way I'd never experienced before.

Caspian's bond had been fully pushed to the side, my body

and heart somehow having enough power to render it useless. It was like they knew it was an intruder and were forcing it out.

Part of me should probably be annoyed with the possessiveness coming through our weird three-way bond, but I found myself oddly satisfied by it. And, for the first time, I found myself utterly alone.

I hadn't brought any of the guards with me, nor had I let the driver drop me off within twenty feet of the place. I walked the winding path through the forest alone with the eyes of Atlas's guards on me. I couldn't see or hear them, but I could feel them.

It didn't bother me.

My loneliness used to stifle me. Render me a useless mess. But now it empowered me. And as I marched right up to Atlas's gates, her clan members were up there, looking down on me.

The gate opened, and Atlas was waiting for me at the door, her eyes never leaving mine.

We hadn't had time to talk about my rejection of her proposal, and I was worried she would bring it up, but instead she merely stepped to the side and motioned for me to come in.

"It's nice to see you in one piece," she said, her voice strangely tense. "I was worried."

"Can you imagine if he killed his princess after she just came back from her torturous time in the witch coven? *Chaos.*"

Either my mind was playing tricks on me, or I finally got a small smirk out of Atlas.

"I wouldn't put it past him. But he's not the one I'm most worried about," she grumbled under her breath. She stepped forward, her hand raising as if to brush my arm, but stopped midway. "Truly. I've been worried about you."

I took her hand and gave it a squeeze. "Thank you for everything. I'm sorry I couldn't marry you."

She shook her head and pulled her hand away.

"It's okay, my love. I think I understand."

The nickname caused the tension in my shoulders to melt.

"You do?" I asked teasingly. The bond was getting impatient, tugging me forward.

She sent me a sly smile.

"Not at all, actually. But I trust you. Now, let's get you to your bonded before they start wrecking my furniture—*again*."

Excitement unraveled in my chest. I could imagine Vesper and Cedar getting so angry with Atlas they decided to take it upon themselves and give her room a new makeover.

Atlas showed me down the hall and through the first waiting room. The castle seemed surprisingly empty, or not, considering that, to them, I was the enemy.

"They're in there." Atlas pointed at the open door, but I stopped at the threshold, giving her a look.

"We should probably talk about General Lee," I said. "I found out something. Though I want everyone to hear it."

"We can discuss it in the meeting after, but first..." She nodded to the door again. "They asked for privacy."

Atlas sent me a lingering look before she turned around and walked down the hallway.

If my heart could speed up in my chest, it would be going a million miles a second.

I walked in and saw them immediately, both standing.

"Have time to talk, Princess?" Cedar asked and motioned for me to take a seat on the couch. I looked at her and then at Vesper, but neither said anything more.

They're probably still upset over the way I left last time. Well, so am I.

"How generous," I mumbled, sitting down. "This is my long-awaited wedding present?"

The memory of Cedar's blood was fresh in my mind. Her taste on my lips. Vesper's fingers moving with mine as we fucked our witch.

I could feel that she was thinking about it too through the bond.

Cedar walked around to the other side of the couch. Slow and languid, like a cat, but I hadn't forgotten how her magic had reacted to our bond. Heat and excitement burst through me.

She placed her hands on the back of the couch, one on either side of me. Vesper simply stared at us before she stepped forward slowly.

"What did your husband say when he tasted me on your lips?"

I knew she was trying to get a rise out of me by mentioning Caspian. We all knew he was nothing to me.

"That you tasted delicious."

She let out a huff.

"Don't tell me you washed me off."

It was my turn to laugh.

"You should know we haven't even kissed once."

Cedar's hands were on my shoulders, rubbing the tension away. Her fingers worked against my sore muscles with precision. I knew I was tense, but I had no idea it was this bad.

"Did someone forget their massage today, Princess?"

Vesper's words were like a sucker punch to the gut, but instead of hurting, it just made that delicious heat brewing inside me all that more potent.

She was letting me know what she was about to do to me. Just like that first night. I tried to move, but Cedar was there, holding me against the couch, her hand coming to circle my throat, forcing me to look up at her.

My breath caught. Vesper was between my legs, pushing my skirt up. She let out a growl when she realized I wasn't wearing any panties and that she could see just how soaked I already was for her.

Cedar's thumb came into my mouth, forcing it open, then leaning down to kiss me just as Vesper's mouth met my cunt.

I gasped. I had been so on edge since bonding with Cedar that I was aching for more.

"Did you miss Vesper's tongue? She's been dying to taste you again."

I couldn't dignify that with a response because Vesper's lips wrapped around my clit and sucked—hard. Her vampire strength was at full play, and the intensity of it had my back bowing.

"God, you taste so fucking good," Vesper moaned on her knees for me. "I missed this."

"This is what you call *talking*?" I forced out as Vesper's fingers played at my entrance.

Cedar pushed my head down so I could see Vesper between my legs. The look in her eyes almost sent me into an early orgasm.

"You look at that face and tell me you could deny her."

I spread myself further, letting my little mouse ravage me.

"As if I could ever... *Fuck*!"

My cries stopped as her teeth sank into my inner thigh. White-hot pain shot through me, Vesper's newborn vampire fangs feeling far sharper than a normal vampire's. Maybe it was just the shock of it.

Or maybe it was just building up since the moment I first saw them and yearned for her to sink them into me. To claim me. To bond me.

The pain didn't last long—my lovers made sure of that. Not only did Vesper pump me with vampire venom, but Cedar was behind me, her hands traveling my body until they slipped underneath the top of my dress, her fingers plucking my nipples.

"Again," I moaned as Vesper started fucking me with her fingers. I didn't have to say anything. She was unstoppable. Curling and twisting them in a way that made me arch off the sofa.

Vesper looked up at us, her mouth covered with blood.

"Our princess is asking you to bite her again, Vesper. Are you going to listen like a good little toy, or...?"

Vesper's lips twisted, and I caught sight of her pearly white new fangs. *Krae, she was so handsome like this.* Human Vesper was something, but vampire Vesper? She was going to destroy me.

"Does your husband know how prettily you beg?" Cedar whispered in my ear.

My breath caught as Vesper's face disappeared between my legs, and I felt her tongue against my clit. She gave me a few pure moments of pleasure before she turned her head to the other side and sank her fangs back into me.

The vampire venom was already taking over. I let out an embarrassingly loud cry that I was sure Atlas and her clan members, no matter how far, could hear.

"I wasn't begging," I hissed, but it sounded far breathier than I would've liked.

"Stop trying to hold onto your dignity," Cedar teased, her teeth dragging across my ear. "Let go, Princess. Come back to us."

Vesper's fingers were destroying me while her tongue lapped at my center, her low growl sending sparks through me. Cedar twisted my nipples and bit whatever skin she could find.

I couldn't stop my orgasm if I tried.

"Good Princess," Cedar whispered. "Doesn't she look good between us, Vesper?"

Vesper showed her head, her mouth covered in my blood.

"Breathtaking."

The emotions I was trying to keep at bay came crashing down in that moment. My eyes stung. My throat constricted. Bloodred tears filled my eyes.

"I missed you two," I whispered, letting the brokenness I felt finally show in my voice.

"Oh, my poor princess."

Vesper got up to wrap her arms around me as Cedar changed her position so she was hugging both of us.

I couldn't stop the sobs from racking my body.

"I'm sorry I didn't come for you," I told Vesper as I leaned into their embrace, the warmth seeping deep into my being.

I don't deserve it.

"It hurt," Vesper said in a low voice. "But I hoped the two of you wouldn't forget about me."

"You know, you can lean on me too, Brat." Cedar's warm breath tickled my ear.

"We're here now. Both of us."

Lean on her? It felt so foreign to hear it. Uncomfortable. In a world that kept showing me I could trust no one, how could I?

I can because it's them.

"Don't go off on your own anymore, okay? Remember, no more secrets. That goes for both of you."

All the warmth seeping from them into me, combined with the vulnerability of their words, was too much for me to handle. The hate was so much easier—the fiery burning feeling that made me act without hesitancy.

This felt different.

Love.

It was the scariest thing I ever experienced. I never once thought twice about my actions. I relied on my feelings to push me forward, to make the decision for me.

But now I couldn't be as reckless because with one wrong move, both would be taken from me.

"I won't," I vowed and pulled away to look at them.

Part of me was scared to do it. It wasn't really the anger I was worried about, but the... betrayal. I didn't want them to hate me, even if it was easier. I wasn't sure if my heart could handle it.

When I met their gazes, though, the feeling in their eyes had the world freezing around us. Much warmer than I could've ever hoped for.

It looked like love.

"I love you," I whispered, my hands coming to cup their faces. I looked at the newly turned vampire and then at the witch. "Both of you. I promise I won't do it again."

Vesper's arms tightened around me, and Cedar froze for a moment, her eyes traveling my face.

"She's not lying. You can feel that in the bond, can't you?"

Vesper's words had Cedar narrowing her eyes at her.

"Vampirism has made you bolder than usual," she said with a hiss.

Vesper gave her a shit-eating grin.

"You like it," she teased, and then looked at me, her expression changing. "Are you willing?"

She didn't have to say anything else for me to understand what she was saying. No matter how dull the bond inside us was now, I could still sense the bit of anxiety and hope she held in there.

She was asking if I wanted to revive the bond.

Of course I do.

In the past, I had hated her bonding me without my permission, even though it was an accident. But now that I had gone for so long without strengthening our bond? I felt like I was missing something. Missing *her*.

"Do you want me to answer for you?" Cedar asked, her fingers ghosting my neck. The low, sultry tone of her voice made me shiver.

"The two of you seem to have forgotten your place," I said, moving, trying to regain some control. I grabbed Vesper by the hair and forced her neck to the side. She let out that delicious little moan that told me she loved how rough I was being with her. "I guess it's time to remind you."

I sank my fangs into Vesper's neck, taking deep gulps of her blood, and our bond flared to life immediately, connecting not just the two of us, but us and Cedar as well.

"Oh fuck," the witch cursed from behind me. Pleasure and lust shot through us. Vesper's hands were on my thighs like they had a mind of their own.

No, wait.

It was more than just her body reacting to the bonding. These wishes were... *Cedar's.*

I could feel the violent need coursing through us. Thoughts were put into my head that weren't mine, telling me to do things like pull Vesper closer, tweak my own nipples, lick the base of my neck...

Cedar's wet tongue was doing just that, our desires aligned.

Her hands were between my legs—*no,* those were Vesper's fingers pushing into me.

The three of us were connected, the bond so powerful that it was pushing aside everything else.

There was no Caspian. There was no one else. Just the three of us, our thoughts, our desires, our love melding together.

There was no stopping us. Fingers were forced into wet cunts. Lips were fastened around nipples and clits. There was no telling where one began and one ended. The blood coursing through us intertwined us so deeply, we were no longer three separate beings but one working together.

I didn't even know we'd stopped until I found myself naked and lying across the couch on the two of them, the buzz from the bond still alive and coursing through my veins when I finally found my wits.

"What did they do to you in there?" I asked Vesper, my eyes shooting to her.

She froze under me, and for once, I wasn't sure I wanted to know the truth, afraid it would hurt too bad.

But for her, I needed to know. I needed to know who would feel my wrath after we made it out of here.

CEDAR

I didn't want Vesper to say it.

I could see how it tormented her, and because of my own trauma with the coven, I knew how hard it was to speak about something like this.

My hand found her arm.

I shifted so I could look at her, but she was looking up at the ceiling.

"Do you want me to…?"

I trailed off, not being able to gauge what she needed in that moment. The bond was strong between the three of us, but she was obviously trying to pull her emotions inward, trying to erect a wall between us.

"No… I got this."

Aurelia pushed herself up on her forearms, looking down at our poor hunter.

"If it's too much—"

"They starved me," she forced out in one breath. "They left me in a dungeon and only gave me blood until… until…" She gritted her teeth, the words coming harder now. "Until I lay there, hallucinating the two of you looking down at me with disgust because of what I'd become."

Panic and pain shot through our bond, but I couldn't decipher who it came from because Aurelia and I blurted the same thing out loud.

"We would never—"

"I don't know when I died," Vesper cut us off. "I think it was sometime after the hallucinations. I stopped sleeping. Started enjoying the blood. It was hard to keep track of everything, and then suddenly I was pulled from the dungeons and given to my new *family*."

She spat the word "family" like it was a curse.

Aurelia cupped her face. Only then did Vesper look at her. There was so much pain in her eyes that it physically hurt me.

I hated the council. Hated how they could be so cruel to their own people.

"We would never be disgusted by you," she whispered. "*Ever. *I'm sorry this happened to you. I'm sorry..." Red tears welled up in Aurelia's eyes. "I'm sorry I couldn't save you when you needed me."

I reached forward, placing my hand on Aurelia's, both of us now cupping her face together.

"I'm sorry I couldn't get there fast enough," I said. "But Aurelia's right. Human or vampire, you're *our* Vesper."

She swallowed thickly. I could see the words circling around in her head, but nothing came out of her mouth.

"We love you. Then and now. Forever," Aurelia vowed. "You're beautiful—"

"Breathtaking."

Aurelia smirked.

"Caring."

"Soft."

"*Sexy.*"

Vesper's lips twisted. It was the first sign that she was coming back to us.

"Does our princess need to prove it to you?"

Her eyes fell to Aurelia.

"*Gladly.*"

I shifted our position so Vesper was lying with her back flush against my front, pillows propped under us. I wanted a front-row seat to this.

Aurelia was already trailing small kisses from her lips to her neck.

"My. Beautiful. Hunter."

Each word was topped with a kiss that got lower and lower until Aurelia was between her legs, arched with her ass up in the air.

Tease.

She looked up at Vesper before licking the length of her cunt.

"You still taste the same."

Vesper let out a sharp breath, and I grabbed her throat, tilting her head so I could lick her earlobe.

"You could never get rid of us, even if you tried," I whispered.

Aurelia gave us one naughty smirk, then descended on Vesper like she hadn't gotten a taste of her delicious pussy in years.

"You feel that?" I asked and started plucking her nipples. "The bond is telling you everything you need to know, isn't it?"

Vesper let out a strangled groan as Aurelia speared her with her tongue. I brought both hands to her nipples, pinching and rolling them between my fingers.

The bond was intoxicating, and if we weren't careful, we might never leave this place.

Fine by me.

All I wanted was to be with them. And anything that could push away those dark, painful memories Vesper was feeling, I would gladly do. Over and over again until they were but a fading scar on her psyche. One that would never meet the sun again and would slowly disappear as time went on.

"Tell me you feel it," I ordered.

"I feel it," she gasped as Aurelia nibbled on her clit.

"Do that again, Princess."

She did, a bit harder, and it had Vesper throwing her head back.

"Fuck," she gasped.

"Tell me what you feel."

"I feel the two of you." She let out a cry as Aurelia sucked on her clit. "Inside me. Together. And you—"

She was cut off by another cry when Aurelia started teasing her clit with her fangs.

"We what?"

"You don't hate me," she said. "You... You..."

I twisted her nipples, hard. Her body began to shake. The scent of her arousal was pooling in the room.

"You accept me. Love me. Regardless."

"Good hunter," I cooed before looking down to Aurelia. "Bite her clit and drink from her."

Aurelia let out a sinful giggle.

"My, my, someone's getting *creative*."

I kept playing with her nipples as Vesper's breathing stopped in anticipation. Then, Aurelia licked her clit and sank her fangs right into the sensitive bundle of nerves—

"*Fuck!*"

Her orgasm was explosive. I closed my eyes, savoring the feeling of it shooting between the three of us. When I felt another burst of pleasure from Aurelia, my eyes opened.

Aurelia was playing with her pussy as she drank from Vesper. I couldn't help the moan that fell from my mouth.

Vesper was still, her body stuck in the kind of bliss that seemed to go on and on until Aurelia finally dislodged herself from her clit.

She crawled up her body until she was straddling Vesper's thigh.

"Dirty girl," I whispered. "Look at how needy your cunt made her."

Aurelia started grinding against Vesper's thigh, her need to come obvious between us.

"Fuck, I can't—"

Vesper's hand went between her legs, pumping her fingers in and out as she watched Aurelia.

It was all too much. Before I knew it, my own hand was shoved between Vesper and me, strumming my clit to try and catch up to them.

Fuck. Fuck. It was too good.

Their pleasure tasted sweet on my tongue, their need and desperation taking my own orgasm higher than ever before.

We came simultaneously, our moans intertwining in our own melody.

Perfect.

Every day I wondered how it was possible that I'd met them. And every day it was still so hard to believe we were here, together. Alive.

Aurelia fell into Vesper, and I wrapped my arms around them both.

We got a moment of pure, warm bliss before Aurelia shot up.

"The meeting," she gasped, panic lacing her features. Vesper pulled her back down, and I wrapped my arms around her so she couldn't move.

"Ten minutes," Vesper mumbled.

"Don't run off so soon, Princess."

"I'm only a princess to you," she murmured.

"That's fine by us."

She would always be our princess, no matter her standing or who she was married to. Just like with Vesper, our feelings for her wouldn't change.

She shifted, a silence falling over us.

"In this meeting, I'm going to ask you to be a hunter again," she warned Vesper.

Vesper nuzzled the top of her head and let out a sigh.

"Once a hunter, always a hunter. It never left me. Tell me what you need, and I'll do it."

"General Lee. He has something sneaky going on. It feels dark and... dangerous. We need to figure out what he's doing. I need you to follow him."

Vesper

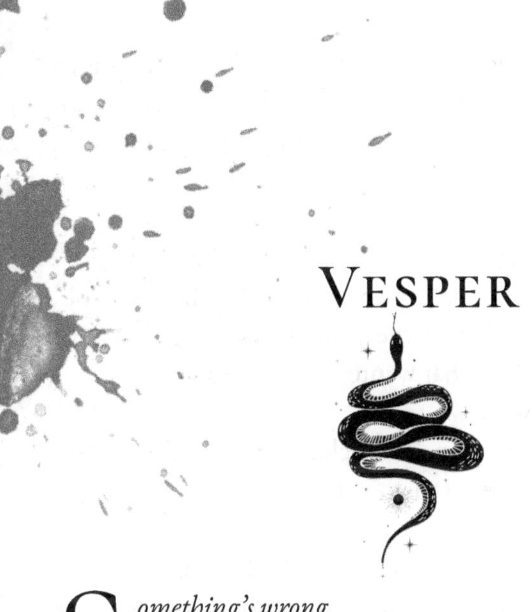

Something's wrong.

General Lee had walked into the place thirty minutes ago, and even my vampire hearing couldn't make out any noises.

Quickly but silently, I snuck over to the other side of the building, keeping tabs on where every single vampire guard was. But none of them even looked my way.

As strange as it sounded, it felt good to slip back into my hunter self. The skintight black outfit was almost exactly the same, the weapon on my belt lighter but intertwined with Cedar's magic. It would do.

Crouching, I watched as the vampire sighed and looked off into the distance, obviously not wanting to be here.

The moment he was distracted, I pounced. My hand covered his mouth while I grabbed the knife and shoved it right through his chest and into his heart.

The other vampires would hear the scuffle and be here in seconds. Steeling myself, I slowly placed him on the ground and listened.

Footsteps came from the right.

I only had a few seconds to prepare before a vampire appeared from the corner of the building. His eyes widened when he saw me, and he reached for his dagger. Quick as lightning, I slammed it into his heart and twisted. His groan was *loud*. Loud enough to call even more attention.

But there was nothing. Not even the sound of the wind.

I had the sinking feeling in my chest that something was off, and my mind had limited it to the general. But there was one other organization out there that wanted to be on top.

One I knew all too well.

An ear-piercing, horrible, nails-on-chalkboard sound reached my ears. I immediately covered them with my hands, but it didn't help in the slightest.

The sound shot through my entire body, rendering me useless, and I crumpled to the ground, my mouth opened in a silent scream.

My vision was getting blurry, but I could make out the dark blobs that silently crossed the space. Two of them stopped by me, looking down. I could see the device in their hands, one that hunters only used on the rarest occasions due to how inhumane the effects were.

My eyes were turning red, blood pooling in them. Pain racked my entire body.

One of them kneeled down, getting close enough for me to register his face. He lowered the sound on the machine just enough for me to hear him talk, but not enough to stop the ringing pain.

A familiar snake ran up his throat. A face that looked so much like my own stared back at me—the only difference was that it had aged over the years.

"Look how far our savior has fallen," my father said with a frown.

"You're su-supposed to be..." I groaned as a wave of pain shot through me. "*Retired.*"

He gave me a twisted grin.

"Yes, well, when my child fucks up, I have to take responsibility, don't I?" He grabbed my face and forced me to look at him, letting out a noise of disgust. "The organization has forsaken you. I am here to remove your title."

He held out his hand, and the person next to him handed him a dagger. One whiff and I could tell it was magical.

No. Horror washed through me. I pushed myself up on unsteady legs, trying to put as much space between us as possible, but hunters surrounded me, five at least, all of them putting their hands on me and forcing me to the ground.

I thrashed, fighting them as hard as my weak body could handle. One of them grabbed my arm, and I snapped at them with my fangs, but another managed to hold my head down.

I should have let Cedar come.

The bond was roaring to life, letting me know they were both feeling what I was and worried about me.

My father came up, the knife aimed right at my throat, before he stuck it in and dragged it down the column of my throat, destroying the tattoo.

White-hot pain flashed up the entire left side of my body. The magic burned as it ate away at my skin. My scream was cut off, the pain too much for me to even make a sound.

Stop. I wanted to scream. *Why me?*

But I couldn't. All I could do was stare at my father as he raised the knife again.

"Do it," I forced out through the pain. My throat was on fire. My fangs were aching to bite into something, but the hunters had me trapped.

My father looked down on me. I couldn't decipher the look because I had never seen it before, but whatever it was, it had him dropping the blade to the ground.

"You're no longer one of us," he said, his voice filled with venom. "You made your bed with the vampires, now you have to lie in it."

The hunters were just as confused as I was. My father was

known to be a ruthless vampire hunter, yet here he was, letting his own child live. Even when our organization specifically called him to end this. To end *me*.

A kind of painful hope unraveled in my chest. It caused bloodred tears to fill my eyes.

All my life, I had wanted my parents to show they cared about me. That it wasn't just about the prophecy. But I had been disappointed and hurt over and over again, both physically and mentally.

But now, for the first time, my father was showing me the mercy I never got as a child.

"I'm going to finish this prophecy," I told him, pushing myself to a sitting position as the hunters started to slowly retreat. "Not for the hunters. For myself and the people I love."

My father motioned for the others to leave. They cast one glance at me before they started disappearing. Behind buildings. Into the surrounding forest. Melding into the darkness like the professionals they were.

Leaving only my father and me.

"How noble of you," he replied. "Maybe it'll make you feel better about betraying your people."

I let out a growl and shakily stood. Pain was coursing through my veins, and my vision was still hazy. They'd taken the sound machine, but the ringing was still there, making it hard for me to concentrate.

"Don't you see they've been betraying us? They're just using our bodies, our lives, to further their agenda. Don't you understand how much pain we went through to get here? Is any of it truly worth it?"

"You're bleeding out, yet you still have the energy to lecture your own father."

I took a step forward, and this time he didn't move. He let me get closer. So I took another step. And then another.

"You're here. You let me live. So you must know it even if you don't admit it. Don't you want more? Don't you want to see your children again?"

His throat bobbed, and his eyes fell to the ground.

"Vesper, I—"

I wobbled, almost falling over before his hand caught me. It was warm and gentle, so much so that it caught me off guard. I flinched, expecting pain, but it never came.

"They turned you against us. Your own children. Don't you see it?"

His face twisted. His jaw tightened.

"It doesn't change anything," he said, pulling me up. "In another life, one where we weren't tasked to save our species from ruin, maybe I could've been a better father."

"You can still try—"

"Enough," he spat, but it lacked the usual harshness. It brought me back to a memory.

I was a child, begging him for something. I forgot what it was, maybe candy or a toy, but I remembered how tired my father had been at that moment. And it made me understand that, while he had been cruel and hurtful, maybe the hunters made him that way.

I let myself fall into him. It wasn't a hug since he didn't wrap his arms all the way around me, but I felt the weight of one lingering on my back.

"Run away," I whispered. "Take Mom and run. Nothing good will come from staying here. If not hunters, then the vampire council—they're using our blood percentage to try to justify punishing us for being hunters. It'll never be safe."

There was a pause before I was pushed back with a force that had me stepping back.

"I'm sorry for everythin—"

It happened so fast, and I was so disoriented I didn't realize what was happening. Blood splattered all over me. My father's face froze in a horrified expression. I looked down at his chest, where a hand had been shoved, holding his still-beating heart.

I opened my mouth in horror, the scream still building in my chest as the person pulled his hand away and let my father's dead body fall to the ground.

General Lee was there, staring at the heart in his hand as it slowly stopped beating. He looked horrible. His hair was a greasy mess around his head. Blood covered his body, but it didn't seem like it was all my father's. His shirt was torn, and I could see the scars Aurelia mentioned peeking out.

They didn't look like scars, though. They looked like open wounds, blood slowly leaking out.

And the smell.

I crawled to my father, my body simply reacting as I bit open my wrist and forced it to my father's open mouth. His eyes were already unfocused and far gone, but that didn't stop me from trying to pour my blood into him. I was so weak, I was shaking.

"The hunters always have to stick their nose where it doesn't belong," General Lee said before tossing my father's heart aside. "Now, what to do with you?"

The scream that had been building in my chest was let out like a battle cry, and I lunged at him using all my strength, but he caught me by the throat and held me up. I struggled against him, but even if I wasn't in my weakened state, there was an obvious dark power rolling off him.

What is he?

From the time he had left my sight until now, something changed about him. And I was...

Scared.

His eyes were red and glowing, and black veins traveled across his entire body. The smell was starting to become overpowering, and every time that dark power brushed across my skin, it burned.

"Unfortunately, Adrian wants obedience. And that means I can't kill you right now, or else the princess is going to have a fit. But that doesn't mean I can't send a message."

I fought against him, kicking and clawing at his arm as he dug his nails into my throat and gave me a wicked grin.

"Say hello to the council for me."

Pain swept through me, and my consciousness slipped away, plunging me into the darkness.

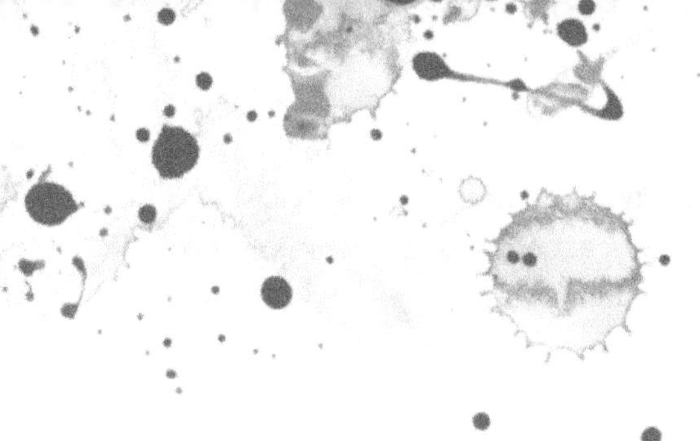

AURELIA

Cedar's hand in mine was the only thing keeping me from rushing into the castle. I took the steps one at a time instead of running like I wanted.

She was at my side, whispering hopeful things, but I couldn't believe a single word. How did this happen?

I knew sending Vesper to follow him was a risk, but I never thought he would deliver her right to the council. Atlas was behind us, silent. Unusually silent. None of us wanted to be here. Any wrong step, and the council could punish all of us. Especially Atlas, since she wasn't supposed to be taking in any new clan members.

But all of that seemed so small. I felt it all happen through the bond, so fresh that I could feel every lick of pain that went through her. Unbearable. The grief that blasted down the bond was something I had never experienced. The only thing similar I could find was when my mother had died right in front of me.

"She'll be okay," Cedar said in a whisper.

"She has to be," I whispered back.

The time it took for us to get to the entrance and finally to the throne room, where Kyan was sitting—more like lounging with her legs over the side—felt like an eternity.

She looked regal as always, with her red-tipped claws, her long silver hair, and some type of coat embedded with red jewels. Her eyes were narrowed, and it was like her body had been sculpted from rock.

She perked up as she saw us, a slow, cat-like smile spreading across her lips as she got up to greet us.

"Aurelia, congratulations on your new marriage. A pity to see you didn't bring the husband today."

"This doesn't involve him." I bowed in front of her, and both Cedar and Atlas followed my lead. "I've come to retrieve—"

"The silver-haired hunter, I know. There's just one issue with that."

She motioned to her guards, and they disappeared for a few minutes. When they brought in Vesper, she looked worse for wear. There was a large scar running down her neck that didn't seem fully healed. She was lethargic, and I could tell it took an immense effort to look at us.

The bond was painful, begging for me to go to her, but I took one step before I was pulled back by Cedar.

"She was finishing her servitude with the Leclair family. So, actually, I can't return her to you, Aurelia."

Atlas stepped forward. "She was transferred to me. This can all be confirmed by them—"

"Which is why I invited them here as well."

The door opened and the Leclair family walked in. They had been noticeably absent from both the engagement party and other events my brother held.

The father came first, the daughters followed. There was a rumor about the second daughter being from an affair he had, but I had never seen her out in public. She had mismatched eyes and scars all over her body, and she never once looked up at Kyan.

"Mr. Leclair, can you please confirm?"

"My daughter made the trade," he said, obvious disdain in his voice for the actions of his daughter.

"Charlotte?" Kyan asked with a sickly-sweet tone.

"That is correct."

There was a pause before Kyan looked right at Atlas.

"Do you think I'm an idiot?" she asked, the smile never leaving her face.

The question was rhetorical, and obviously no one would actually confirm or deny.

Kyan looked around at all of us, waiting for someone to answer, but no one dared to speak. Then she turned to me, her eyes already red, a warning sign of how mad she was, before they finally landed on Vesper.

"Do you have anything to say for yourself, Vesper Monroe? I like the new look, by the way."

Her voice was harsh, contempt dripping from every syllable. The last part was dropped as an obvious insult, no doubt because she knew what happened to Vesper. Anger boiled in my veins.

"As you can see, it's true. So we'll just take Vesper back—" Atlas said, taking a single step forward, keeping her head bowed.

"I wasn't talking to you," Kyan spat, then looked back at Vesper. "They made a deal, you were transferred, and somehow you're now under Aurelia's care? What a coincidence."

"It was a wedding gift," Atlas offered. Kyan was getting angrier and angrier every time Atlas responded. "You know how the princess likes her toys."

Kyan's lips pulled into the slightest bit of a smirk.

"As does the whole vampire world. Vesper, do you have anything to say for yourself?"

I couldn't understand why she kept addressing Vesper. And I knew that with one wrong word out of her mouth, she would be hurt even more than she already was.

"It's as they said. I had no say in the matter. This was all a deal between them."

Her voice was so weak. I could feel how much effort it took for her to speak. Cedar was feeling an immense amount of guilt, no doubt because she listened to us and stayed back.

"Were you unhappy with our arrangement?'

I tried to send her a wave of caution through the bond, as she wasn't looking at me anymore.

"I don't know anyone who would like indentured servitude," she replied, and panic grew in me.

A muscle in Kyan's jaw twitched.

"Apologies for her crudeness. Vesper is—"

Kyan stopped me by holding up her hand.

"Well, I do not appreciate her candor. But I will allow it. Once. Vesper, General Lee sent the body of your father along with you. It was actually in my mind to go after the hybrid vampires of your family. Now tell me, where are the other three?"

Her father? The pain coming from her felt like a punch to the gut. Her grief was now starting to make sense.

Vesper let out a growl and tried to fight the guards holding her, but it was no use.

"Don't spoil the fun, Vesper. I'm just teasing. I can find them myself."

A wave of relief shot through me. *Thank Krae she's not going to push it.*

"Atlas." Her tone was sharp, forcing all attention back to her. "You may have been exiled from our family, but it seems you still have the brazen confidence you once had."

A tremor of shock went through the whole group, landing right in my chest. Only when Atlas clicked her tongue and tilted her head to the side to meet my gaze did I realize that she wasn't looking down because she was scared of Kyan.

She's mad.

I knew the rumors about Atlas coming from a royal family, but we had never discussed it. This was something new altogether, even if not totally unexpected for me.

There was shock from both Cedar and Vesper in my bond, but their eyes were on me. Like I had been keeping something from them, when, in reality, I had just guessed.

Looking at Kyan and Atlas now, it was almost laughable that

anyone was oblivious to this. The ridiculously long hair, their love for jewels, and their attitude all matched. The only real thing we needed to figure out was why she got exiled in the first place.

Them being so harsh with her accepting new people into her clan also made sense now.

"There are no rules against me taking an indentured servant," Atlas told her. "We made a deal. We saw it through. That was it."

Kyan pushed herself from the throne and walked slowly down to Atlas, who, this time, met the vampire ruler dead-on, a low growl forming in her chest.

"*Cute*," she said with a smirk, and in the blink of an eye, she had Atlas on the ground, her face pressed into the rune on the floor. "You have embarrassed us by going around me so blatantly, and for that we have some changes to make."

She pulled Atlas up by her hair. From my position, I could see droplets of dark vampire blood fall to the ground.

"I have ignored the complaints that you have been running wild without someone to tie you down. Both clans and families alike were worried. Too much power, too many vampires, zero ties. I think it's time we fixed that."

Tied by marriage.

Kyan let her go and smoothly got up and walked straight to the Leclair family. I thought she was going to grab Charlotte. After all, Atlas had told me she only got Vesper because she promised to date Charlotte.

They would've been a good pairing.

But she went straight to the black sheep of the family instead.

The girl stepped back, obviously shocked that the royal was standing right in front of her. Luckily for her, Kyan only smiled at her and held out her hand.

Hesitantly, the girl gave it to her.

"Rose Leclair," she said in a purr. "So adequately named."

She brushed her hand down the side of Rose's face, the one with the scars.

My heart twisted at the look of embarrassment that spread across Rose's face. Kyan was being extra mean but disguising it as flattery, without fooling anyone.

"I hereby declare that Rose Leclair and Atlas Nox are to be wed. But because Atlas has been so disgracefully exiled from the family, there won't be any royal customs, nor will Rose be accepted into the family. Instead, Rose Leclair will join your coven and rule by your side. Any objections?"

She looked back specifically at Atlas for this one. But instead, it was Rose and Charlotte Leclair's father who spoke up.

"We are honored, Your Majesty. Never in our wildest dreams did we imagine a marriage hand-picked by Your Majesty. Though Charlotte is a clearly better option for Atlas. Rose is nothing more than a weak human mutt that has cursed our bloodline—"

"Careful, Leclair, or I may think you consider yourself above me. Did you mean to correct me?"

"No, never. I apologize. I only meant—"

"That your daughter, the one you fostered with your own lascivious ways, is not good enough for an exile of the royal family?"

Answering that question would be digging his own grave, and he seemed to know it, so he mumbled a quick apology and stepped back. If I wasn't so worried about Vesper, I might have found this whole thing laughable.

Charlotte managed an obviously forced smile when Kyan took a look at her.

"Congratulations to the new couple. It is true that originally I wished to marry Atlas, but I see that we are ill-fated."

Kyan, satisfied with the answer, took Rose to Atlas's side. Atlas rose, not looking at the girl even once.

"Such a *beautiful* couple," Kyan spat and then turned to saunter back up to her throne. As soon as she sat down, she sneered at us. "Now get out of my sight and don't think of disrespecting my ruling ever again, or next time I'll take all of your heads."

Vesper was thrown to the ground, and Cedar and I were there to help her up in seconds. My heart ached for her, but we stayed silent as we exited the grounds, walking back to Atlas's car that was waiting for us.

My Little Mouse. We'll take care of you now.

VESPER

"Drink," Aurelia said with a hoarse voice.

Bloodred tears filled her eyes. Pity and pain radiated from her through the bond.

Cedar was by my side, one hand holding one of mine, her other wrist bleeding, held over my mouth. But I was holding back.

The hunger was ravaging my body, putting violent thoughts in my head. I wanted to sink my fangs into her and drain her blood more than anything. But I didn't want to lose myself in it. And even though Aurelia was with us, I was afraid to lose control.

I was barely holding on, my body feeling weaker with each second.

The world passed us by in a blur. I thought we were in a car, but if I was being honest, I couldn't be sure. All I could see were the panicked and hurting faces of Cedar and Aurelia.

When the first droplets of Cedar's blood entered my mouth, my entire body froze. It was so sweet. And with my body being on the brink of nonexistence, it tasted like the most delicious thing I'd ever had.

I grabbed her wrist, my grip weaker than usual, but enough to force her wrist against my mouth and bite down on it.

She let out a pained gasp, but her cheeks quickly started

turning red as I pumped venom into her. But she was fighting the effects this time.

"We will have a feeder waiting for her," Atlas said, her voice breaking through the tension between the three of us.

Atlas is starting to get on my nerves.

There was only one thing I wanted more than Cedar's blood.

Her. My eyes darted to our sweet, traumatized princess. *Her too.*

I wanted them both. *Right now.* One riding my mouth. The other between my legs.

I couldn't think of anything else.

"I doubt she'll want one," Aurelia replied, her hand coming to brush my matted hair.

So gentle. When were we ever this gentle to each other?

Against everything in me, I removed my fangs from Cedar.

"Wait! It's not enou—"

"When we get back, I'll take from the reserves," I said, my eyes flitting between the two of them.

I can't risk them. Every time I was near death, theirs were the only two faces I saw. And I knew one thing for certain: I never wanted them to look at me this way ever again.

It hurt more than anything General Lee could do to me.

Before pushing Cedar's wrist away, I licked the wound, coating it with venom. Then, as a little gift, I planted a kiss on her pulse.

She looked away from me. Aurelia caught the act, and a small smile spread across her face, finally breaking the pitiful look she was giving me.

"Wounds," I said and pushed myself into a sitting position, with Cedar and Aurelia helping me up.

It was a car, likely a van, with a partition that separated us from the driver and had more than enough room for the four of us in the back.

My heart soared.

We were finally together again. These weren't the best circumstances, but if the council knew about it and didn't forbid it, we were in the clear.

At least for now.

"They were wounds, not scars," I clarified, looking at the group. The memory of General Lee's hand holding my father's heart was still fresh in my mind. My eyes stung, but I tried my best to push through. "I caught a glimpse of them before it all went to shit."

Aurelia's brows furrowed.

"My source would have mentioned it if they were open."

"Did you see what he was doing there?" Cedar asked.

I shook my head.

"I was about to go in. I was taking out the surrounding vampires guarding the place when the hunters came."

"I'm sorry about your father," Cedar whispered, her hand on my back.

"He was shitty," Aurelia said with a huff. "One more enemy gone." I couldn't hide the way my heart sank at her words, and her face twisted up. "Why do you feel like that?"

"I..." I ran my tongue over my fangs, Cedar's blood still there. "I don't know. He was going to kill me but pulled back and..."

My hand came up to my neck. There would be a scarred mess where my tattoo used to be, my outcast status visible to everyone. I flinched when my fingers brushed across it. It was sore and still open, but not actively bleeding.

The pieces started clicking.

"It's magic," I told them. "His wounds. They felt and smelled weird."

"How would they heal then?" Atlas asked, calling our attention back to her. She had a long lock of her hair between her hands, her eyes on it as if it were more engrossing than our display.

She probably doesn't want to watch Aurelia with us. Dark satisfaction unfurled in me.

"A witch can make and heal the wounds," Cedar replied. "He has to be working with one."

Aurelia made a noise.

"We don't have any in the castle, so whoever did it in the first place must be healing him. The real question is, *why* is he using magic on himself?"

There was an uncomfortable feeling in the bond. Like dread slowly seeping into us.

"Did you happen to see what was carved on it?" Cedar asked in a small voice.

I shook my head. "I was too busy trying not to die."

Atlas let out a scoff.

"And see where that got us."

"We are going back to the Castle palace," Aurelia cut in before I could attack the dark-haired vampire who finally had the nerve to look at her.

"That's not a good idea," she warned. "Your brother is going to be furious."

Aurelia sat back against the seat with her arms crossed.

"Word will get back to him about your gift anyway. It won't look good if we delay this any longer. And I need to warn Caspian."

Atlas's jaw twitched.

"General Lee won't kill me," I said, and everyone turned to look at me. "Neither will her brother. He said he needed Aurelia to obey, and killing any of us would make it difficult."

"He may be bloodthirsty, but he's lazy," Cedar concluded. "He had General Lee there, likely doing the harder strategy work, whatever that may be. And he has his inner circle, the ones who are enforcing what he wants. Has anyone actually seen him kill anyone since... Levana?" Her voice got thick toward the end.

"Only in his *sparring matches*. He's killed guards, and more recently moved on to his inner circle," Aurelia answered her. "He had me do most of it. Up until now, as far as anyone is concerned, he hasn't been the one to kill anyone outside the family."

"He's making sure you're the one to step up if anyone wants to challenge him," Atlas offered. "Didn't you learn anything during your time under your father?"

A growl ripped from my throat. Aurelia placed her hand on my lap, quieting me.

"She's right, unfortunately. He's trying to separate me from everyone. It makes it less likely for people to side with me if there's an uprising."

But an uprising was exactly what we were trying to accomplish. We needed something to turn people against him. Adrian only killing the vampires who followed him wasn't enough.

We needed something shocking. A kill that would make a statement.

"I have an idea," Cedar said.

I turned to her with a smile.

"Scheming witch! I like where this is going."

She sent me a smile that had my stomach flipping.

"First, let's get through this, hm? Adrian will want to meet us first. After that trial, we can consider everything else."

I knew what awaited us wouldn't be easy, but the dread coming from Aurelia told me it might be harder than I imagined.

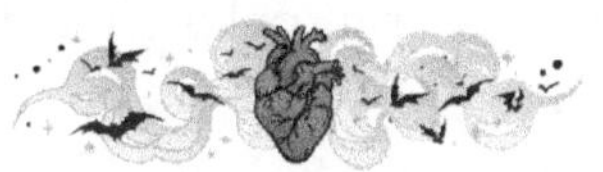

"And somehow the strays have made it back," Adrian said from the nest of a bed he built for himself, feeders surrounding him. "Let's hope this time they're on a tighter leash, or I may need to get rid of them myself."

My body was still weak, and the bastard was having Cedar and me kneel on the ground as Aurelia stood before him.

I had seen Adrian only twice in my life, once when he killed Levana and then at the engagement-turned-wedding, but having him so close now was giving me the same feeling as General Lee.

There was something evil about him. Especially in the way he looked at his own sister. I had seen those same eyes before, and it hit me again that his were nothing like his sister's—or even their father's, which never looked that... *malicious.*

"We won't have a problem," Aurelia declared, looking back at us.

I almost lost my balance but quickly righted myself before anyone could say anything. Adrian smiled, then looked us up and down, no doubt taking in our uniforms.

This part had been Aurelia's plan. We had even gone as far as to dress in the new guards' uniforms. It didn't escape me how many times I'd played this same role, all of them feeling like different realities.

"They follow me, and now that I have sworn my loyalty to you—"

Faster than I had ever seen a vampire move, he appeared in front of her.

Fast. Too fast. How did he move so—

Aurelia gasped as his hand wrapped around her neck. It didn't look like he was hurting her, but that didn't convince my body that it was right.

I pushed myself forward, needing to get his filthy hands off her. Cedar's hand on my arm, pulling me down, was the only thing that gave me pause.

I couldn't stop the growling, though. Red covered my vision. My body wouldn't go back into position, but at least Cedar's hold on me kept me still.

"Is that true, dear sister?" Adrian asked, dropping his voice. "Because somehow, in a matter of a few days, you married someone I didn't approve of *and* came back with guards that I know would rather have me dead."

I could feel her panic. Her anger. I wanted to squash him for what he was doing to her.

"Let's not start a war we cannot finish," Cedar whispered.

"Well put," Adrian said, having heard her. "Sister?"

Her anger spiked.

"I am prepared to show my loyalty to you," she vowed. "In any way you deem fit."

Adrian smiled cruelly at her, his fangs shimmering in the dim lighting ahead.

"And if I ask you to birth an heir for your husband? Or ask you to rent yourself out to royal family heads? Better yet, let's arrange it. I know the Solei family is dying to get their revenge. What do you say?"

Disgust rolled through the three of us. Another growl spilled from my lips.

I almost attacked.

"Don't try to scare me with that bullshit," Aurelia hissed and pushed him away from her. "You need me for things far more important than that."

"Oh?" He raised a brow. Red flickered in his eyes.

But Aurelia wasn't fazed. In fact, she brushed invisible dust off her shoulder.

"They're whispering about you," she said with a sigh. "Saying you're too unstable to lead. *Crazy.* Not just families here and there, but people in the council."

What is she doing? Why is she goading him?

"You think I care about that? Try again, sister."

She looked at her nails. "What if I told you one of those damaging your reputation is a traitor, hiding in your mists and feeding intelligence to the council?"

That got to him, just like she said it would.

"No one would dare," he spat.

She shrugged. "Okay, guess I'm not needed for anything. I'm going to Caspian for some heir-making—"

"Damn, you really know how to be fucking annoying."

She turned to him with a smile.

"Runs in the family."

He let out a growl, not bothering to hide his anger.

"Get me their head by the end of the week."

Satisfaction rolled through the bond.

"I'll do you one better. Tomorrow, at the Blood Rites. Let's make an example out of them."

His expression changed for the first time, awareness evident on his face, but curiosity was the overwhelming emotion.

Apples from the same tree. Back in the day, this trick would have worked on Aurelia as well.

"Don't make promises you can't deliver."

Aurelia started retreating. Each step back was another step closer to us.

"I will deliver, don't you worry. Now, if you'll excuse us..."

She waited for him to say something, but he merely shrugged and climbed back onto the nest of his bed, the feeders already waiting for him.

Before we even left the room, he had already sunk his fangs into one of the girls' necks.

We walked the hallways, following Aurelia as she led us in silence. The castle was the same as ever, but there was a chill to it that had me looking over my shoulder. My vampire hearing couldn't pick up anything, but it still felt *wrong.*

We aren't safe here.

"My room," Aurelia ordered, turning to us. "Blood, then tonight is just for us. Tomorrow, the Blood Rites are at sundown. It should be enough time for you, right?"

I turned to Cedar, who nodded.

"More than enough." She took my hand in hers. "But first, we have *a lot* to discuss."

From the looks on both their faces, there wouldn't be much *discussing* on the menu for tonight.

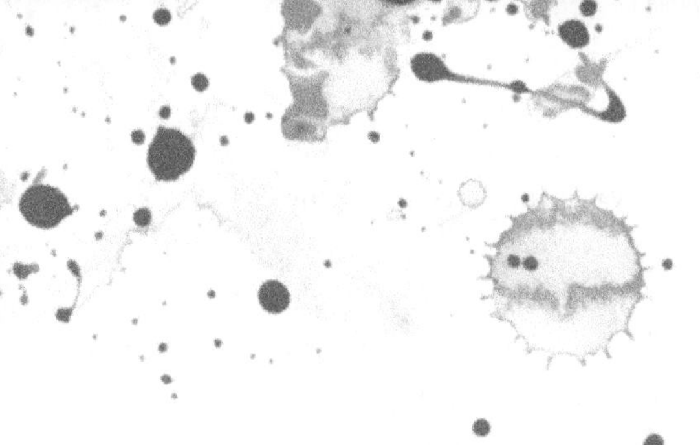

AURELIA

"Once a toy, always a toy," I said with a sigh as I slid the large fake cock into Vesper's cunt. Her mouth popped open, a wild growl spilling out. The cock was strapped onto me, giving me full control.

My fingers were on her clit, playing her. She arched her body, an obvious plea for me to quicken my pace, but I wasn't about to listen.

Cedar was holding Vesper down with red magical vines on my bed, her legs spread from me as I fucked her nice and slow. There were a few pillows behind her, her upper body at a slight incline so she could watch us. The witch was behind me, her hands trailing my body.

One plucked my nipple as the other teased my ass cheek.

"Look at her *writhing* for more," Cedar taunted with a chuckle.

I gasped when her hand came to pluck my other nipple. Wetness was gathering at my core, but she made no move to put me out of my misery.

The bond intensified everything. I could feel every moment of pleasure and frustration pouring out of Vesper, and I knew Cedar could feel how much I wanted her to bury her fingers in me.

She was enjoying this. Watching. Commenting. Maybe even more so being part of it.

"Poor..." I thrust into Vesper hard, then pulled back. "Little..." *Thrust.* "Mouse." *Thrust.* The sound of her wetness mixed with her growls and moans was intoxicating. I wanted to see just how far I could push her before she'd truly lose it.

"Let me go." Vesper yanked at the bonds, but they were unmoving.

"Don't you remember this was your idea?" Cedar asked, her hand finally slipping between my legs from behind so she could sink her fingers into my wet cunt. It stalled my movements. "We didn't want your new vampire strength and bloodlust to hurt our sensitive princess."

"Sensitive," I huffed and quickly started up my thrusts again. Cedar kept up with me, timing her thrusts with mine, fucking me while I fucked Vesper.

I let out a gasp when I felt another fake cock at my entrance.

"Come on now, Princess, keep fucking our little hunter, and I'll fuck you. That's the deal, hm?"

"I remember us once agreeing on tying Little Mouse up on the bed so I could fuck her while she ate you out. But we can shelve that for later."

"It's a date."

Her words sent a jolt of excitement through me.

I watched Vesper open her mouth, probably to say something snarky, but when the witch pushed the cock inside me all the way to the hilt, my eyes closed.

"Oh Krae," I moaned and bucked against the feeling. Vesper let out a breath as it caused the cock inside her to move.

"Nice and slow for Vesper, Princess. And for you..."

I jerked forward as Cedar began pounding into me with the cock, my hands just barely catching me before I fell onto Vesper.

I found myself unable to move as pleasure washed through me.

"Move, Princess," Vesper commanded, but I couldn't. Not

when Cedar's fake cock was hitting my cervix so hard it had me seeing stars. Then, just like that, it stopped.

"Vesper, flip her."

The vines disappeared from her arms, but her legs were still locked in place. Vesper was pulling the cock out of her and flipping me so that I was lying flat on her.

Cedar's fingers ran down the cock that was now glistening with Vesper's wetness, and she looked me in the eyes, a playfulness there before she slowly lowered her face and...

"Holy shit!"

"Fuck!"

Both Vesper and I cursed as Cedar took the entire cock in her mouth. Sudden heat flashed through me. My cunt convulsed. A need like I'd never felt before ran through me.

Red vines wrapped around both of us now, strapping me and Vesper together. But her arms were still free to play with me.

My nipples. My clit. Vesper was everywhere.

Cedar pulled back, licking her lips.

"Dirty little princess. You're dripping all over Vesper."

She ran her hands down my folds, then Vesper's. I hadn't realized this position left us both bare to her, one pussy on top of the other.

She undid my strap slowly. *Painfully* slow.

"Faster," I panted as Vesper pinched my nipple and threw my head back when Cedar lined both cocks with our cunts. "I can't... This is..."

The bond was going crazy. The pleasure. The heat. Our feral need for each other.

And then she slammed the cocks into us. Vesper was already close to losing it, but that was the final straw. Her teeth sank into me, spreading fire down my neck and straight to my core, and my orgasm ran into the three of us like a wave, taking us all under.

"Fuck, this bond..." Cedar said, out of breath, but she kept her pace, fucking both of us through the shared orgasm. "You both look so fucking delicious. Indecent. So good together. Fuck, I could come just by watching."

Vesper drank gulps of my blood, her venom spreading from my head to my toes, warming my body.

It was all too much. Too hot. Too mind-blowing.

I went limp as another wave started to crash through me. My cunt violently convulsed around the cock, my scream trapped in my throat.

Vesper came with me, a low groan exploding from her chest.

The red vines vanished, and Cedar carefully pulled the cocks from us, letting Vesper and me catch our breaths. She chuckled and lay down on the bed beside us, watching us with an amused look.

Vesper and I moved in tandem, her moving down between the witch's legs and me grabbing her face and forcing my lips to hers.

She still tastes like Vesper.

I pulled away to look into her green eyes.

"You take care of us so well, my love," I whispered, pushing the hair from her sweat-covered forehead. "Let us return the favor."

Her heart skipped a beat at the nickname. Warmth flooded the bond, but it was chased away by something sour.

Doubt.

Vesper was feasting on her nonstop, the ravenous beast Cedar had restrained coming back to repay her in kind.

It allowed me to take Cedar in for the first time with her walls completely down. She had no chance to resurrect them, not with Vesper's tongue on her cunt and me gently caressing her face.

"Do you doubt my feelings for you?"

Something else showed through the bond. Panic. Fear.

"I... *Fuck*. Vesper..."

She tried to push me away, but I was there, pushing her into the bed, caging her there.

"Can you not feel it?" I asked, running my finger down her chest where we all felt the pull of the bond. "You're in here too.

The object of my devotion, running through my mind and heart every moment of my existence. I should hate you for how important you've made yourself to me."

She arched into me. I kissed down her neck, my tongue licking her pulse.

"But I can't bring myself to. Don't you see it, witch?"

The sour feeling lingered, but it was being overpowered.

"Slow down," I ordered Vesper. Her growl ripped through the room. "Try me again, hunter, and I won't let you come for weeks."

It would be fun too.

Her growl lowered but didn't stop.

"Gods damn it, just stop. We'll make her come. Just..." I teased her neck with my fangs, pulling a sharp gasp from her. "Tell me to stop if you don't want it."

I wasted a moment, licking her pulse. My fangs ached with the need to bite into her.

She groaned, never telling me she wanted me to stop.

"Good witch."

My fangs sliced through her skin with ease. Sweet, fragrant blood exploded across my taste buds. In my haze, I almost forgot to linger so the venom would enter her system.

"This can't be real," she moaned as the venom worked its way inside her.

The shot of pleasure through the bond had Vesper and me both moaning.

"Aurelia... Please, I can't stop myself..."

I pulled myself away from her neck so I could look into Cedar's eyes as she came.

"Go on, Vesper."

Seeing the witch come for us was a vision. Her magic flared around us, the heat brushing across my skin.

"Feel this. Feel us. Don't brush it off." I grabbed her chin and forced her to look at me. "You belong here with us, my love."

When her orgasm finally subsided, Vesper joined us on the

bed, all of us a panting mess. No one spoke for the longest time, just enjoying the fact that we were finally all together again.

Then Vesper sat up.

"Hey, why didn't I get a cute pet name like that?"

For the first time in what felt like a millennium, true laughter spilled from my chest.

It wasn't long until Cedar joined in, and Vesper was left to stare at us, though I noted the small smirk on her face.

Whatever came next, I would cherish the time with them.

They were worth everything.

Cedar

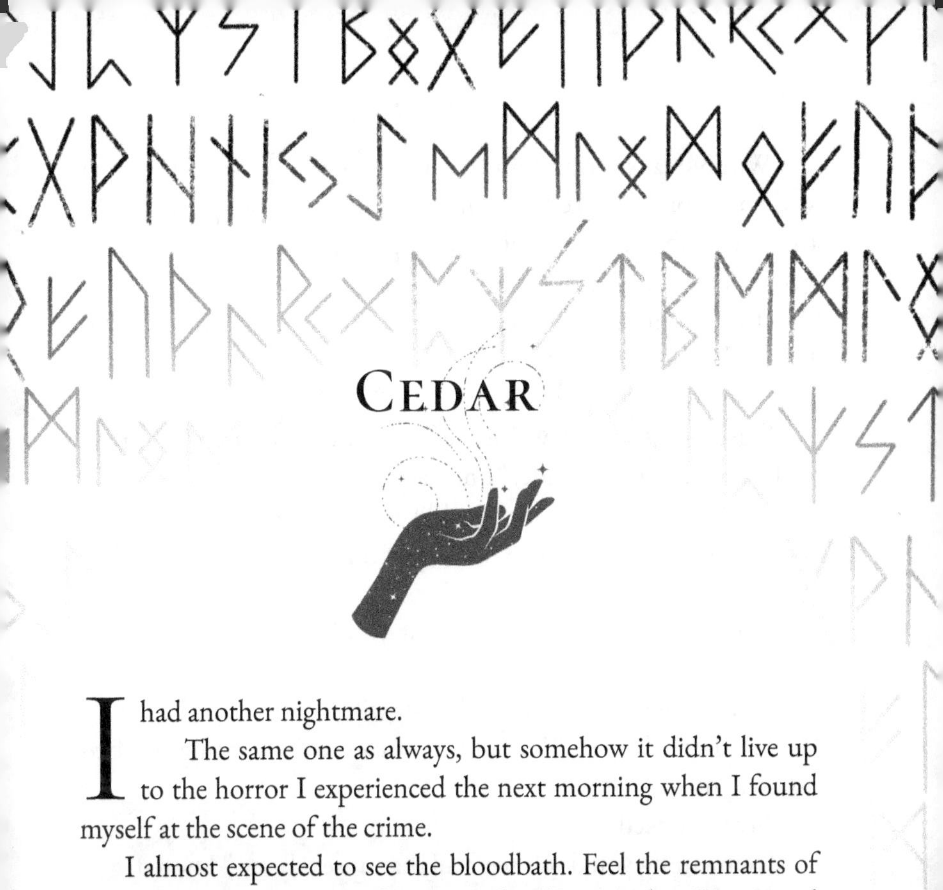

I had another nightmare.

The same one as always, but somehow it didn't live up to the horror I experienced the next morning when I found myself at the scene of the crime.

I almost expected to see the bloodbath. Feel the remnants of magic. Anything that would prove what happened to Vesper and her father.

But there was nothing.

That made it all the more sinister.

I wasn't alone, not after what happened to Vesper, but neither Aurelia nor I wanted her to come. So I opted for someone much less desirable.

"Are we sure this is where it happened?" Caspian asked from behind me, the sound of his feet brushing against the ground hitting my ears.

"Are you saying Vesper lied about it?" I wasn't even trying to keep the hostility out of my voice.

He let out a sigh, almost like he was annoyed that I was having a temper tantrum or something.

"I'm saying she was hurt pretty badly, so things could've gotten mixed up. I don't smell any blood or magic."

Without answering him, I continued along the path Vesper said she took. I walked around the building, noting that while there were footsteps, Caspian was right. There was no lingering magic, let alone blood or other vampires, in the area.

It wasn't until I got to the door at the side of the building that I paused.

There's something inside.

"Also, I don't think we've been formally introduced," Caspian said, coming up to my side. "I'm Caspian Hart."

The bastard offered his hand like I would actually shake it. I merely looked at it and then back up at him.

"I know who you are."

"But I don't know much about you," he continued with a smirk.

"Well, maybe you should ask your wife."

He didn't budge. "I would if you weren't warming her bed every night."

My jaw ticked.

"Something you don't seem all that upset about," I noted.

He shrugged and slipped his hand back into his pocket. The entire time he was with me, I had made a point not to look at him, but now that I was forced to, I realized he was quite casual for his status.

"This arrangement between us is mutually beneficial." His smile dropped, his face turning serious. "I never wanted this. My sister was set to take everything, and then... He killed her." His voice shook toward the end.

"I'm sorry," I said, and this time I meant it. He gave me a pitiful smile.

"And because of my rise to fame, my lover dropped me. He was okay with keeping me in the shadows as a nobody, but as soon as everyone's eyes were on me..."

I didn't know what made him feel comfortable enough to spill all this to me, but I was starting to get slightly uncomfortable.

I felt for the man, but that didn't help me get over the fact that he was legally married to Aurelia.

In the eyes of the vampire world, he was the one for her, and we were the ones forced into the shadows. Even if we were back together, it still hurt.

"Seems like we're all in a shitty situation." I looked back toward the door and lowered my voice. "Something's in there. I can feel it."

He made a humming sound.

"Magic? I can't smell anything."

I raised my hand, ready to open the door, but paused. Signals were going off in my mind, but the stupid part of me ignored them and pulled the door open.

That was a mistake.

One that would've cost me my life if Caspian hadn't wrapped his arms around my torso and jerked us away from the building with his vampire speed.

I felt the explosion of magic before I saw it and recovered fast enough to create a barrier to protect us from it.

That magic collided with mine and sent us spiraling backward. Caspian and I were thrown against something, with him taking the brunt of it. I had to keep up my magical shield while the explosion hit us for a full ten seconds before it died down.

"What the fuck?"

We both looked at the building. Most of the exterior was still standing, but the walls were cracked, and chunks had fallen from it. I pushed off Caspian and ran to it, hoping to see whatever was inside.

Magic. Dark magic. *Old.* The same type I felt on the coin that Atlas had once used to communicate with Vesper. The same type I felt in my nightmares as my coven leader drained the life of my parents. Whatever General Lee was hiding in there, it was something that should never have been in his hands to begin with.

I ran inside. Caspian was yelling at me to come back, but it didn't matter now. The trap was gone.

There used to be a staircase there, but it was mostly gone, so I could look down at the ruin left by the explosion. And, in the middle, a single burned body.

It was suddenly hard to breathe.

This wasn't just a trap to protect General Lee's secret and kill whoever tried to uncover it. They were taking care of the loose ends, including the witch who had helped them along. Though "helped" was probably the wrong word. I didn't know any witch who would willingly help vampires do something so dark.

I had an inkling as to what they were doing down here, but I didn't want to jump to conclusions. Because something this horrific would open the floodgates into a possible all-out war between witches and vampires.

I forced my shaky legs to take me to the lower level and take a look at everything more closely.

The runes are similar to the ones I see in my nightmares.

It could only mean one thing. I jerked to the side as my stomach hurled, all its contents coming up, and Caspian came up behind me, his hand patting my back in an unusual display of compassion.

"This isn't good, right?"

I shook my head and wiped my mouth before looking back at the witch, who was unrecognizable.

Well... almost. Their features and body were mangled, but their robe was one of the magically treated ones that all coven leaders gave their dogs, enhanced to withstand an explosion like this.

But what made it even more sickening was that it was a robe I recognized.

A robe I had worn most of my life.

The White Lotus.

And I knew that, if the body wasn't as destroyed as it was, I might recognize and have worked with that person.

"This is the worst possible outcome," I said and paused, trying to give myself enough strength to even say the words. "If this is how he's getting his powers, we'll never be able to defeat him."

"So witches are giving them to him?"

"They aren't giving him anything." I turned to face him. "He's stealing their life force and using it to make himself stronger. Plus, he seems to know what he's doing, which means this is not the first or second time."

Caspian's face dropped, and he looked back at the body.

"What are we to do then?"

Sickness swirled in my stomach again.

"We follow the plan and hope that one of them gets angry enough to kill the other. There's no way we'd survive one, let alone both."

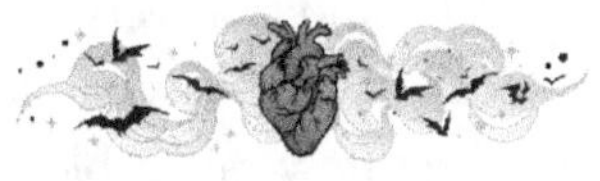

I pulled at the itchy fabric of my outfit for the evening.

Caspian and I were a little off after our *excursion*. The whole point was to go and find the witch who was helping them, but now that they were dead and I had confirmation that the general had likely taken the lives of many witches, we weren't sure what to do.

I filled in both Vesper and Aurelia, and just like us, they had a moment of realization that we might be in over our head. But our princess was the first one to snap out of it.

It will work. I know my brother, and I know how to force his hand.

And so, trusting our princess, we got ready for the night. Caspian had graciously provided us both with outfits, maybe because he felt bad for what we experienced that morning—or because he was just a kind vampire.

Regardless, we accepted them anyway.

Mine was a full dark green ensemble with glitter and gems

placed in a very particular but obviously witchy way that made me stand out like a sore thumb.

Even if somehow the entire kingdom hadn't heard the rumor that Vesper and I were back, that would be clear now. Though, from the looks of it, people were less worried about having a witch in their midst than they were about the new king.

"Weird that the two bodyguards are dressed up for this," Vesper muttered, tugging at her own clothing.

I looked at her, my eyes roaming her slim figure dressed in black with deep red accents. The majority of her chest was out, highlighting the scars and the now slashed-out tattoo on her neck, like they wanted to call attention to where she came from.

She looks damn good in that, though.

Her eyes met mine, slightly reddening at the iris.

The bond meant that I could feel every emotion coming from them. Including the bloodlust that was still lingering at the back of Vesper's mind. No matter how much blood I gave her or how much human blood she drank from the reserves, it never left.

Her injuries were too severe. Every ounce of blood was going into healing her body, and while she looked fine, I could tell that she still couldn't stand for long. She sure as hell would not be able to fight.

I fucking hate all of it.

I felt for her. And I hated that I had some part in it. Not only did I not go with her as backup, but she wouldn't be a vampire if I had made it to her sooner, so they wouldn't have targeted her. I knew the hunters. I read about them in our archives. More than that, I knew Vesper. I knew how she was brought up. How her entire world was killing creatures just like her. It was my fault—

"Stop blaming yourself," she whispered, her eyes narrowing on the princess. "I'm fine now."

"Are you?" I couldn't help but push back. All the emotions from what I witnessed earlier and the panic and fear were getting to me. Which was probably why I added, "Do you not hold a single ounce of hatred toward me for what you've become?"

A burst of pain told me I shouldn't have said anything. I made it a point of telling her I didn't care about her being a vampire, yet here I was, ruining it because of my own unstable emotions.

And because I knew she might be harboring some hatred toward herself and her new condition.

To me, she was the same Vesper. I didn't care about any of it. Vampire Vesper, human Vesper. Both were mine.

"This is not the time or the place," she hissed. "Let's focus on the princess, and if you still want to hash this out, we can later."

That put an end to our conversation and forced me to look in front of us. We were in the throne room again, a place I was getting sick of.

The magical explosion opened up my senses, forcing me to take in things I previously hadn't. I had overlooked the lingering bits of magic embedded into the stone of this place. It felt... corrupted. Disgusting. Its tendrils slithered up, wrapping around our ankles and brushing across our hands.

Almost like it had a mind of its own.

It made me want to crawl out of my skin. It was similar to the magic I felt in General Lee's hideout. Something about it didn't feel right.

I didn't think anyone else could feel it. The vampires didn't feel magic the same way we did. They could smell it, but if it wasn't actively coming from a witch, would they even know? They hadn't allowed witches near the Castle family in ages.

Maybe this is why.

There was something depraved going on here. But what I hadn't told the others was...

My eyes shot to the new Castle king, but his were already looking my way intently. I knew he didn't like Vesper here, but me?

I'm a threat. Or I'm going to be used next. Neither thought sat well with me.

My ego told me not to look away first, but the rational part of my brain forced my eyes to the front, looking over the sea of vampires who had shown up for the Blood Rites.

The sun was setting. The doors of the throne room were open, letting the golden rays shine in. Right in front of the stairs below the throne, there was a large goblet that was almost the size of a whole person. And inside, dark vampire blood.

There were texts about this in our archives, but this was the first time I or anyone else in my coven was invited to witness it.

"Thank you everyone for coming," Aurelia said, stepping forward with a smile that twisted cruelly on her face. "Both our loyal Castle family members and..." She motioned to the side where the vampire heads of various families and even some clan heads stood. They were segregated. It was like the room had been split in half, with low-level family members on the left and important vampires on the right.

Atlas and her new fiancée were surprisingly absent. She was probably pissed at the arrangement and taking it out on us.

Though if a fight broke out and she was here, we would undoubtedly still lose.

"Our esteemed guests," Aurelia finished, smiling even wider for them just before she walked down the steps.

"As you know, it is customary that when anyone joins the family, they add their blood to the goblet, then drink from it, tying themselves to us. But now that we have a new king, it's time *everyone* pledges their loyalty to us—through blood." Aurelia held her wrist to her face and bit into it in one smooth motion before she held it over the goblet, letting it fall inside. "I may no longer be part of the Castle family, but I pledge my loyalty nonetheless."

Caspian walked from his place off to the side to do the same, looking at Aurelia with a warm smile. There was a bit of jealousy coming from Vesper, but I was actually starting to feel relieved that she had someone by her side.

My heart twisted.

Our bonded was spilling her blood for the maniac she called her brother. It meant she was officially and irrevocably tied to him. The Blood Rites were more of an assembly than anything else, but at the end of the day, it was another bond. Another thing that tied her to this kingdom.

To him.

What can he do with all that power? If a bond between the three of us is this powerful, what does it mean for them?

"I have one more present to welcome in this new era," Aurelia added and walked to the side where they were waiting. "I promised my brother one thing. Proof that there is a traitor in our midst. Someone who seeks to ruin our family's rule before it even starts and has been secretly sharing information with our enemies."

Whispers started, with vampires looking from side to side, trying to figure out if the person they were standing next to was the very traitor.

"General Lee, will you please join us in front?"

Gasps shot throughout the room. Some cowered, others almost seemed to be looking at the general with hungry gazes, trying to catch everything.

The family stayed suspiciously quiet.

All eyes were on the general as he stood next to the king like he always did. He was done up in a deep black robe and button-up ensemble. I glared at him, not able to keep in my hatred.

I could feel the disgusting waves of dark power rolling off him, especially now that it was coming to light.

He gave Aurelia a smile that made my skin crawl.

"Are you accusing me of something?" he asked, puffing his chest. "Kyan wouldn't take too kindly to you accusing her favorite and most loyal general."

But Aurelia didn't care about the threat. She just smiled.

I watched Adrian, trying to figure out if this would be the thing that pushed him off the edge, but surprisingly, his facial expression hadn't even twitched.

"Then why don't you come down here and prove me wrong?"

He puffed up again, but the whispers had already started. The doubt had already begun to sink in.

This is it. If he truly had the rune on his chest and had been siphoning the magic and life force from these witches, putting his blood in the goblet would taint it. Maybe even kill vampires who drank from it, depending on how many witches he'd actually taken.

Magic and vampires didn't mix well, which was why there were so very few cases of witch-vampire hybrids. Levana had been a special one.

"Yes, why don't you go and prove it, hm?" Adrian asked, a sly smile on his face.

They held each other's gaze for a moment before the general turned and started walking down the steps of the throne.

"Now, all I ask is that you," Aurelia motioned to the goblet. "Pledge your loyalty."

It wasn't that the general was expected to pledge his loyalty to a new king, but the way he froze sent a burst of suspicion through everyone in the room. It was obvious in the way they narrowed their eyes at him.

At this point, I wasn't even sure if him being guilty of anything mattered. He simply wasn't doing it—to a king who went crazy over the simplest things.

I looked at Adrian and saw that his hands were already digging into the side of the throne.

Sweat dripped down my brow. The general was so close to Aurelia that if anything happened—

"My loyalty is to the council," he said. "Kyan would not be happy if I—"

"But aren't you here because you believe in my brother's cause? In his rule to bring back the Castle family from ruin?"

This finally got a reaction from the royal side of the room, not so much in whispers and gasps, but in the shared glances between them.

"My sister's right," her brother said and stood. "You said you were loyal to me, so now prove it. In front of everyone. I'm sure Kyan will understand one day."

The general turned around, panic on his face. *It's happening.* I inched closer to Vesper, needing some type of stability in this whirlwind of panic.

"Your Majesty, listen—"

"Is there a reason why you don't want to pledge?" Adrian asked and tilted his head. "What my sister said is true. You were here to help bring the Castle family back from ruin. We don't have to lie in front of our friends and family."

The general was getting more nervous. His eyes were shifting, and he looked like a man who was about to flee.

"Like I mentioned, Kyan—"

"Is not here." Adrian disappeared and reappeared in front of him. Lee's eyes were getting red, but there was no sign of magic. No black veins traveling across his face and neck. "Now pledge your loyalty or lose your head."

If he's not using the witches, what is he doing?

"Wait."

Aurelia and Caspian went to his side, and in one swift movement, they yanked his shirt open. I stepped forward, my hand reaching out to stop them, but Vesper grabbed my wrist.

"Don't you dare touch me, you animals!"

My heart stopped in my chest. Ice-cold fear ran through my veins, freezing me to the ground.

Run. Run now. Not safe.

My entire body was urging me to get the hell out of there and to safety. But I couldn't move. Couldn't breathe.

Because right in the middle of his chest was a rune, carved into his skin, still open, but no blood was dropping. Almost like it was... *festering.* Black veins spread out from around it slowly, reaching up to his neck but stopping before they were visible.

It was one thing to see it on the ground, but seeing it in person, seeing my fears come to life, was something else entirely.

My mind flashed to the rune on the floor of the council's

throne room. To my nightmares. They were all connected. *We* were all connected.

No one here seemed to know what it meant, but they could tell something was wrong, and all of them backed away as if scared.

Can they smell it?

Some eyes shot to me, making the connection. Connecting the dots and thinking that a witch had done this to him. Maybe even me.

Adrian turned to me, a sinister smile spreading across her face.

"I guess your little witch pet is going to be useful. How about you tell everyone what this is?"

This is why they dressed me up like they did. They were putting me on display so I could answer this one question. Aurelia and Caspian were sending me messages with their eyes, and through the bond, I could tell what they needed me to do.

But I was still caught off guard because Adrian asked the question like he already knew. Like we weren't revealing anything to him. Aurelia promised to deliver a traitor, but was General Lee truly one?

And, more importantly, if Adrian knew about this, how did he know?

Who taught them? The White Lotus themselves?

"It's a soul siphon," I forced out through the knot in my throat.

"And what does it do?"

My eyes traveled to Aurelia, who gave me a pitiful look. We needed to force his hand, so I needed to play this up. I needed to twist it in a way that would leave him no choice but to take action.

"He has been stealing the souls and magic of witches to make himself stronger. Stronger than any other vampire out there," I replied. Flashbacks of my parents in the middle of the rune back at the coven flashed through my mind. The similarities were too striking. "You don't want his blood. It will poison everyone here and inject dirty magic into them. Their bodies won't be able to take it."

That was when the general knew that things weren't going to go well for him. He tried to escape, but her brother was there, holding on to him.

"And why would you need to do something as radical as this? What does Kyan feel about this?"

I was finally starting to see Aurelia's plan. The general had two options: he would either confess that the council had been stealing the souls of witches in front of everyone and threaten to pull us into war, or admit he had been doing it for himself, and if that was the case...

"She doesn't know," he said, his eyes looking ahead.

"So you did this for yourself? Why, when you already have such a good position? Unless... you want to overtake someone more powerful than you?"

This was it. This was how Aurelia was going to pit them against each other. Even through my fear, my pride for her skyrocketed.

Adrian was said to be crazy. Truly and deeply deranged. He killed his own people left and right for no reason. Now, if he let the general go without punishment, it would seem weird to everyone here. Weak.

His hands were tied.

In seconds Adrian had his hands on the general's head, attempting to pull it from his shoulders, but magic burst from him. I clapped my hand over my mouth to stop myself from gagging as the feeling of it washed over me.

Vesper was ready to take off toward them, but I took her hand, unable to stop the tremors.

"Don't! He's too dangerous, and you're not healed."

She shot me a look. Anger burst through the bond.

"But Aurelia—"

"She's got it. Look."

She and Caspian were already moving toward the right side of the room and away from the fight. Everyone was inching away from them, not wanting to get caught in the crosshairs.

The general pushed her brother off, his movements fast. Almost too fast for my eyes to make out, but I could tell that they were evenly matched. Her brother recovered fast, grabbing his clothing and forcing him to the ground. More magic started wafting from him, and I had to hold Vesper to steady myself.

This much magic... Dozens, if not hundreds, of witches.

How could this happen right under our noses?

Lee pushed himself up with ease and sent a punch straight to Adrian's stomach, who just let out a crazed laugh.

"Don't do this to me," he yelled. "Don't let them get in your head. You know why—"

"I know you want to overthrow me," Adrian cut him off and pushed him away.

That's when I saw it. General Lee was changing. The veins started spreading through his body, his eyes starting to glow. But not the red of a normal vampire. It was green. It was magic.

Magic that went straight into the new Castle king and sent him flying.

A move like that would have killed any other vampire, but not him. He got up and ran at the man, sending his fist flying to his face, backing him up right into a trap.

The Castle guards finally joined in and grabbed the general. Their strength was no match for his, but there were enough to push him down to his knees.

Adrian laughed.

"I'll spill everything!" the general yelled. "If you think this is sickening, the family has been doing much worse since the beginning of—"

"Shut your mouth."

Grabbing his head, Adrian placed a foot on Lee's chest and pulled. The general let out an animalistic scream as the guards held him, some even falling to their knees to try and keep him in place.

"Such a fucking pity."

This time, when he pulled, the general couldn't fight him. It took an immense amount of strength, but he did it, just before he waved the head around, leaking magical blood, like it was a trophy.

How many lives were stolen for this magic? How many witches had their magic sucked out of them until their souls gave out? How many of them screamed to our gods for help, but no one answered?

It was scary to think about. But the most frightening part was how easily her brother killed him. Because it meant that he, too, had done something to change his body. A confirmation that the vampire we were dealing with was far from ordinary.

He turned to me, his smirk in full force, and threw me the head. I caught it by reflex, but as soon as I did, a sharp wave of nausea ran through me.

"I'm sure you two know a good drop-off place for that. The council or the covens, I don't care. Make sure you send a message."

"Yes, Your Majesty," I forced out. I was going to throw up.

The head was plucked from me by Vesper, who held it to her other side and as far away from me as was allowed in this situation.

I had been so concerned with my own reaction to the magic that I hadn't realized what I had been feeding into the bond. I had been forcing them to live my disgust. It couldn't have been easy for them.

I definitely didn't want her holding that thing either.

"It's not safe. The magic—"

"Let me handle this," Vesper whispered.

I looked back at Aurelia's brother, feeling my stomach drop.

Is there another reason he allowed me to stay by her side?

I sure hoped not.

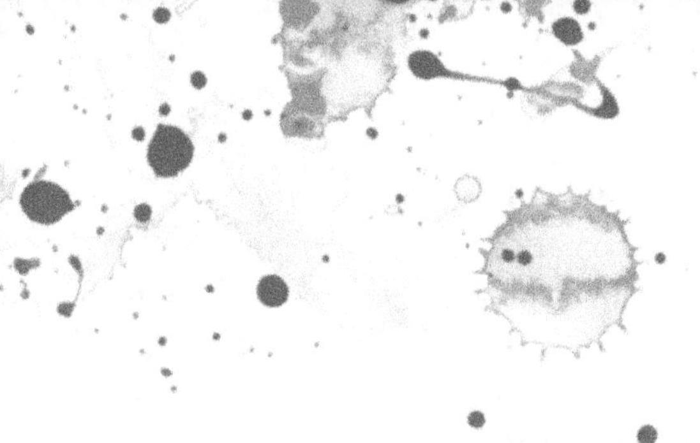

AURELIA

I looked over the deep grooves in the body before me, my stomach twisting more and more the longer I looked at it.

One would think the general's death going off without a hitch would please me, but I felt like we were toeing a line. Every moment felt like I was holding my breath, fearing one wrong move would send us all tumbling to the wrong side.

General Lee's body was the most grotesque thing I'd ever seen, and the longer I stared, the harder it was to look away.

I had seen many vampires die. My mother. Our people.

But none of them looked like this.

The wounds were carved into his chest, and they felt fresh but somehow old at the same time. Jagged edges. They were deep and still open, but there was no blood coming from them.

I reached out to touch the skin, the urge to feel it overpowering me. *Calling me.*

"Stop!" Cedar ordered, her hand finding my shoulder and jerking me away.

I snapped out of the trance then, my mind and body catching up. I hadn't realized how close I had gotten.

All of us were lingering in the side room, the Blood Rites having ended hours before. Adrian fucked off to do god knows what, but I didn't truly care when I had this *monstrosity* in front of me.

Atlas had joined us on my request. She had to sneak in from the garden so Adrian wouldn't see her or notice she'd come, since he would no doubt be likely to attack her for her absence at the ceremony. I had sent my husband away to work on some cleanup and make sure the four of us had enough time to talk, and now that he was back, he stood to the side, not wanting to get too close to the body.

We needed all the backup we could get for something like this.

I grabbed our witch's hand, needing something to steady me. There was still a constant flow of disgust and fear coming from her whenever she looked at the body.

After her explanation, I could understand why. General Lee had been doing the unthinkable.

"This is…" Vesper started, standing by my side, looking down at the general with a frown. She was trying to send calming waves to both of us through the bond, but it was a lost cause. The situation was unraveling into something far more horrifying than I ever could have imagined.

"Grotesque," I finished for her. "I didn't know this was even possible. That someone would stoop as low as…"

I shook my head. Even after I exposed him and everything fell into place, I don't think I truly understood the magnitude of what the vampire had done. To himself and others.

My eyes fell to Cedar for what felt like the millionth time. From the moment I showed everyone his wounds, she had been on edge. Not just anxiety, but fear. *True fear.* I'd never seen her like this. Even when her own coven hurt her. When we ran for our lives. When we watched Vesper get taken away from us.

She feared what the body meant. I could sense it in her. Even without the bond, it was easy because her entire body was tense and ready to run. Always facing the door.

"How many witches does it take to do this?" Vesper asked, looking at Cedar, and her fear spiked further.

"At least a dozen, I'm guessing."

My heart dropped.

Atlas looked at her. "You're *guessing*? Aren't you our expert here? Maybe we picked the wrong witch."

For the first time, Cedar looked to the ground, almost like a sign of submission to Atlas. Anger stirred to life in my veins.

"You don't speak to her that way," I hissed. Atlas glared at me but softened almost immediately after. I knew it was due to her soft spot for me, but I didn't give a damn.

I wouldn't allow anyone to talk like that to my lovers. Ally or otherwise.

"What I mean is that you're the only witch in close proximity. Are you telling me you know nothing? If we are going to figure out the risks of this whole thing, we need information."

Nervousness built up in Cedar. I reached out to grab her hand and found her shaking. My heart broke for our witch.

"All I know is that if vampires are doing *this*, I am in danger. Every witch is. Once they realize they can harness our power, they will do anything for it. No matter the consequences."

Vesper stepped forward, taking Cedar's other hand.

"What else can you tell us about this?"

"I think..." Cedar took a deep breath. "I think my coven is connected to this."

The news felt like a bomb.

"What do you mean?" I asked, my stomach dropping.

Her eyes shifted to mine before they went back to the body. But the words weren't coming out.

"The witch's body, right?" Caspian asked, finally coming closer. "I saw your reaction earlier."

He walked toward her and placed a hand on her shoulder. Surprisingly, she didn't push it off, but from the way her body was hunched forward, I guessed it was more because she lacked the energy than because she enjoyed his touch.

She nodded.

"Was it someone you recognized?" Vesper offered, her other hand coming to touch Cedar's and my joined ones.

Cedar sent her a bitter smile.

"The body was too destroyed to know," she said. "But our cloaks were magically treated to withstand even the most powerful magic."

"We won't let anything like that happen to you."

It was Caspian who delivered that line, bringing out a flood of warmness from me.

My life had been filled with men trying to hurt me. Steal from me. Bind me to them and use my body for whatever they wanted.

He was a refreshing change, and at that moment, I was glad I picked him.

"As heartwarming as this is, can you give us anything else?" Atlas growled.

"Just because you're pissed that you have to get married doesn't mean you can take it out on us," Vesper spat. "You think I wanted to be starved to death and turned into a vampire? You think Cedar wanted to spend every night living the same recurring nightmare after what her coven did to her? You think Aurelia wanted to be sold as a broodmare? Grow up, Atlas. No one wanted any of this."

Atlas's eyes turned a brilliant red.

"It's your fucking fault all this happened," she hissed. "All I wanted was to help Aurelia. I regret taking you in every day. All you've done is cause me trouble—"

"Both of you, stop!" My tone left no room for discussion as I stood between them. During the word sparring, they had inched closer to each other until they were a mere foot away, somehow forgetting about the dead body between us. "If you can't keep it together, I will be forced to treat you like the children you're acting like."

They glared at each other, neither of them willing to lose the game of pride.

I put one hand on each of their chests and pushed them away.

That got their attention, and they both looked down at me. I gave them a warning growl.

"Now, Cedar, if you'd be so kind as to finish telling us what you know."

She nodded and let out a shaky breath. I reached out and held her hand through it. Caspian was by her side, looking at her with the utmost concern.

"The only knowledge I have is what I spent years accumulating. The nightmares. The visions from the seer. About my parents."

"Visions?" Vesper asked. "You never told me..."

Bitterness and pain filled the bond.

"I didn't know it at first. He was trying to tell me something. I can see that now," she said, looking at the hunter with a pleading gaze. "My coven must've used a similar way to steal power. That's how my... parents died. He was showing it to me over and over again, forcing me to look. The rune was slightly different, but in my heart, I know it was meant for the same thing."

"Do you think your coven and the council have been working together?" I asked.

Cedar gave me a shaky nod.

"They're involved. I saw the rune on the floor in the room with Kyan. No one could do that except for a witch. So I guess it's your turn, Atlas. What can you tell us about your previous family?"

Atlas crossed her arms.

"They've worked with witches, that much I know. But I was not at the point where I knew much about the inner workings of the council before I left, so I can't help much there."

We were at a standstill. All the information we had was out in the open, but there was no clear path forward, and we still had a decaying body in front of us.

"On the bright side, without him, getting to my brother will be easier. And we can finish this prophecy once and for all. Even if we don't know much about what they're involved in, it's a start."

"I can ask the witches," Cedar said after a moment.

"*No.*"

"You're not going back there."

Vesper and I spoke at the same time, protectiveness flaring in the bond. Her face was a picture of exhaustion and anxiety, but for a moment, a small smile broke.

"Not my coven. There are others out there. More witches I can ask. I have a... *lead* I think can give us some answers."

Something was rumbling in my chest. I didn't want to say it. As the person in charge of seeing to my brother's downfall, I knew what I needed to ask of her, but I didn't want to. Not when this was already affecting her so badly.

"Ask, Princess. I see you wavering,"

Of course Cedar can see right through it.

I sighed. "We need to recruit the witches. I was originally going to ask you that, but after seeing how this affected you... I didn't want to push you too hard. Nor do I want to put you in danger again."

"I know, but we need the help, don't we? On top of that... The body should be returned. Your brother requested it be used as a message, but the covens may be able to figure out who he killed in the process and let their loved ones know."

"It will start a war," Atlas hissed. "And if they figure out the council is involved...

"Not if she says it was him alone," I said. "That was his story, and we will stick to it."

"We should still send a message to the council," Atlas insisted. "Let them know we are onto them."

Vesper snickered.

"Seriously? You're going to put us in danger just because you want to get back at them? Are you crazy?"

The comment set Atlas off. She rushed at Vesper, her hands grabbing her shirt.

"You know, I never fucking liked you. I smelled it from the beginning."

"Again... Grow. The fuck. Up." Vesper enunciated each word, almost like she was goading her.

In a second, Caspian was on the other side of Atlas, pulling her away, while I did the same to Vesper. *Fucking children.*

Aurelia gave Vesper a sharp look, and through the bond I could feel the anticipation for the punishment she was going to deliver for this outburst.

"The head goes to the council, the body to the witches," I hissed. "I will deliver the head with Vesper—*alone*—and Cedar will go to the witches."

"I am coming—"

"If you can prove to me that you will *not* fight Kyan and behave, I will have you come. But remember that our fight is with my brother, *not* the council."

Atlas held my gaze, her chest puffing. But then she stepped back.

"Kyan is still mad at me. Maybe it's better if I don't come."

"What is that about anyway?" Vesper asked.

Atlas looked like she was going to fight her but held back.

"I was born into the family in charge of the council. Kyan is a cousin, never supposed to be in charge," she admitted. "Everyone was looking forward to the day I would take over, but..." She looked away with a frown. "I didn't want it. I knew my family was up to some shit, but I never knew it was this. I ran. I kept my identity hidden and started my clan. I never looked back."

"Is that all?" Cedar asked. "Kyan seems to hate you."

Atlas's jaw clenched.

"I may or may not have killed her lover."

It was so silent you could hear a pin drop.

"Maybe we should get a messenger to drop it off."

"Agreed."

"Yep."

Vesper

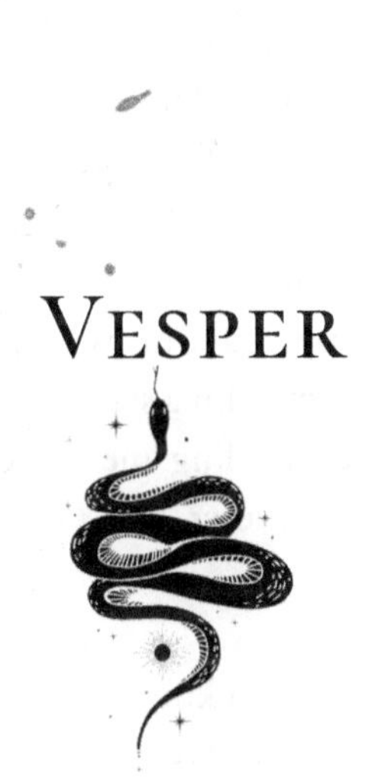

"Vesper!"

Tate's arms wrapped around my middle, and I froze. I'd been unsure of how he'd feel about the new me, but I couldn't help but melt into him when he squeezed me even harder.

The wind tousled my hair, so I pulled him to me, afraid that his still-human body might catch a cold.

It had taken some intricate work to get a message to them, but I was glad it worked out. We decided to meet on the outside of the property, close enough for my absence not to garner unwanted attention and far enough that no one would be reporting hunters gathering.

It was quiet, save for the sound of the other hunters Gabriel had brought with him, stationed just over the tree line. They were setting up a small camp, murmuring about what their leader was up to.

"I missed you," I whispered into Tate's hair. "I'm glad you're safe."

"It's you we should be worried about, always finding trouble," he grumbled and pushed himself away from me. Tears shone in his eyes, betraying his true feelings.

My poor, sweet little brother. He didn't deserve any of this, and it sucked that I had to tell him our father had died in a note. I could tell it was bothering him. The bags under his eyes were deep and told me he had been crying far more than usual.

This life was too hard for him. Part of me was glad he wouldn't have to go through what I did growing up, but that didn't mean I was any happier about us losing a parent.

I ruffled his hair and sent him a smile.

"Trouble seems to be finding me these days," I said with a sigh. "Are you hanging in there? Has Gabriel been treating you well?"

He gave me a sly grin.

"Well, if you *really* want to know, the organization sent us on a mission to capture these crazed rogues that were shooting—"

"Oh god, here we go again," Gabriel interrupted, coming up from our right. "He's fine. If anything, I think he likes living the nomadic lifestyle. What happened to never wanting to see me again, huh?"

He hadn't changed much, though my eyes narrowed on the tattoo on his neck. I didn't expect bitterness to flare at seeing it intact, but I couldn't help it. That wasn't the only thing getting on my nerves.

Anger flared in me no matter how hard I tried to clamp it down.

"Times change, but more importantly, you're taking him on missions?" I growled.

Gabriel shot me a look.

"We have to keep up appearances. Jobs don't stop when our father dies, our sister is cast out, and our mother is missing."

My slow-beating heart threatened to skip in my chest.

"No sign of her yet?"

Gabriel shook his head.

"I'm guessing Father knew that mission might be his last, so he prepared for Mother to go someplace far away."

Tate's grip on me tightened. I looked down to see tears welling in his eyes.

"That's exactly why he should be kept away from those missions. We don't know what the hunters want with him. Or if the vampire council will take you next. And yet you—"

"Ouch, Vesper! Lighten up, will you?"

I jerked away from Tate, realizing I was squeezing him a bit too hard with my vampire strength.

"Sorry," I muttered and looked back at Gabriel. I hated the pitiful look that crossed his face.

"How have you been handling... everything?" Gabriel asked, his tone shifting and his expression changing. It was hard for me to believe he cared about me, but it looked real.

"I'm back with Aurelia now, so better than being at the beck and call of some royal vampires."

"Don't act like you're not at your princess's beck and call," Tate teased.

I ruffled his hair. "You'll understand when you're older. I'm fine, really. I'm just... worried you two might be next."

"They are trying," Gabriel said with a sigh. "But we kill everyone they send, and you know the organization isn't about to let *all* their best hunters go."

I flinched, but it wasn't because of the word "hunter." It was because I wasn't one anymore. The identity I had aligned myself with for so long had suddenly and forcibly been taken away from me. It was hard to imagine a world where I wasn't a vampire hunter.

"It seemed to be common knowledge to everyone but myself that the organization uses hybrids."

"It's their worst-kept dirty secret." Gabriel clapped his hand on my back. "We're just glad you made it through."

I let myself simmer in the rare warmness between us.

When will I see them again? Will I?

What we were about to do would change the world as we

knew it. There would be deaths, and how many of those would be the same people we fought by and loved?

"Now," he said and cleared his throat. "Tell me what you need."

I looked down at Tate. He had grown since I'd last seen him, his face and body filling out, and his hair was longer. His boyish look was slowly disappearing.

I wanted to stay in this moment forever. Just being with the two of them and acting like nothing was going on outside our little bubble. But I wasn't here to see them. Just like Cedar had to get the witches on board, I was the only one with a connection to the hunters. Even if severed.

"We are going to finish the prophecy. Kill the last in the Castle line. But... he's getting stronger, and we don't know why. You remember, he beheaded the witches and was going on a rampage, killing everyone in sight without breaking a sweat. We can *feel* how much worse it's gotten now." I looked at Gabriel. Originally, I didn't want to tell him about what the general had done with the witches, but I couldn't hold it back. "His right hand, someone from the council, was caught sacrificing witches and taking their powers. Cedar said it was over a dozen."

Tate's gasp had me grinding my teeth. I hated how much of this he had to witness.

"Is that what her brother is doing too?" Gabriel asked.

I shook my head.

"His body would need to have a rune carved somewhere," I said. "From what we've seen, he doesn't have it."

He loved to show off his chest and back in robes, especially when he was with his feeders. If there was a rune, we, or one of the staff, would've seen it by now. Plus, in order to heal it, he would have to have a witch around, but Cedar hadn't mentioned another one.

"Can he get the magic another way?" Tate offered. "You know, like maybe drinking witch blood instead?"

I shook my head.

"If that were the case I would have magical powers too."

I paused when I realized the information I had just shared. Tate gave me a small snicker while Gabriel smirked.

"Look at my sister go," he joked. "A lover of every type. All that's missing is a human."

I let out a growl.

"Fine, fine. I'll shut up," he said, hands raised. "As far as using witches' magic that way, I'm not sure I've heard of anything like it."

"Are you sure?" I asked. "You were with the coven for a long time, and we know they're connected to this."

"My involvement was limited to seeing the prophecy through. I didn't linger around when we weren't working together on it."

"Oh! Maybe he's drinking other vampires' blood! Or killing them and eating their soul!"

I gave Tate a look.

"What are you reading nowadays that has you thinking that?"

"It's called *Dark Hunger*, and it's an epic comic where the main hero has been fed vampire blood all his life and slowly descends into—"

"Okay, enough!" Gabriel cut him off with a sigh. "Sorry we can't help you, and you came all this way—"

"I need something else," I said, turning serious. "He may be getting more powerful, but that doesn't mean we are giving up. We are recruiting. We need the hunters' help."

Gabriel looked at me for one long moment before grabbing Tate's arm and jerking him away. "Nope. We like our lives, thank you very much."

I reached out and took his other arm.

"Keep Tate somewhere safe, but I *need* the hunters. At least a good handful. There is no one better on this earth to kill a vampire like him."

"It's not our problem," he spat and tried to pull Tate away again.

"Wait! You can't just leave her like this!"

"You colluded with the witches to control my life and oversee the prophecy, but you can't even offer aid when we are trying to get it done?"

At that, he turned around.

"I am not putting our lives on the line! I worked with the witches to make sure you were protected during the prophecy. That you could see this whole thing through. But what you're talking about? This is madness!"

"I'm just asking for a few hunters," I forced out. "Why is this such a big deal—"

"Because you won't win!" His words settled over us like an icy blanket. "You won't win, Vesper. Not against someone like him."

Suspicion rose in me.

"You do know more than you're letting on."

He looked down at the ground.

"When it was Aurelia, I had hope. But him? I don't... I'd rather you abandon all thoughts of the prophecy and move on with your life. No matter the cost. If what you're saying about all this magic-stealing stuff is true, I... I don't have hope."

I stared at him, unable to comprehend the sudden switch.

"That's it, just like that?"

"Just like that," he said and tugged Tate along. "For all of our sakes, let's make this our last meeting until this is over."

Tate looked back at me with a frown.

"Stay safe!" he called back. "You can do this! With or without the hunters' help!"

I sent him a small wave.

Thanks to my new vampire hearing, I caught the last bits of Gabriel's muttering.

"Don't encourage her," he hissed. "She'll get herself killed."

"I have faith. She got this far, didn't she? Just think about it, okay? We have more than a few heads who would love a chance to get back at the vam—"

They were far enough away for me to hear anything else.

With a sigh, I looked up at the sky, wondering how on earth I was going to tell Aurelia I failed.

Cedar

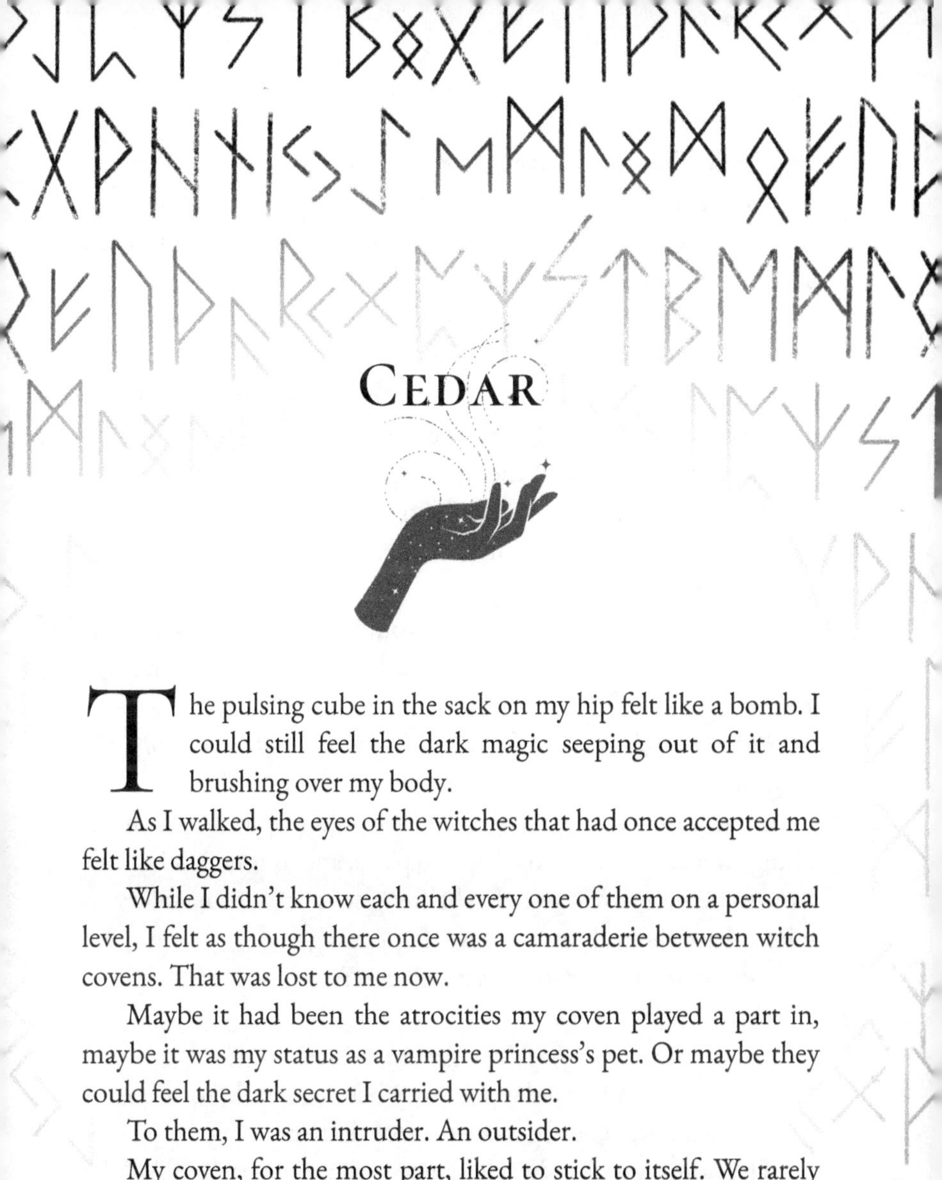

The pulsing cube in the sack on my hip felt like a bomb. I could still feel the dark magic seeping out of it and brushing over my body.

As I walked, the eyes of the witches that had once accepted me felt like daggers.

While I didn't know each and every one of them on a personal level, I felt as though there once was a camaraderie between witch covens. That was lost to me now.

Maybe it had been the atrocities my coven played a part in, maybe it was my status as a vampire princess's pet. Or maybe they could feel the dark secret I carried with me.

To them, I was an intruder. An outsider.

My coven, for the most part, liked to stick to itself. We rarely took the chance to interact with others, probably because our leader didn't want our crimes known to the public. I could see that now.

But this one... They knew me.

It was one of the few located in the heart of the city closest to the Castle family. They put up barriers around their territory that would repel anyone who would do them harm and all humans.

Except if they were wanted for something.

Levana had used their territory to lure Vesper to her. She and I had been the only two to deal with this coven and, to be honest, the only two on the coven grounds.

While I didn't know their official coven name or the name of the attack dogs they kept, there were one too many Edelweiss scattered about. On street corners. Street signs. On top of the entrance to what looked like a normal office building.

I swallowed down all the nervousness as I looked up at it. It was taller than all the other buildings around it and its very tip seemed to brush the clouds in the sky, almost as if it were a finger gently running across them.

There was no guarantee they would let me in. There must have already been rumors about what happened between me and mine.

But what they don't know is that my coven is helping the vampires.

Or at least it seemed like it, and I wouldn't put it past them. Things were all starting to click into place, and as much as I didn't want to be here, I felt an overwhelming sense of responsibility to at least warn them about what was happening.

And try not to start a war while I'm at it.

Easier said than done.

Just go in. Drop it off. Make a quick exit.

It was about a half a day's journey here and back, so at least if I was locked out, I could get back before dinner.

The bond was already aching and pulling me back to Aurelia and Vesper. I didn't want to leave them, not now.

We had agreed that I wouldn't point fingers at the council. I was just a messenger, nothing more, nothing less.

I just hope people still choose not to shoot the messenger.

Pushing myself to go, I was shocked when the doors all but fell away when I put my palm on one and pushed. I jerked forward, the sudden nothingness in front of me causing me to lose my balance.

My gasp caught in my throat when the scene changed in front of me, blown away by the sheer beauty of it.

Inside wasn't your normal office building. It didn't look like an office at all. I was transported directly into the forest with three towering waterfalls surrounding me. The sound of the water rang in my ears, and even the smell was clean and fresh.

Beyond them were tall mountains with bright flowers scattered throughout. A small breeze carried the scent of them and the water. It tickled the hair on my neck.

The floor below me changed from dirty concrete to flowing water. My heart jumped, afraid of falling in, but the cold splash of the water never came.

Is all this really possible?

"Cedar, my poor, sweet witch, you've been the talk of the town."

I forced a smile on my face and looked up to see a woman right in front of me. Long, white-silver hair, a heart-shaped face, pink painted lips, and a smile that looked like she truly pitied me. Her light blue eyes told a more sinister story, though. Her blue and white dress matched the surrounding water and flowed off her curvy body like the current below.

The power radiating from her was unmistakable. But it wasn't harsh, like my coven head's was. It was smooth, feeling just like the stream below us.

The gentleness scared me even more than the harshness of the magic back at my coven. Their cruelty was expected. However, her magic lulled me into a false sense of security, making me want to trust her without her doing anything to earn it.

"I would guess as much," I said and bent my head to her. "Morgan, it's nice to see you in person. I don't believe I've ever had the pleasure."

Her smile widened.

"Still so smooth with your words. Was that how you got not one, but *two* bonded to you?"

Heat washed up my neck. Of course she knew. Morgan was

the coven head and liked to remain elusive. While her location wasn't a secret, not many were granted entrance into her place.

Myself included.

"I didn't know the witches knew about that," I muttered.

Her eyes twinkled. "We know about everything, my dear. Even that dangerous box you carry."

Panic and fear flooded me.

"No. None of that. I won't hurt you."

But others may was what she left out.

"I suppose you know what it contains then." I reached into my sack to pull out the magic artifact that held the body of the monster who hunted my people. It pulsed with that same dirty energy I felt in the throne room.

Only when she plucked it out of my hands did I realize how heavy it made me feel. How sickly. My stomach lurched, and I had to clamp my hand over my mouth at the suddenness of it.

Morgan looked at it with a sadness that I couldn't bring myself to show, even though I felt it. It was a different kind of pain. One that sunk into your bones, scarring you so deeply that every time you saw another witch, you would be reminded of its existence.

"Disgusting creature," she said, handing it off to the side where an assistant appeared, seemingly out of nowhere, and took it from her before disappearing again. "We will do the work of trying to figure out the witches he stole from. Thank you, Cedar. I am sure the families will be happy to get some closure."

I bowed my head to her and took a step back, ready to make my swift exit, but she stopped me.

"Is there something you want to ask me?"

I froze, feeling like a mouse caught in a trap. The door was right behind me, but it felt like miles away.

The sound of the waterfall intensified.

My heart pounded in my chest.

"Are you a seer?" I breathed, feeling dizzy.

"I am many things," she admitted with a chuckle, taking my hand gently as she guided me further into her realm. "A coven leader. A mother. A protector. Most importantly, though, I know you want to know something about that Castle leader. So ask, my sweet witch."

I let her sit me down on a chair that looked transparent, the same current running under it, while she took another opposite me.

I sank into it with ease. My muscles relaxed, and for the first time in months, I felt like I could drift off into a deep sleep.

Not one plagued with nightmares.

"We haven't seen any markings on him, but he is getting stronger."

Her smile never changed, like she knew exactly what I was going to ask. Because she did. I had seen that look on the seer in my coven many times over.

"Then it isn't witch lives he is taking," she said. "And I think you know that."

I gritted my teeth. *Do I, though?* I wasn't so sure I knew much of anything anymore.

"I don't know much about these rituals."

"Don't you?" she asked, leaning forward. Her eyes dug into me. "In your memories, isn't there something you witnessed that might provide you with some answers?"

My parents' murder flashed before my eyes. I clenched my fists against the rage building up in me. I was so comfortable in the chair, mind unperturbed by anything else, that the memories seemed clear. More painful than before.

"That was different. My coven—"

"*Ex*-coven," she corrected. I didn't know why that sent a pang through my chest.

"He didn't have markings either," I said quickly.

Morgan just stared at me. Long enough for me to realize what I had said.

I cursed and looked down at the ground. A stray fish caught my eye. Unease traveled through me. Vesper and Aurelia tried to fight it through the bond, but it was too much without their presence.

"I don't want to go back," I whispered, hating how weak I sounded.

I was weak. I couldn't save Vesper by myself. Couldn't save Aurelia. I was a burden to them both, and now I was sitting with a coven leader talking about things I really shouldn't.

"But someone is waiting for you. He went through a great deal to save all three of you. Don't you think you should return the favor?"

I looked up at her to protest, but my eyes caught sight of something that had been banned for at least a decade. A single orb, bright red fire raging inside it.

My mind flashed to the dream the seer sent me.

The coven will burn.

Was that a message for me? A warning? And was Morgan giving me the keys to something unthinkable?

"If you want to enact your revenge, it's possible. But I ask that you save him." She gave me a long look, then whispered in the most broken voice. *"Please."*

Only then did I see the resemblance between her and the boy in my dreams. It wasn't the color of their hair or their eyes, but their features. The way they looked on with a soft, knowing gaze.

"His mother?"

She shook her head.

"His aunt. I watched my sister die to save him from that monster you once called coven leader. Our entire family was born with the power to see the future and has been hunted since. I am asking you to save him for her. Bring him back to me."

My mind stalled. Had the seers been leading me to this moment in an attempt to get one of their own free?

Now I'm starting to know how Vesper felt when she realized her entire life had been controlled by people behind the scenes.

"If I do this, will you join us?"

She stayed silent for a long moment.

"You know the answer to that."

I did. The witches never got involved in things that didn't concern them.

"Does he know how to stop it?" I asked. "The coven leader?"

She pushed the orb closer to me.

"I guess you'll have to find out for yourself, won't you?"

Did I want revenge so bad that I was willing to do this? I had been so busy with Aurelia and Vesper that I hadn't had time to realize what my parents' murder meant to me.

The rage was simmering below my skin, just waiting for a chance to burst out. If I could see it, I was sure it would have a similar hue to the orb in front of me.

"This is some sort of trick." I was trying to convince myself. A last desperate chance to talk myself out of it.

But I was being pulled in by the desire to burn it all down. To make them pay for hurting my parents. For hurting me. The people I love. He bled us dry until there was nothing left as he starved the people in the coven, hoarding power and using us as his watchdogs to keep the peace.

Even against our own people.

He didn't care about us. If anyone went against him, he would see that they were taken down, in or outside the coven. It was one of the reasons why I couldn't show my face around here often.

I was among the ones sent out to kill others. Just like Vesper, murder and darkness were attached to my entire being, no matter how much I tried to deny it.

Levana wasn't known as a witch killer. She could move with freedom. Come into this coven and befriend them.

I wasn't afforded the same liberties.

It was my last dirty secret. My lovers didn't know. It was the one thing I kept hidden away in the recesses of my mind, trying to help me forget.

They deserved to pay. And the coven leader in front of me seemed to read my thoughts with ease.

"A helping hand is all," she said with a smile.

"You're asking me to kill more of us than I already have. Doesn't it make you feel sick?"

I was trying to get a rise out of her, but she didn't fall for it.

"What makes me sick is all the beatings they put you through as a kid. The scars still pumping full of his magic, and I know they bother you, even now that you've escaped his clutches. That at night sometimes you sneak away when the others aren't paying attention and try to scrub your body clean of them."

I sat straight. My ears started ringing. "Stop."

Vesper and Aurelia didn't know about what I did in the shower when I was alone, and I was too ashamed to say it out loud.

"It makes me sick that they forced you out in the cold. That they put you through rigorous training when you were just a young girl. And my poor nephew, all alone. In chains. Never seeing the sunlight. I see the real monsters, Cedar. I've seen what they've done to you and what they will do. You would be doing us all a favor."

My eyes dropped back to the orb.

"Is this a prophecy?"

My hand was already reaching out, my fingers brushing over it.

Energy surged through me.

"I would call it a nudge."

I pulled back, my stomach twisting, and stood, looking down at her.

"I will get the information my own way. If I have a chance, I will save him. But that is not my focus right now."

Her smile never wavered.

"Go on now, sweet witch. Your lovers are getting impatient."

I bowed my head and turned to leave, but she gave me one last parting gift, her voice trailing after me.

"If you change your mind, the orb will be at your fingertips."

I left the fake office building with a shiver running down my spine.

Maybe it's time I leave the witches for good.

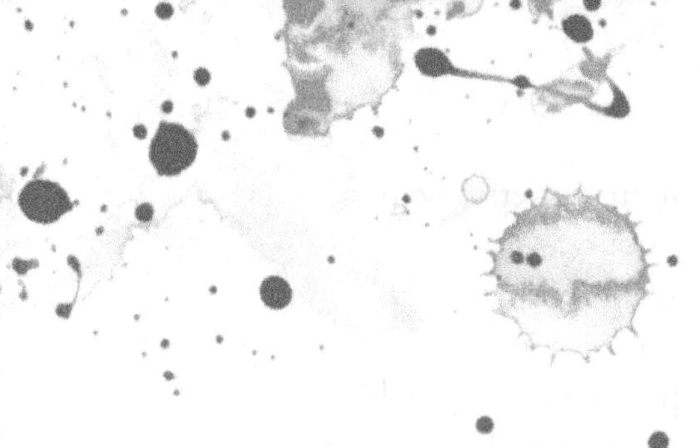

AURELIA

Cedar was keeping something from me. I could feel it in the way she averted her gaze.

Is she feeling guilty about something?

I prodded the bond, but nothing gave. Vesper was an open book with her emotions, but Cedar was getting better at hiding them from me.

I felt something happen when she went to deliver the body of the general, but we never got an answer from her. Days later, she hadn't divulged anything.

Until now.

We were all gathered for a secret meeting with the other royals. Our numbers had almost tripled since the last one, with more and more people seeing just how crazed my brother was becoming.

The ploy with the general helped. Regardless of his twisted actions, Adrian's reaction was extreme. Crazy even to some. And that scared people.

The unpredictability.

That was why the royals tolerated my father. While he might have been cruel to his own people—his daughter and wife included—he would never make waves. Not with the royals.

But my brother didn't care about that. All he cared about was his own power, and the more powerful he became, the easier he was to snap at a moment's notice.

My eyes shifted from vampire to vampire, taking in every single one of them. Their mannerisms. The small things they gave away when they thought people weren't watching.

I had no idea if I could trust any of these people.

But I have to try.

We had moved from one permanently wet and smelly place to another, this time with a longer table that could house most of the heads. Their right hands stood behind them, brushing shoulders with the people they'd never dare be caught in a room with before.

I sat at the head, chess pieces spread out before me. The king and his bishop stood together, pawns surrounding them.

"Fredrick first," I said and looked at the familiar face. It pleased me to no end that Dalia was able to convince her lover to join. She stood behind him, her true husband next to her. They were the first to call me out on my supposed loyalty to Adrian, so I knew they would be safe.

"We caught three seemingly rogue vampires canvassing the edges of our property last Saturday," he said, his low tenor spreading through the tense room. "We didn't know they held the Castle uniform and patch until after."

I nodded.

"Any discernible features?"

He shook his head.

I knocked three pawns down.

"Solei," I all but barked the name.

Stormy eyes met mine. The old vampire, the same one who had wanted to breed me and my mother for our distant relation to our goddess, sat at the far edge of the table. Atlas was sitting next to him, making sure he didn't do anything funny.

It had been her idea to bring him, something I was not all too happy about. But because of the stunt I pulled, he had missed out on one of his most prized possessions. Rumor was he blamed my brother for not marrying me off fast enough. For playing a silly game and losing.

Being in the same room as him was sickening, but what was the saying? *The enemy of my enemy is my friend...* or some shit.

He made sure to glare at Vesper every second he could, not forgetting the person who had led to the demise of his bloodline.

"The one in his shadow paid me a visit," he grumbled. "Talking something about blood contracts or whatever."

I raised a brow at him. The one he was talking about was one of the last of Adrian's people. Most of the others were already dead at his hands.

To be safe, we needed all of them gone. For this to work, I couldn't leave a single stone unturned.

"And yet I saw him just this very morning," I hissed. "So *why* did you not find a chance to kill him?"

"Because he mentioned something interesting," he said. "That there was a use for *vampire* blood instead of human blood."

Murmurs broke out, vampires looking at one another.

"Vampire blood?"

"But what about blood bonding?"

"One-sided?"

"Or we just kill them."

"It doesn't taste as good."

"Not as fun either."

I slammed my hand on the table to stop the gossiping. They were moving into dangerous territory, and if we didn't put a stop to it, I was worried at the ideas they might come up with on their own.

"What did he say exactly?"

He shrugged. "Just a mere suggestion. Asking if I ever considered switching the feeders for some hybrids or full vampires. Then he left."

My head was starting to thrum. Anger and annoyance were pulsing through our bond, making me all that more reactive.

Fuck the Solei.

"And you still let him live," I growled.

"He didn't do anything."

I imagined jumping up over the table, lunging at him, and tearing his heart out. I imagined crushing his head between my bare hands. Taking out his throat.

I hate this fucker.

Before I blew up, I moved on to the next.

"Elora."

She looked up at me, looking stronger than I'd seen her in years. It had been immensely painful to see what her husband did to her. I didn't know what changed, but I was glad something had.

After this was all over, maybe I would be able to help her.

"I have been whispering to my husband, but he is still unwilling to go against him openly. Lucky for us, we were also approached about blood contracts, and one of them got a little... handsy. The muscular one, tall, with the chain."

I knocked down a knight. It wasn't one of the more powerful vampires who seemed to gather around my brother like flies, but it was good enough.

"Do you see that, Solei?" I asked, looking back at him. "If there is a will, there is a way. Do I need to question your reason for being here?"

He sneered.

"My reason for being here is to get rid of that bastard for messing up my plans."

"Oh, yes, the plans of forcing me into marriage and raping me so I could have your disgusting little rat children," I said with a twisted smile. "Poor you."

Vesper's growl shot through the room.

His fists clenched at his sides, but he didn't move, telling me this truly might be his only chance to get rid of Adrian.

"Vesper."

"The hunters refused."

There was a sharp inhale from somewhere in the room. My fingers dug into the table, leaving indents.

"Why?"

"Too risky."

I scoffed. I shouldn't have expected much from the brother who had sold out his own sister for dubious reasons, but it was still a blow. Having the hunters on our side would have made all the difference.

"Cedar."

"The body has been delivered. The witches do not seem to have it in their mind to attack the council."

"Anything else?"

"They want me to go back to my clan, tie up some loose ends..."

She trailed off at the end, causing me to look up at her.

"And?"

"And my old coven leader may be using the same type of ritual to make himself stronger. Just like Adrian, he doesn't have any markings on his body, at least that anyone's seen. But I do know he drains witches for power, so there is a chance he knows how to put a stop to it."

Is this why she is looking at me like that?

Guilt ran through me. Because of our plan, she would be forced to go back to the clan that abused her and murdered her parents. It was our only chance to try and stop either of them from gaining more power, and Cedar would pay the price.

If she makes it out alive.

My immediate reaction was to say no, but I couldn't, not in front of the group. Not if I wanted to seem like the cold-blooded leader I was supposed to be.

"I don't suppose he will give that information willingly."

"No, but I have some ideas on how to get it out of him."

I would talk to her about this later. Vesper shot me a look, and the bond told me how displeased she was with this information.

You and me both.

We had barely made it out alive, and she was insinuating she would go alone. Even if they both went, I still wouldn't feel comfortable.

Her coven was even worse than my brother in some ways.

"Anyone else has an update?' I asked, turning back to the group. Hands raised. "If it's not about killing any of his people, information on his dealings, or any *credible* rumors about his next plans, I don't want to hear it."

A few vampires had the nerve to lower their hand.

I sat back and motioned for the others to continue, but the entire time, my mind was on the witch at my side.

I will do whatever it takes to make sure she doesn't go back there.

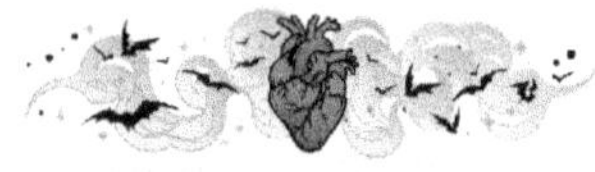

"You're not going," I said, sitting on the cold counter in the bathroom while she washed her face.

She was wearing nothing but loose pants, leaving her breasts bare. Not like it mattered, since she'd be naked in mere minutes and there was no one else here but Vesper and me.

But fuck, it was a delicious distraction.

Vesper was on the other side of her, leaning against the counter.

"What is this, some type of ambush?" she asked with a smirk. It was reminiscent of the old her, the witch who had somehow snuck into my guard. She had been so playful then, but between our escape from my father and her coven, she lost that part of herself.

I bet the nightmares don't help.

They had slowed in frequency over the last week or so, but that didn't mean they were gone for good. Vesper and I watched her during the night, trying to calm her, though nothing really helped until the nightmare was over.

Cedar wiped her face with a towel. I grabbed her wrist and forced her to look at me.

"It's too dangerous," I said. "I don't care what the witches told you or what your coven leader knows, you aren't going back."

With a sigh, she inched closer until she was between my legs, her face so close to mine it made me lose my thought for a few moments.

She was so beautiful. The green eyes. The freckles splattered across her face like stars. It was a wonder I didn't notice her the very first time I saw her.

"Is my poor princess worried about me?" Her hands ran up my arms. "Or is this your way of saying I haven't been paying enough attention to you?"

"Don't try to distract me," I hissed. Vesper came up behind her, her arms sliding across her torso, and it was Cedar's turn to shudder. She tried to keep a straight face, but I could see and feel the desire flashing across her face.

I leaned forward and left open-mouthed kisses on her chest.

"You're staying here," I said decisively. "We will find another way."

She let out a shaky breath when Vesper's hands slipped into her pants.

"What a delightful ambush."

"We love you, Cedar. We don't want to see you hurt, and we can't..."

Vesper couldn't find her words, but I could. I had been ruminating on them since the day they came to my engagement party.

"Lose you," I finished for her and pulled Cedar's nipple into my mouth.

She let out a moan.

"I may need a bit more convincing. After all, the ceremony is in two days, and we are still outnumbered."

"Leave that to me," I whispered and bit down on her nipple. I could feel the pleasure shoot through the bond as Vesper started playing with her clit.

"Don't be stupid," Vesper warned. "Don't leave us."

She turned to the side and captured Vesper's mouth in hers.

My cunt pulsed at the sight of them. They fit so well together. Beautifully. Vesper's pale skin and deep scars shone in the light. She opened her eyes, catching mine as they devoured each other.

Because of the prophecy, I had both of them.

For the first time in my life, I was feeling true warmth. Comfort. Love.

When they parted, I grabbed Cedar's face and forced her lips to mine. We melted into each other. The kiss spoke so many words for us.

I need you, said a flick of her tongue.

I love you, said her lips as they moved against mine.

Please don't leave, said our bodies as they pressed together.

I couldn't remember the last time I had gotten so lost in a kiss. And when she moaned into my mouth because of Vesper, I swallowed it all greedily, taking it as if it were my own.

I wanted to show her how much I wanted her. Needed her. And with the words seemingly failing me now, I focused on the next best thing.

Our bodies.

"Beautiful," I said breathlessly as we pulled away from the kiss. My hands ran down her body, and instead of my usually harsher ways for pulling pleasure from her, I focused on being gentle.

My fingertips were light as I caressed her chin, then her neck. The bond was spurring to life. We had no problem feeding it every single night we were together, but there was something more about this moment.

It felt... intensified.

I placed my palm where the bond should be in her chest and watched her watch me.

"All ours," Vesper whispered, her lips on Cedar's shoulder. "You're important to us."

A knot started forming in my throat. *Vesper found the words after all.*

"Is that so?" Cedar asked.

Vesper slipped her hand further into her pants, bringing her fingers to her pussy from behind. I made quick work of pushing them down so I could see it as she slowly began fucking her.

My fingers were light as I circled her clit, and she leaned back, putting her weight on Vesper, finally letting herself indulge in us.

"Don't tell me you can't see it? Feel it?"

Doubt crossed into the bond, telling me Cedar might not feel we really wanted her. Or that we didn't feel as strongly about her as we did about each other.

"My poor witch," I cooed and placed a sweet kiss on her chest. The bond stirred. "Stop doubting us. You belong here, with us." She let out a deep moan. "You were made for us."

"We were inevitable," Vesper continued. "The three of us. The universe made us like this, puzzle pieces meant to fit together."

Cedar's head felt back.

"Eyes on me, my love."

Her head snapped up at the nickname. I could feel it then, the warmth spreading between us.

I slipped my fingers through her folds, pushing them in with Vesper's.

"This is what you want, isn't it? Both of us?"

"Yes," she forced out.

We pushed our fingers in deeper, curling and twisting them.

"Do we make that pussy feel good, my love?"

Her mouth was open, but nothing came out, save for a gargled moan.

With two of my fingers and two of Vesper's, she was being stretched further than ever, but fuck, did she take it well.

Her cunt was hot, pulsing around us as we slowly fucked her in tandem.

"This pussy is ours. You're ours. And we're not willing to let any harm come to you. Never again."

"Never," Vesper vowed, her fangs brushing Cedar's skin. "I'll kill anyone who ever harms you."

"Why? Why me?"

"Because you're you. A beautiful lotus that bloomed in even the coldest conditions. Born from tragedy, just like us. A survivor. A fighter. But most of all…"

"No one else would ever do. No one but you," Vesper finished.

"Ours," I said as I pushed my fingers further into her.

"Oh gods," she muttered. "You two feel so good filling me up."

"Do you need any more proof of us?" Vesper whispered, her fangs getting dangerously close to her neck.

"Bite me," she begged. "Both of you."

I didn't need to be told twice.

Vesper took one side of her neck, I took the other, and both of us bit down.

A symphony of moans and pleasure shot through us. Cedar's magic exploded, caressing us in warmth, finally also deciding to accept us fully.

I drank gulp after gulp until I was able to pull myself away to look at her beautifully flushed face. Her cunt pulsed around us, her orgasm tearing through the three of us.

"You are not an outsider here," I whispered, and her breath told me I hit my mark. *She really was thinking this.* "You are not just someone we picked up along the way. You were meant to be here, with us, and that is where you will stay. Do you understand?"

She nodded.

"I understand. Now, please, let me touch you."

Vesper detached from her neck. "No, witch. We aren't done with you," she said. "Tonight, it's all for you, and we'll keep going until there's not a single doubt in your mind."

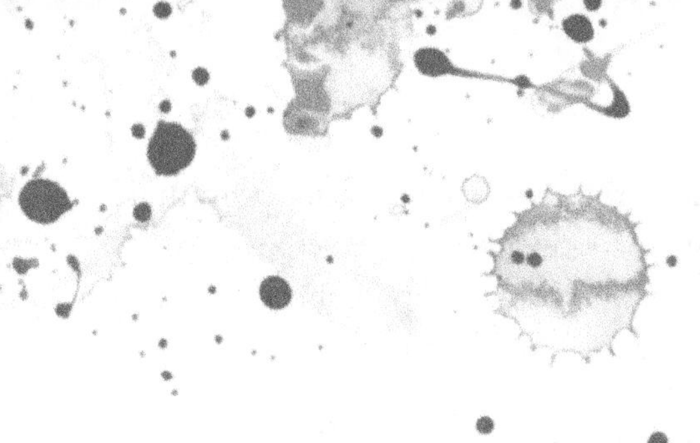

AURELIA

The Underground was a dark and dingy place that made my skin crawl.

It wasn't accessible to most vampires since those here were on the rougher side. It was rumored to be filled with mostly criminals and rogues who were cast out from society and said to house some being hunted by the organization.

But luckily, thanks to my connections, I had found a way in.

Many feared the horrors that waited below. But I needed exactly that.

Adrian was about to be unleashed onto the world. The prophecy dictated that the Castle family needed to be ruined when the bloodline came to maturity, and the ceremony was only a day away. If I couldn't finish it, I was positive that a lot more horrors awaited us.

So, whatever was rumored to be in the Underground was probably the type of disturbing creatures I needed.

The real question was if they would want to work with me.

Thanks to Caspian, I had more than enough resources at my fingertips, but who knew what they would want? Or if they would even care?

"Who knew the Underground was actually underground?" I grumbled as I almost lost my footing on a loose rock.

This entrance was at the base of a mountain, likely an old mine shaft they had repurposed for their dealings. It was dusty and smelled like old blood.

I had left Vesper and Cedar at home, telling them I was going to meet Caspian, and gave them a task to find something in the palace. Since I didn't let Cedar go to the witches, we were running on the little information we knew.

And because we were assuming this had to be some type of witch ritual, I asked them to find runes. I wasn't sure if they truly bought it, but it would at least give me some time. I needed to keep my feelings in check so as not to disclose anything through the bond.

I was starting to doubt if Adrian truly was using a witch ritual. *Especially after what Solei said.* But I didn't have time to entertain silly notions such as that.

I wrinkled my nose as I walked further in.

There were no lights, with likely all their people relying on their vampire senses to make it in safely.

"Sometimes the best disguises are the simplest ones."

A voice came from the darkness. I squinted, but even my vampire sight felt useless here. I could make out their movements as they walked, but the darkness seemed to cling to them, creating a shadow of a person.

Then I smelled it. A pungent, burning smell of wood.

"I didn't know they accepted witches," I noted and tried not to freeze when the voice spoke right by my ear.

"We have creatures you never even thought walked this earth hidden away. But one thing's for sure: we don't accept your kind, *Princess.*" The voice was clearly feminine. Her hand reached out to touch me, and I turned to face her.

The sunlight coming from behind her blocked out the majority of her features, but I could make out the white-streaked short hair and glowing red eyes.

"You found this place, which means someone has a big mouth. Either they decided you needed our help, or they sent you as..." She was suddenly behind me again. "*Bait.* Which is it?"

"I'm surprised you don't know. After all, you are the ruler of this place, are you not?" I asked, ignoring a shiver. "There is a thorn in my side, and I am in the process of getting rid of it. I came to inquire if the Underground would like a stake in it."

The chuckle she let out had the smallest bit of fear spiking in my heart. She sounded almost as crazed as my brother.

I just hoped she was more willing to listen than him.

After all, she would get the most out of this.

"I never said I was the ruler," she said.

"Don't try to act modest now," I answered with a smile.

She scoffed.

"We don't want anything to do with the above-ground world. All you do is fight us. Harm us. Throw us away like trash."

Her hatred feels real.

"I see you care for your people," I told her as her magic surrounded us. It went around my arms. My legs. Throat. Then it squeezed. "I care for mine too, that's why I'm doing this."

"I don't take kindly to *liars.* Try again."

She squeezed harder, making it difficult to think through my panic.

"It's truly a part of it," I forced out, my hand coming to grasp at nothing.

"But not all," she hissed. "One more time, *try again.*"

"For the people I love!" I said hastily. "For us. I want to end this prophecy and live the life we deserve."

She let the words linger in the air as if tasting them.

"There it is," she cooed. "The selfish princess. But still, the Underground wants no part in this—"

"I don't want your people to get hurt. I don't want any more lives lost. That is why I *need* you. Please. We have others. Royals. Hunters. Another witch. But numbers are everything. I'm... *I'm calling a Royale.*"

There was a pause, then she let out a booming laugh, her red glowing eyes coming up in front of me.

"A *Royale*? You against him? You'll never win."

The Royale was something only royal vampire siblings could call. A duel to determine the rightful ruler of the throne. It became more common after the fall of the hunters when the vampire population boomed. Clans and royal families started producing heirs left and right, and when the time came for someone to sit on the throne, too many people wanted it.

They solved it in the simplest terms that would leave no question.

A fight to the death.

The last secret I am keeping from my lovers.

It was the only way I knew to get his defenses down. It would just be me and him.

"I won't, which is why I'm recruiting."

"And breaking the rules?" She pulled away with a raised brow. Her surprise must have made some of the magic disappear, as I was able to make out her scarred face.

"I either break the rules, get cast out, and win, or..."

My throat closed of its own accord. I had considered this possibility, but I was having a hard time saying it out loud.

"Or you die, and everyone else jumps in to avenge you. So sweet. Didn't take you as a sacrificial lamb. Though you were the hottest gossip when you sold yourself to your husband."

She turned her back on me. An insulting gesture that told me that, even with her back turned, I posed no threat to her.

"But that still doesn't tell me what's in it for us."

"Land," I said. "Inside a barrier where no one can find you. It must get stuffy here."

If that piqued her interest, she didn't show it.

"Last I checked, you weren't in a position to offer Castle land."

Nor would anything to do with Castle property appeal to them. Once a family was plunged into ruin, no one wanted the remnants for at least a millennium, for fear of what curses the land might hold.

"I'm not," I admitted with a smirk. "My husband's land. He's terribly bored with the fortune his family left him and is willing to give it up."

"The Hart family," she mused. "He does have a good section, and it's near the mountains, so we could extend our Underground there..." She rubbed her chin. "How much?"

My smirk widened.

"All of it."

She froze and turned to me.

"You're lying."

I puffed my chest and put my hands on my hips.

"I know you can tell I'm not." *Or at least I think that's what her freaky power does.*

"And the people?" she asked, her voice coming quicker.

"Just like the Castle family, they will be let go and free to roam to whichever clan or family suits them."

She let out a hum. "Maybe you're not as cruel as the rumors have you out to be."

"My people have suffered under my family, then were used by Prince Icas, only to now fall under the rule of my brother, who has been murdering them left and right. They deserve freedom."

"I want them."

My heart sank. My fists balled at my sides.

"No."

Her smirk was so wide that I caught not one, but *two* of her shiny canines, giving her a total of four on each side.

I've never seen a vampire with a mutation like this. It scared me to think I had no idea of what type of creature I was dealing with.

"Even if it's the difference between your life and death."

"Even then," I said and stood tall. My people were nonnegotiable. I might not be their princess anymore, but I would do what I could to help with their suffering.

She held my gaze before delivering another one of those skin-crawling laughs.

"I told you, Princess; we have other creatures in our depths and have no use for your kind. I just wanted to see your reaction. I will provide some of our strongest, but don't expect an army."

Relief washed through me. Even if I couldn't win this... *they could.* It hurt to think of what would happen to Vesper and Cedar when I was gone. Especially when we had just been reunited again.

"My husband will see to the land. Show up tomorrow, and it's yours."

I walked past her, not willing to stay any longer in such a claustrophobic place. It felt like the walls might collapse on me.

"Just a warning, Princess. If we see this Royale going south, we are backing out. Silently and without warning. Even a *whiff* that it is doomed, and we are gone."

"I would expect nothing less from a ruler who cares for their people," I said and continued my exit.

"Good luck, Princess. If fate allows, maybe the world can finally see what true nightmares lie below the surface."

Cedar

One more day.

    One more day, and Aurelia was off to meet her husband. I was part jealous and part nervous. Tomorrow we would end this, for better or for worse.

Hopefully for the better.

I still felt like I wasn't contributing enough because I wasn't going to the coven. Vesper had been beaten up by the general and still went back to her hunter brother, after all.

Both of them had made a very interesting case for me not to. Apparently, tag-teaming me was an easy way to get me to submit.

But there was just too much on the line.

Now we were going crazy, searching the entire palace for the remote possibility that there could be a rune hiding somewhere. But the longer I stayed in the castle, the surer I was there was no magic involved at all.

Vesper and I had split up, with her taking the upper levels of the castle and me the lower. Hours later, and there was no hint of magic. Nor any sign of what Aurelia was doing through the bond.

My mind was going crazy.

Did she send us on a wild goose chase to distract us from her real purpose?

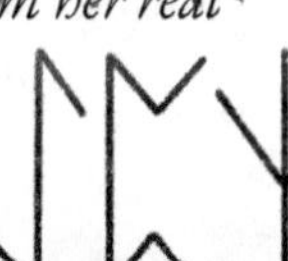

The palace was unusually quiet. No sign of her brother or any of his guardsmen.

My brain started feeding me images of her being tortured. Of her brother figuring out our plans and taking her hostage. Or maybe Solei, who eyed her with so much disgust it made my skin crawl. Maybe he'd found a way to take what he was owed, just like her father did.

I couldn't let it get to me, not until I had searched every nook and cranny. I tried to trust that she was doing this for a reason. And maybe we would learn something, and I wouldn't feel like such a useless piece of trash.

The dungeons were the last place I needed to check.

I had avoided the area and had only come down here once when I was a simple guard who infiltrated the palace. Vesper had been taken, and even back then, it had been hard to see her tied up and hurt. But I was focused on my job of seeing the prophecy through while trying to ignore my feelings when she was obviously so intertwined with the princess.

Us being together had only been a fantasy then. Now, I had them both. It was very real, and I wasn't willing to let them go.

I snuck down the hall, my eyes skimming over the piled vampire bodies in each cell. My stomach flipped. Bile started rising.

What the hell is all this?

The first cell was bad, but one look at the next one, and I found another pile of bodies. Horror filled my body, and it pushed me further. There was no way each cell could be full of death like this.

But the further I got, the higher the piles of bodies got. There seemed to be no end to them.

Where is he getting all these vampires? Is he culling the Castle family?

Then I felt it. Something that was but a small wisp of magic during my first run here now felt like a full-on tidal wave.

It's coming from below.

I followed the feeling, going further into the dungeons. It was potent, old magic, not as disgusting as the general's, but it felt *wrong* nonetheless.

It wasn't until I stopped at a large iron door at the end of the hallway that I realized what I had stumbled upon.

Feeling my anxiety, Vesper was probing the bond, but I pushed it away. I wouldn't get her involved until I was sure.

I found it.

I found what her brother was doing to make him stronger. And it was locked behind heavy iron doors that looked to be centuries old.

A sick hope filled me.

My hands ran over the carvings as I tried to further feel the magic.

And hopefully not get thrown back by an explosion this time.

The smaller carvings depicted the goddess Krae. Some had her praying, some kneeling, but all of them surrounded one huge carving. In it, she was holding her hands out as if inviting me in.

It wanted me to touch it. Wanted me to open it. It was so strong, I could almost hear a chanting in my mind.

When wrongness stirred in my chest, I found myself backing away, my body catching on quicker than my mind.

This is wrong. Something is wrong.

Alarm bells were ringing in my head.

This is unguarded. Why is this unguarded? It shouldn't be. If anything, the dungeons should be filled with people trying to protect the very thing I was about to open.

Run.

But when I turned to do that, someone was behind me.

Him.

I stumbled back, away from Adrian, as he looked at me with the same expression he had in the throne room.

There's nowhere to go. I'm trapped.

"I needed a witch anyway, but you're a day too soon," he said with a sigh and ran his hand through his hair.

"What's behind there?" I asked and tried to move further away, though I knew that putting space between us was only delaying the inevitable.

I'm going to die here.

Panic shot through the bond. I could almost hear Vesper's panicked yell through my mind. I still couldn't hear Aurelia, though.

"What?" He looked up as if he were thinking. When his eyes met mine again, they were completely red.

My stomach sank.

"Who?" I asked, my voice shaking.

His smile widened.

"Don't worry, you'll see what's behind the door, but first... Let's take a nap."

Pain shot through my neck. My magic didn't have enough time to react to his speed.

Time slowed. My body felt heavy. Blackness started closing in.

"We'll have use for you yet, little witch. See you when you wake up."

Against the screaming in my head, my world turned black.

VESPER

Something's wrong.

Part of the bond went silent. I could finally feel Aurelia, and it was getting stronger, meaning she was getting closer. But Cedar's part of the bond was gone.

It wasn't like when she was asleep at night. We could still feel her then, feel her fear and pain.

But this... There was nothing there.

The bond still existed, nestled inside me right next to Aurelia, but it was dormant. Cold.

I finished my work in the upper floors and bolted down to the foyer. The bond was pulling me to her. Our panic feeding into each other's.

By the time Aurelia rushed through the doors, I felt like I was going to jump out of my skin. Her hair was tousled from her run up into the house, her dress dirty at the hem, and she smelled of blood and magic.

"Where were you?" I asked and grabbed her by the arm.

She looked over my shoulder, then back at me.

"I was meeting my husband," she whispered. Most of the time, when she was with us, she called him Caspian. None of us liked his official title.

I thought she was doing something to prepare for tomorrow. But why couldn't we know about it? And why did it have to be now?

Did she send us on this scavenger hunt knowing we'd find nothing?

I couldn't feel angry because of how panicked I was.

"The bond... It's—"

"I know," she said in a nervous whisper. "Where was she? Did she find—"

"Oh good, you're finally back from *visiting your husband*," Adrian said, suddenly at our side. Dread rose in me so quickly, I jerked away from him, automatically trying to take Aurelia with me.

His slightly red eyes met mine, and he gave me a smirk that showed off his sharp fangs.

In my panic, I had moved to face him, pushing Aurelia behind me.

"Forever the protector," he said in a cheery voice that felt more like a sneer.

Aurelia peeked around me, her hand brushing across my arm. It was her way of telling me to stand down without actually saying the words, but I had trouble moving. Especially when Adrian looked at me with such disdain.

Before this, he made the effort to hide how much he truly hated me, but it seemed that he was done playing.

It made me worried. For both my lovers.

"I wanted to go over some details with you about tomorrow." His eyes fell to Aurelia. "Do you have time for a feeding?"

"Yes," she said quickly and stepped around me. "I'm parched."

Her brother gave me a long look.

"Is your *toy* joining?"

I opened my mouth to say yes, but Aurelia beat me to it.

"No, she hasn't been performing well. That's why I had to stay so long today." Her tone was extra snooty, and I tried to pretend like it didn't hurt me, but I knew she could feel it in the bond. "She will retire until she is well enough to serve."

Adrian let out a snort.

"It's because you tire her out. It wouldn't be like this if you'd chosen a born vampire."

I clenched my fists, trying to keep the growl from rising up in my chest.

"Maybe for the next one," Aurelia casually commented as she allowed herself to be pulled away. Just as she was about to disappear, she gave me a look that told me how sorry she was.

Keep it together, I told myself. *You have bigger things to deal with than her shitty attitude.*

I waited until they were out of sight before I started trying to follow the remnants of the bond, but because of how dormant it was, I couldn't pinpoint an exact direction.

So I did what I would do as a hunter. I focused on the lower levels, where she had gone. Taking one of the staircases down, I went further into the palace. I remembered doing this another time, sneaking around, trying to kill the princess.

Back then it had been risky, but this time if I failed, it wasn't just my life that would be on the line. It could mean trouble for all of us.

My footsteps echoed in the empty hallways. The upper floors still had some workers mulling about doing their job, but there was no one here.

Weird.

Every moment that passed had me more worried about Cedar. I was constantly looking over my shoulder, feeling like I was being followed.

Where are you?

The sun had set over five hours ago. The coming-of-age ceremony would be happening in a mere six hours. Aurelia wouldn't be coming to help.

I need to find Cedar.

We've been living in enemy territory and plotting against him. Maybe he finally figured out what we're trying to do.

It scared me. I had already been so close to losing both of them. I couldn't let it happen again.

The silence in the bond was the most frightening thing I'd ever felt.

It feels like Cedar is truly gone.

I couldn't let my mind wander to what could be. It only made the fear in my stomach that much worse. I felt like I was going to throw up.

I walked the lower halls, visiting the old quarters where the guards were. It was mostly empty. Whether that was because of our work taking out his people or because Adrian himself had decided to use them as practice, I couldn't tell.

Suspicion rose in me, and I couldn't shake it.

I listened carefully, making sure my footsteps were as silent as possible.

There were still some guards hidden in the rooms. I could hear them sleeping. But none so much as stirred as I walked past.

I inhaled deeply, trying to find the smallest scent of my witch, but there was nothing. Logic told me she had to have been here, but I couldn't find any sign of her.

I took to the rooms, peeking in, but after the fourth or fifth door, I started to get antsy. The longer I spent searching, the worse I felt.

All the anxious thoughts in my mind started to feel real, so I skipped the rest of the bedrooms and headed straight for the dungeons.

Just as I was about to go down the stairs leading to it, footsteps reached my ears.

I hurried back, ducking behind a corner just as two guards made their way up. I held still in case they sensed me, but they seemed too involved in their own conversation to even notice me, so I decided to get a good look at them.

They looked to be in Adrian's inner circle. Maybe the only two still alive. They had been on our list to take out. And, more importantly, if they were here, I assumed Cedar would be too.

"The bodies are starting to smell," one said, wrinkling his nose.

"They don't even have any blood anymore," the other one huffed. "All of them have been drained dry, so I don't know why he's keeping them."

The other one twisted his neck and rolled his shoulders as if he'd been doing some heavy lifting.

"Well, you know the princess. She'd start asking questions if a bunch of bodies started showing up."

Bodies?

There was a small laugh.

"And, you know, she would never lower herself to come to a place as dirty as the dungeons. Honestly, he was pretty smart to think of it."

The other vampire sighed and looked down the hallway. I quickly ducked back behind the corner, counting the seconds until he spoke again.

"You know... During the ceremony tomorrow, maybe we can sneak down and get some of that *special blood*—"

There was a muffled thud and then the sound of someone crumpling to the ground.

"Say that one more time and I'll feed you to him," one threatened the other. "Then you'll just be one more body down there. Got it? You're lucky you've made it this far."

"What the fuck, man! I thought we were joking around."

"I don't joke about things that would cost me in my life," the other said before I heard their footsteps, thankfully leading toward the opposite end of the hallway.

I glanced over just in time to see the other vampire get up shakily. I expected him to follow the other, but instead, he stood there grumbling.

Oh come on.

The bond was stirring. I was close enough.

Cedar is down there.

I don't have time for this.

As fast and as silently as my legs would carry me, I closed the space between us. He didn't even have enough time to realize what was happening before my hands were on his head and I snapped his neck.

I didn't stop there. The anger, panic, and nerves were too much. It caused me to lose control.

I pulled the head clean off and carefully caught the body before it fell to the ground and alerted anyone else. Hauling it over my shoulder, I made my way down. Blood was spilling behind me, but at this point, I didn't care.

Something was dangerously wrong here, and if I didn't hurry, I was afraid that Cedar would become one of the bodies they mentioned.

The smell hit me immediately. It might not be obvious to those without a super sense of smell, but I could make out the dozens, if not hundreds, of dead bodies stuffed in the cells.

Quickly, I put the guard in the first one, trying not to let myself get too distracted by the mountains of dead vampires.

They had been slaughtered. Their necks slashed. Body parts pulled apart. Arteries cut.

They wanted every single drop.

Special blood.

Most of the wounds seemed to have been made to get as much blood out as possible. I walked down the cells, pausing at one of them when I made out a vampire I had seen during my first day in the castle. It was a family member.

Actually...

My heart dropped into my stomach. A lot of them were either guards or vampires from the Castle family. Some even part of Caspian's present.

The disgust was almost unbearable.

Why is he doing this?

But the more I thought about it, I realized that I hadn't seen many feeders around. A handful maybe, but there should have been dozens for a family this large.

Is he drinking vampire blood instead?

Impossible. He had to be doing something else with it, but I didn't have time to think about it now.

Instead, I kept walking, going further into the dungeons than I'd ever been before. I followed the hallway until it started slanting down and turning.

That was when I heard it.

Small, melodic whispers, barely audible, muffled by the thick dungeon walls.

They came from the same direction as the bond. I kept going but came to a sudden stop when I reached the door. Krae was on it, reaching for me, and my breath was stolen from me when I felt the power of whatever was behind it.

Cedar is in there as well.

The bond pulsed, pulling me closer.

I walked forward with careful steps, my hand reaching out to touch the carvings on the door. Power zapped at my fingertips.

It told me to back away. To run and hide.

But I wouldn't. Not this time.

There would be no more running and no more hiding. I needed to face what was in there, so I pushed it, needing to use more strength than I anticipated.

Inside was a large, circular room. It was huge, and light was streaming in from the top as the sun started rising. Cedar was right near the entrance, unconscious. I lunged toward her, taking her in my arms and pulling her to me.

Her skin is so cold.

I held her tight, rubbing my hands up and down her arms in an attempt to warm her up. She didn't have any visible markings, but I could tell her power had somehow been zapped from her.

She stirred but didn't fully wake.

The melody started up again, and my attention was pulled to the middle of the room. Chains that connected to either side of it came together there, binding thin wrists.

A person. A woman, to be exact, with long hair that fell over her face as she hung from the chains. She was on her knees, her white dress stained with so much blood it was starting to turn black in places.

Her soft voice carried across the room.

What the fuck?

As if sensing me, she looked up, her eyes meeting mine. Black veins ran up her face, down her arms, and into her hands.

Cedar woke up with a gasp, grabbing onto me. She forced me to look at her, fear crossing her features.

"This is bigger than we thought. It's not just him. Her father too. All of them have been gaining power through her. We have to let her go. We have to tell Aurelia she—"

The singing got louder, pulling both of us to the women in the middle. She slowly got to her feet, swaying unsteadily.

"Aurelia..." she moaned. *"Stay fierce."*

Her singing sounded more haunting now. Like a child's lullaby, but with a dark edge to it.

"Hush now, little princess, don't you cry,

Daddy's coming soon, so wipe your eyes.

You know how he listens for the smallest sighs.

Hush now, darling, don't make a sound.

Daddy doesn't like it when your tears are found."

Horror hit me like a tidal wave.

Is this...?

There was no possible way the woman trapped in the dungeons was who I thought she was.

"It's her," Cedar forced out, her hands holding my shirt. "It's her mother."

The women swayed before looking up at the rising sun.

"Today's the day. You've come to save me, sweet hunter," she sighed, then looked right into my eyes. "The prophecy is coming to fruition and finally... We will be free."

I sat there, unable to move, as realization hit me.

The prophecy is way bigger than anyone ever imagined.

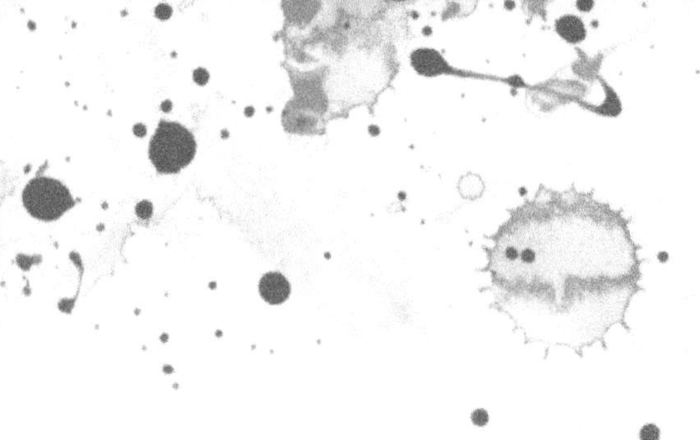

AURELIA

here are they?

My hand lingered on my chest. Underneath my dress, I held the one gift Cedar and Vesper had given me. I always kept it on me, though I tried to keep it out of sight, especially when we had company.

I put it on today. I would need the strength.

I looked around at the crowd gathering. The royals were in place, most of them not looking at me. The Underground had yet to show up. No sign of any witches. And no hunters.

Most importantly, no Vesper or Cedar.

Just like on the day of my wedding, I was alone, but instead of feeling betrayed, I felt something else.

Fear. For them.

I first felt it when the bond disappeared. Slowly, it started back up again, but it was weak, meaning our witch was alive... But what happened to her? What happened to Vesper? Why did neither of them send anything through the bond?

More importantly... *What do they have up their sleeve?*

It had become our pattern. Anytime they were gone for a period of time, and I just so happened to get in trouble, they would swoop in and save the day. This time, we couldn't make mistakes. As much as they wanted to save the day, I had it all planned, and if it didn't go perfectly...

I went through all of it in my head.

I got rid of his closest people.

I brought in the clan heads.

I got the Underground's help.

And, last but not least, the Royale.

If any of these things fell through, I was afraid of what it would mean for us.

I was standing on the elevated portion of the throne room, looking down at all of them as they gathered.

Usually, the coming-of-age ceremony was handled by the king or the head of the family, but since he was both at the moment, I was asked to step in.

I was holding the family's prized sword, the one my father used to rule over the vampires and whoever dared defy him. It was encrusted with his favorite gems—rubies—and polished, though not enough that you couldn't see all the battles it went through. If I looked closely, I could still see flecks of blood on the handle.

It felt heavy in my hand and vibrated with a dark power.

I had never been allowed near the thing or allowed to touch it. The women of the Castle family weren't deserving of this rite. We were married off instead. *That* was our ceremony, one where we had to wear an uncomfortable dress and invisible chains around our hands and feet.

The men got to be worshipped like kings, their value goddess-given from the moment they were birthed. It didn't matter if they accomplished anything at all, just that they had the *chance*.

How unfair was it that, no matter how much I gave to this family, they and the vampire royals would never see me as equal?

I will change that. I couldn't let myself back away now. I knew from the moment I kneeled in front of him that it would lead to this.

When Adrian walked through the doors, wearing his gaudy king outfit, attention was on him immediately, everyone turning and watching as history was made. But Vesper and Cedar were still nowhere to be seen.

His red eyes scanned the crowd before they landed on me, then they never strayed as he walked down the red carpet to the throne room.

The crowd fell away, and it was just him and me. His eyes told me he had me right where he wanted me. At his helm, doing his bidding.

But that's where he is wrong.

He stopped just at the stairs, then kneeled in front of me. I was supposed to walk down and hand him the sword as a way of showing that the family was entrusting him with our future.

But I wasn't his family. Not anymore.

Nor was I his little pawn.

I kept the sword in my hand and pointed it directly at him. Whether Cedar and Vesper were here or not, I needed to do this. I needed to stand on my own and take him down once and for all.

For us.

"I may no longer be a Castle," I said, letting my voice carry across the room. "But I am here to refute your claim to this family."

He slowly lifted his head.

"Little sister, what are you doing?"

I took a step down. A murmur went through the crowd. All eyes were on me.

I could feel the murderous intent rolling off him, but he kept that damn smirk on the entire time.

"You do not belong on the throne."

He raised an eyebrow at me.

"Because I'm a bastard child? Come on, I thought you were more accepting than that." His voice held an amused twist to it that had a few people chuckling awkwardly. "Or maybe..." He rose to his feet. "You just want it for yourself."

I tried not to react to the obvious insult.

"No one should inherit this throne," I spat at him. "We are

built on violence. On kidnapping and forcibly impregnating the women of this family. We take. We maim. We murder. And I know that if I allow it, you'll kill us all."

There was a two-second delay before he threw his head back and let out a booming laugh. Those who were on his side started laughing as well, joining him. Mocking me.

He wanted to get a rise out of me. He wanted me to back down. But only because he knew, even if there was only the tiniest chance of it, that he was going to lose today.

He wanted me so angry, so ashamed, that I wouldn't see what was in front of me.

But this had been my whole life.

From the moment I was born, my father had used me as a tool. Abused me. Not just in our home but in front of others as well. He put me in my place more times than I could count.

I was used to people looking down on me, thinking I was nothing more than a pretty little jewel to adorn whatever king I was given to.

They wanted my power, and they thought owning me would give them that.

Never again.

"You can't do anything about it," he said, glaring at me before taking another step forward. But he wasn't the only one. I met him right in the middle and pointed the sword at his throat. "Do you think that sword will kill me? Did you not learn anything while you sat here, bathing in the riches that should've been mine? All that money and time spent on your useless schooling, and this is how you decided to defeat me? It doesn't matter what weapon you hold; you're alone standing against me, and you will fall."

"What makes you think I'm alone?"

I raised my hand, motioning for a group to step forward.

This is it. Everything we've been waiting for.

For this, I needed blind faith. I couldn't give in to the doubt that was swirling around my head.

But only when the sound of silence hit my ears did I look up to see that not a single person had stepped forward.

I looked through the crowd, meeting the eyes of every single royal head I could, but none of them would dare look at me. All the fear and doubt in my soul had come to a head. My fears were being realized.

No one came for me.

"You think I didn't know what you were trying to do?" he asked in a whisper, then added, louder, "You think I didn't know you were trying to get my own people to overthrow me?"

He grabbed the sword with his bare hand, not even flinching as it sliced through the skin, his dark, disgusting-smelling blood falling to the floor.

He pushed me back, forcing me to walk up the steps backward.

"You got to them," I said, the realization making me feel numb.

Has every single one of them betrayed me?

I tried to look around him for Vesper or Cedar, but his hand was on my face, forcing me to look at him.

"It was a cute little game you were playing. Once a silly, stupid princess, always a silly, stupid princess. And you want to know the best thing about it?" He leaned forward, his lips at my ear. "No one is coming to save you."

In that moment, I truly believed him.

Time and time again, I had been shown I was all alone and the world I had been born into didn't care about me.

After my mother died, there was no one to protect me. My stepmother and stepsister had acted like I was a vile curse brought upon the family. The prince I was to marry wanted me only for my ability to produce heirs.

Why would it be any different now?

"That's where you're wrong, *my king.*"

The last two words dripped sarcasm, and I recognized the voice behind them.

Little Mouse.

Fate was reminding me I wasn't alone anymore. I was bound to two individuals who would give their life for me as I would for them, and both of them had burst through the doors in front of us.

They're here for me.

Cedar looked pale and was limping as she walked down the aisle, and I was so overjoyed to see them, I didn't realize they were holding something.

Someone.

Someone I had thought of every waking moment since her death. The same someone that filled my dreams.

The ghost of the last descendant of Krae was between their arms. They had to hold her up as she dragged her feet along the long, bloodred carpet.

I couldn't breathe. I couldn't move. My brother was two seconds away from killing me, but all I could think about was that my mother was alive.

She's alive.

And then she looked up at me with those beautiful greenish-gray eyes I'd missed so much. I hadn't realized I had forgotten the color of her eyes until that very moment. She was skinny, looking as if she was only moments away from going crazed.

I wanted to rush to her. I wanted to hold her in my arms. Hug her. Apologize to her. More importantly, I just wanted to go near her so I could make sure she was really who I thought she was.

How, in this unbelievably cruel universe, did they deliver the one thing I had been missing?

But I used it for what it was.

A distraction.

Adrian had turned to look as well, so I used the moment to push the sword into his chest. When he inevitably caught it with the other hand, I used my foot to push him off the throne platform.

He landed with a thud, and Cedar sent out her magic around him, circling his body.

But it wouldn't be enough. I could tell she was weakening as her magic flickered, so he was able to push out of it with ease. Vesper pushed my mom into Cedar's arms and headed toward my brother, but he was too fast.

Evading her, he was in front of me in seconds.

I was prepared for it, though. I shoved the sword forward into his torso.

"I am calling a Roya—"

His hand was suddenly around my mouth, and he was forcing me to the ground, even with the sword still shoved into his body.

"Let's not be hasty now, shall we?" he said, using his other hand to pull the sword out. It cut through his skin with a sickening squeal, and more of that disgusting blood fell all over me.

He let out a pained groan, but that was the only indication that he'd been stabbed right through the stomach.

"Unfortunately, I can't let you be some sacrificial lamb, no matter how much I want to fucking kill you right now," he whispered. "They were kind enough to free your mother, so I need someone to take her place."

Hands that were not his pulled me up. When they got me into a standing position, I realized that both Vesper and Cedar had been taken as well. My mother was on the ground, unable to stand, but still looking at me.

"Stay fierce," she mouthed.

"Can't you see?" I yelled as they tried to pull me away. "The queen isn't dead! My father tried to kill her and then stowed her away—"

"To do what exactly?" my brother asked. I watched in horror as the wound on his side started knitting itself together.

"You're stealing her power," Cedar said, fighting the guards.

He might only have a handful left, but they were loyal to a fault. No matter what they were watching unfold, they held us like it was their lives' most important task.

They didn't see the betrayal. To them, the woman in front of them was just a random washed-up queen who deserved nothing from them.

Maybe I had been wrong about everything. Maybe the people had never loved my mother, because how on earth would they just let her lie there otherwise?

Anger burned within me, and I reached for her.

"Mother, I'm here! Mother—"

"What are you waiting for? Take her away," Adrian hissed. As he motioned for someone to step forward from the crowd, I saw someone else I recognized. None other than the coven head that almost got us killed. "Poor little witch thought that she could get away," Adrian teased, going up to Cedar and grabbing her by the chin before throwing her off to the side and toward her ex-coven leader. "Take her out of my sight," he ordered.

"*Gladly.* We have some catching up to do."

Horror unfolded in my chest as I watched them disappear, leaving nothing but a cloud of red smoke behind.

Just when I thought it couldn't get any worse, another boy was brought in from a side hallway, the last two guards holding him. There were chains around his neck, wrists, and feet.

They pushed him forward so hard, he fell to the floor before us.

Tate.

"I knew you would try to do something to ruin this for me, but little did you know that every single one of your allies sold you out. No one is coming for you. No one is going to save you. You are going to die here, and if anyone so much as dares cross me..." He gave me a meaningful look. "I have the kid."

The guards carried me and my mother away. I tried to talk to her, but the moment I did, I was reprimanded with a slap to the face.

I looked at Vesper, who was staring at Tate with a heartbroken expression. I couldn't bear it. The bond was running wild.

Cedar is gone. And now they're making me leave Vesper behind.

We underestimated him. We thought we were clever enough —I thought I was clever enough. But he proved me wrong. It wasn't just that he was stronger or faster than any other vampire. It was that people obeyed him without question.

I waited until we were down in the dungeons to talk to my mom. She was sitting there, surrounded by piles of dead bodies, but her eyes were on me. I hastily crawled to her, reaching out and hesitantly touching her.

I was afraid she might disappear if I didn't.

"What did they do to you? Where have you been?"

She gave me a smile that calmed all my fears.

"I've been right here," she said, and lifted her hand to cup my face. "They fed off me. Kept me alive as they drained my blood so I couldn't fight back."

It was all starting to come together. I couldn't believe it.

"Was it just your blood they were drinking?"

She shook her head and gestured at all the dead bodies around us.

"There were a few powerful visitors too. They came and went but were never kept for long. Maybe a week or two, until they felt the power waning, so they got rid of them."

"This is how they're getting stronger?"

She nodded. "For some reason our blood—the blood of Krae —sustains them most. There's a reason why our blood doesn't taste as good to each other. It was the goddess's design that we did not feed off each other for fear that we would become too power-ful. But Aurelia..." She grabbed my face between her shaky hands. "This is not over yet. The prophecy can still be completed."

"I don't want to hear about the prophecy anymore—"

"You're right. This family was never supposed to last. Your father and his father tried to do the same thing—to run from the prophecy. In order to do that, they have been stealing our blood for decades."

I stood straighter.

"What do you mean?"

"I mean that this family was supposed to have died out long ago. They stole us. Murdered our people and impregnated our women. But no more. The three of you can do this, I am sure."

"But Mother—"

"Hush now. Rest while you can. This isn't over."

I wanted to fight her, but I couldn't because, for the first time since I was a child, she started singing to me. Slowly, my body lowered so that my head was in her lap, and she was stroking my hair.

My eyes met the bodies piled in the cells, and my heart started breaking in my chest when I met very familiar eyes looking right back at me.

My stepmother and stepsister never got away after all.

I closed my eyes and let my mother's voice carry me away.

CEDAR

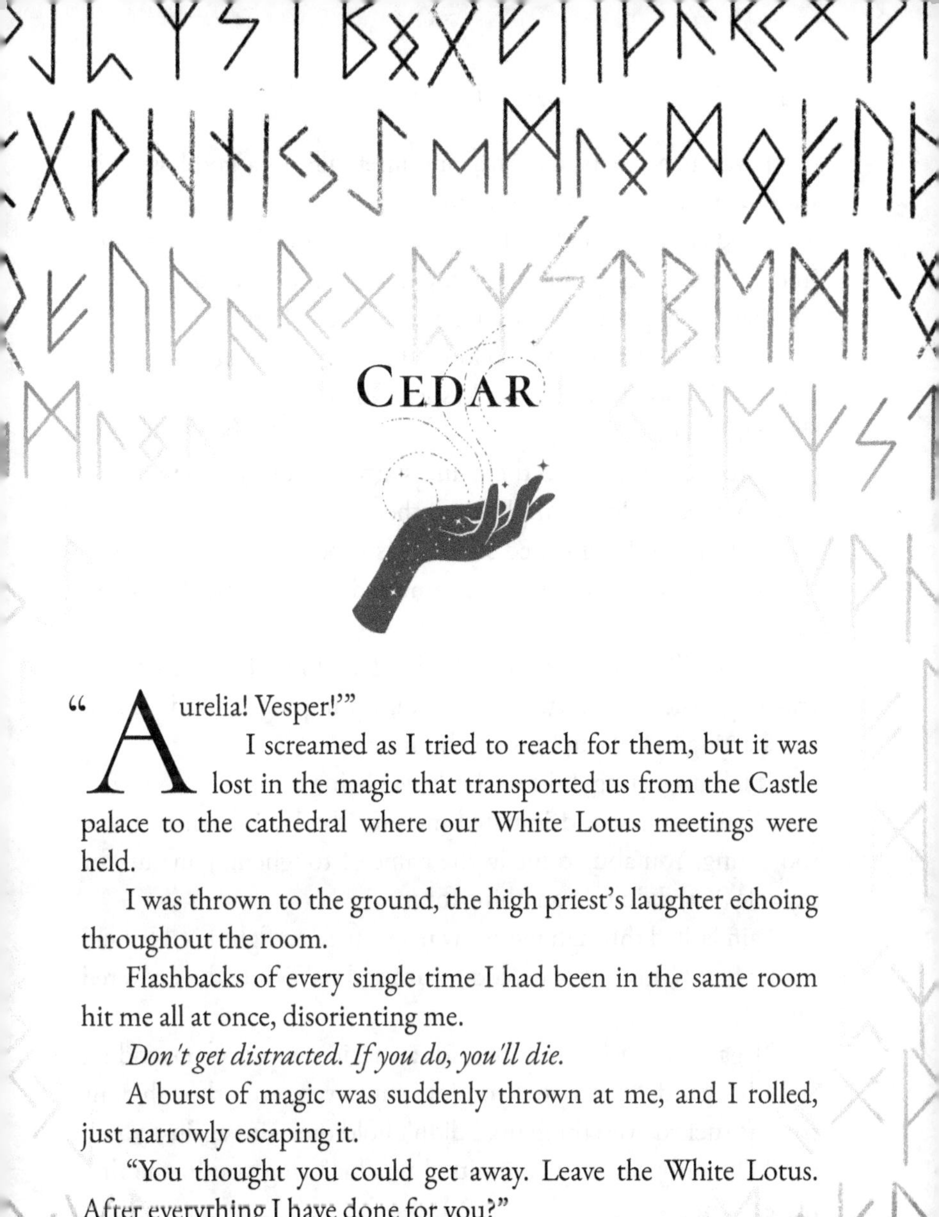

" **A**urelia! Vesper!'"

I screamed as I tried to reach for them, but it was lost in the magic that transported us from the Castle palace to the cathedral where our White Lotus meetings were held.

I was thrown to the ground, the high priest's laughter echoing throughout the room.

Flashbacks of every single time I had been in the same room hit me all at once, disorienting me.

Don't get distracted. If you do, you'll die.

A burst of magic was suddenly thrown at me, and I rolled, just narrowly escaping it.

"You thought you could get away. Leave the White Lotus. After everything I have done for you?"

I forced myself to my feet. He was facing me, his magic spilling out. But it wasn't only his magic. He was standing on top of a rune that gave him the power. The same rune that stole our magic from us as he whipped us.

The statues of the gods were behind him, all of them looking down at us. Watching, but not intervening. Just like always.

Helma, please.

I was at my wits' end, begging internally to a goddess while the enemy was right in front of me.

I had always waited for the gods to answer me. I was dedicated in my prayers. I prayed to them my entire life. I believed they were the ones pulling the strings. That they could help me.

It was why I stayed for so long, thinking they would show me the way. It wasn't until I met Vesper and Aurelia that I started to think differently.

I stopped praying to them and started focusing on my lovers and what we could accomplish together.

Still, the gods remained silent. Was it because they had abandoned us for the atrocities we committed? Or because they abandoned *me*?

"You killed my parents," I hissed at him. His magic was crawling inside me. After years of him pumping it inside me, it was starting to wake up just for this moment.

It felt disgusting. Like my body was being invaded.

"You took me and initiated me into the White Lotus. I was too young. You abused me in the name of toughening me up for my role. You didn't do anything for me."

Pain lashed through me as my magic tried to fight his. He held up his hands, his magic exploding around us. White dots covered my vision.

"I gave you a home," he said, a magic whip now extending from his hand. "I accepted you into my coven, even though your parents fucked everything up. I didn't hold their sins against you."

"The only sin they committed was believing you in the first place."

He let out a laugh. Only then did I realize how similar he and Aurelia's brother were, both overtaken by the madness of power.

"Why did you even align with him?" I had to quickly roll out of the way as he tried to whip me. My entire body screamed at me to stop. I tried to call for my magic, but it was backfiring. "Wasn't this whole thing about the prophecy?"

"You still know nothing!"

He tried to hit me again, but only got my foot as I dodged. White-hot pain shot up my body. His magic was attacking mine, and I wasn't strong enough to fight it.

I tried to call forth anything, but the light that came from my hands quickly disappeared, leaving me all alone. Powerless.

If I don't come up with something quickly, he may take over my entire body, steal my magic, and leave me to rot.

"You sent us to watch Vesper. To make sure she saw the prophecy through. Why did we get so involved when you were just going to ally yourself with him and throw away everything we worked—"

"Because I wanted it for myself!" he screeched and sent out a blast of magic that knocked me off my feet. "Because for years and years, I helped them take other vampires' life force. I watched as they grew powerful only to be stuck with the shitty magic all of you fed me. It wasn't *enough*."

The air was knocked out of me.

We were more intricately connected than I ever imagined. This didn't just span my lifetime—this had been going on for decades.

This was why the runes had looked familiar at the castle and the council. He was the one behind the scenes, helping them with everything, telling us we were there to enact the prophecy when he was using us to take back the power he thought he was owed.

"But the family didn't trust witches," I said and pushed myself up, shockwaves still running up my body. "Let me guess— after you did the work, you were ousted." I let out a laugh. "You thought you were going to have the first coven to make good with the vampires because you taught them this *disgusting* magic. You didn't care that they were using witches or their own people."

"Because they were going to give it all to me!" he bellowed. "That was our deal. I would do the work, they would act as my guinea pigs, and then I would take it all. But they went back on their word, and they kept that stupid woman locked up."

It all comes back to this. The one bloodline everyone has always thirsted after.

Ice-cold realization froze me to the ground.

"You want them to die so you can take their place. Why didn't you just take Aurelia when she was here?"

He gave me a smirk.

"I had a plan. Keep her here, eventually gain her trust. To them, it would look like I was still on their side, but when it was time, I would have both her and her mother to feed me."

The euphoric expression on his face only made me more nauseous, especially after having seen what really went down in the dungeon. Even imagining Aurelia bleeding out for him...

I will never let that happen. I will burn everything to the ground first.

"You'll never stop, will you?"

"Why would I? I deserve what is rightfully mine. And I will take it. I don't care who stands in my way. Including you."

That was all I needed to know. My mind went back to Morgan.

She knew nothing would be enough until I got revenge. Because the witch in front of me was crazy with the need for power. There would be no changing him. And if he was left in this world, we would always be on the run. Always trying to save ourselves from anyone wanting to use Aurelia's blood.

I held out my hand, focusing on it. Calling the orb to me.

I could feel it around me, the water rushing down my skin, soothing me.

And then it blinked into focus. There was a split second when I thought he realized what was going to happen, but it was too late. I called forth the last bit of my magic, pushing it into the orb before giving him one last smirk.

"You won't be taking anything. From me or anyone else. Ever again."

I slammed the orb into the ground as he lunged for it. It shattered as soon as it hit, the magic exploding outward in a fiery blast.

The fire magic caught onto anything and everything. I dragged myself across the floor before I could push myself up to run away from it. The flames licked at me, desperately trying to eat me alive.

But I didn't check where I was going and found myself trapped under the statues of the gods as the entire cathedral started to go up in flames. My coven leader was screaming in pain as they came at him with a vengeance.

They seemed drawn to him.

This was our revenge.

Mine. Morgan's. Morgan's sister. And the revenge of every single person he had ever wronged.

The smoke started to choke me.

I'm not going to make it out of here alive.

This was what the seer warned us about. The coven was always going to burn. It had been set in motion long ago, and I played right into fate's hand.

My chest hurt as I focused on the bond.

I wish I could see them one last time.

And then I felt it behind me. The low rumbling of ancient magic. Something I had only felt in passing.

I looked behind me to see that the gods had shifted. Their glowing eyes were on me. I almost dropped to my knees right then and there.

A shackled little boy appeared from the fire. It was like it made way for him, not burning even a hair on his head. He looked up at me with a melancholy face.

"You finally made it," he said.

"I did. Am I going to die here?"

He smirked at me.

"The gods have other plans for you." He took both my hands, turning me just slightly so I was facing the entrance of the cathedral. The fire was waning. It was set to attack the coven leader, and him only. Now that he was lying in the fire, charred to bits, it had done his job.

"Thank you for coming back."

I turned to look at him again, but he too had disappeared, and with him the rest of the fire. The only thing left was the ashy remains of the high priest.

I fell to my knees then, my mind trying to make sense of it all, but I only allowed myself a moment.

Vesper and Aurelia need my help.

My magic was trying to recover, and for the first time, I was able to access it without the lingering bits of his.

It was pure and all mine.

My body hurt, begging me not to move. But I didn't have that luxury.

Just as I stood up, the door opened.

Gabriel stuck his head in, his eyes going wide when he saw me.

"Thank god! I thought the kid was trying to trick me."

Of course the seer sent him. And I was grateful for it.

"You're my ride, aren't you?"

Gabriel sent me a stiff smile. "I am. The hunters have changed their mind. They're sending me, but I need your help."

I nodded and pushed myself to move. I stopped at the entrance to look back at the gods, but they had gone back to their original positions as if nothing had happened.

But I felt it. The gods hadn't abandoned me. I understood it now. They would come when they were needed.

I'd been using them as a crutch, pushing all my thoughts and wishes onto them and blaming them when nothing came true.

I had to take the first step, and they would be there to catch me if I fell.

They were here for me now. I sent them a silent thank you before turning around and leaving with Gabriel.

Wait for me.

VESPER

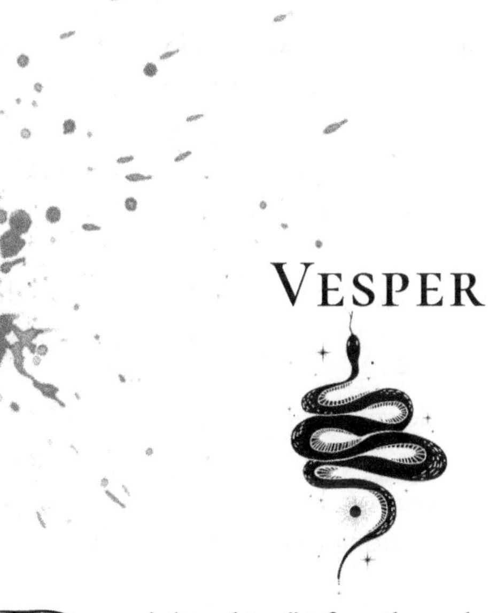

"**D**on't hurt him," I forced out through my closing throat. *How did this happen? How did everything go from hopeful to over in less than a day?*

"I won't... if you behave. After all, you're the one I need to worry about, right? The one with *poison for blood*."

He picked up the sword from the ground and pointed it right at the side of my neck. The one that used to have the snake tattoo.

My eyes shot to Tate behind him. He was hurt. Blood coated his skin, and there were multiple cuts on his face and body. His right eye had started swelling.

Where the hell was Gabriel when they took him?

"Let's stop pretending," I said. "Yes, I am the one who was sent to kill Aurelia."

I had forgotten we had an audience until there were gasps behind me.

Right. Not everyone knew my first goal here was to kill the princess.

"But not her anymore, right? She doesn't belong to this family, so now I am the singular Castle bloodline. You're here to kill me, aren't you?"

I stayed silent, unsure if answering would make him more

crazed. I could see it in his eyes, in the way he looked over me in fast, jerky movements. He wanted me to react so he could kill me.

I gritted my teeth.

I couldn't let him. He separated me from the people I loved and took my brother as insurance. I had no choice but to appeal to him.

He pushed the sword against my neck. I winced as it sliced the skin and drew blood.

"I asked you a question."

"If you knew it all, why did you accept to marry her off?"

He laughed. "Because there is no pawn more powerful than a woman with Krae blood. Come on, let's not be stupid here. I'm not the only head of family wanting to take advantage of it. One other was even in your ranks."

I snapped my head behind me, my eyes looking for the one sick lowlife I knew was no good.

Solei. He was there, right at the front, dressed proudly in a royal coat, his head held high.

But my anger dissipated when I started to look at the crowd. People were scared. The Castle family members were on the left, none of them looking pleased at this outcome, especially after seeing their queen rise from the dead and their last hope being taken away by the guards.

The royals were better at keeping their facial expressions in check, but I could read them from a mile away. They didn't like where this was heading, no doubt some of them now realizing how badly they'd fucked up.

"And you were going to sell her right back to Solei, weren't you?" I asked, turning back to him.

"Cunning snake, aren't you?"

Something was telling me to stall. I just needed to keep him going, and if I couldn't, at the very least try to keep the murders to a minimum.

"What do you want from me?"

His eyes lit up, and he dropped his sword.

"I want to see how far you're willing to go for the people who love you," he said, turning back to ascend the steps to his throne. "Apologies for the outburst! You all know my sister can have quite the temper, but don't let it spoil your mood. I have an announcement!"

Confusion gathered among the group, but no one dared to even whisper.

I narrowed my eyes at Adrian. Something didn't feel right. I had been feeling a sinking dread all day, but even now, as everything fell apart, it was still there. Meaning this was far from over.

He smiled and lifted his arms.

"Everything you heard is true, but let me explain." He walked back and forth, making sure to look every vampire in the eye. "My predecessor was focused on being the most powerful vampire so he could rule over all vampire families and clans. He didn't want anyone to be more powerful than him."

He slammed his hand against his chest.

"But I am going to write these wrongs." His voice echoed through the silent throne room, and light fell in through the stained-glass window behind him, making him look like a god. But I could see how insane he was. "I am here to bring the vampires together so we can focus on the real issue. Does anyone know what that is?"

He looked around, thinking someone would actually answer him.

"*The humans.* The humans! The council has long since forgotten who holds the most power. They have been working with the human authority and the hunters to give us arbitrary rules we have to follow. I'm tired of it, aren't you?"

There was a moment of silence before some of the royal family started to echo him.

His eyes were wide as he looked at them, and his features slowly started to change, becoming sharper. More animalistic. When he smiled, this time there were two sets of sharp canines.

He's going to start a war.

My eyes met Tate's, both of us starting to understand what was really happening here. The prophecy was bigger than all of us. If this vampire, the last of the Castle bloodline, was allowed to rule, war would ensue.

A war that could end all of us.

"So that is why, for my birthday present this year, I am declaring war on the humans. War on the hunters. And war on the council."

Murmurs broke out from the royal family's side. The rest of the vampires were so scared I could smell it.

He stared at them, anger twisting his expression.

"Clap! Why aren't you clapping?"

As some hesitantly started clapping, he took a step back, a lazy smile spreading across his face.

"Trust me, and I will do this for you. For all of us." He let it sink in, enjoying the cheers and reluctant claps. Then he clapped himself, silencing the entire throne room. "And now... Let's celebrate!"

Music started playing. Human feeders started filtering in. The suddenness of it all caught everyone off guard, but Adrian didn't notice. He was grabbing his feeders and laughing joyfully.

People started moving and acting like this was just a normal day while Tate and I stayed in our places. It felt... surreal.

Until Adrian caught my eye. He took a seat on his throne and pointed at his feet, the command obvious. I was scared. More scared than I'd ever been in my existence.

He wasn't a normal vampire anymore. Whatever he was doing had changed him, and rules didn't apply to him anymore.

I need to survive. For Cedar. For Aurelia. For Tate.

With one last glance at my brother, I walked up the steps, coming to stand next to the Castle king. Power radiated off him, and it took everything in me to stay there.

He wanted me to degrade myself. To show everyone he had a vampire at his beck and call. One of his sister's, no less.

I have to do it.

I lowered myself to the floor.

He let out a small huff of a laugh, his hand coming to pat my head. I was keenly aware of how his fingers were sharp and elongated as he ran them across my face and head threateningly.

One of his claws nicked my face.

"Good dog."

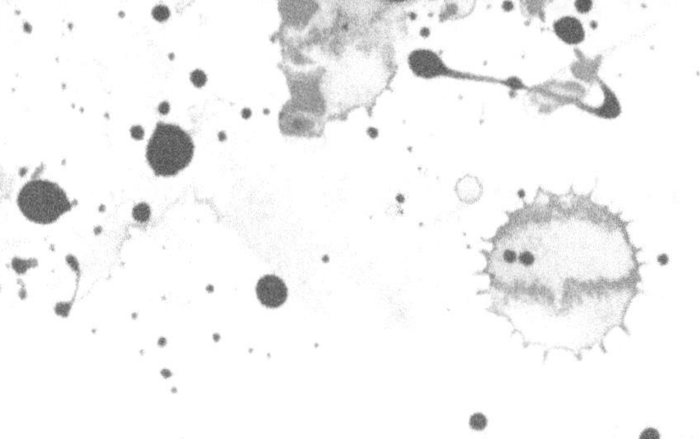

AURELIA

I wasn't quite sleeping. This was a sort of… lulled rest. The world around me felt soft and warm as my mother hugged me, my mind contentedly blank as she hummed her songs to me.

I never imagined this would happen. My mother, coming back to me. It didn't feel real. None of it did.

"Aurelia," my mother called sweetly. "It's time."

I sat up slowly to look at her. She met me with the sweetest smile and then turned to the gates of our cell. I followed her gaze and gasped.

Vampires were there, pulling at the doors.

The Castle family members. Four of them, slowly peeling the door open and holding out a hand to us.

They came. My people. I thought we were doomed when they all watched us get taken away, but for the first time that day, hope renewed in my chest.

"Vesper and Tate? Cedar?" I asked them in a quiet whisper as I carefully reached for my mother.

"Vesper and Tate are fine," a woman said. "Cedar…"

"The witch hasn't been seen, Princess," a man spoke. "But we have to hurry. He's distracted by the party, but we don't know for how much longer. We need to get you out of here."

I nodded and tried to bring my mother up with me, but she refused.

"Mother—"

"Come back for me," she said quickly. "I am too weak to move at the pace you need me to."

Panic rose in me. I couldn't lose her. Not again. Not when I just got her back.

"Mother, you need to come. I have no idea what they will do to you if they find out—"

"They will do nothing. I am too valuable to them." She smiled and ran her hand down my cheek. "Go, my sweet child. And remember what I always told you."

Stay fierce.

I nodded. It pained me to step away, especially so soon after I just got her back, but I forced myself to keep going.

"I promise to come back for you," I vowed.

"I know you will. I always knew."

Bloodred tears filled my eyes. *Trapped for years, but somehow she always believed in her daughter.* I blinked them away and turned to let the others take me away from the dungeon.

"All the guards are with him," one of them whispered. "They're likely too few to have them roaming about."

I nodded but said nothing else. We continued in silence until we came to a fork in the hallway. Right would take me back into the house and the throne room. Left led to the garden.

We went left.

"Thank you," I said, calling their attention back to me. "For restoring my faith in vampires."

They paused and turned back to face me.

"We would do anything for you, Princess," the woman said.

"All we want is your safety," the man added. "Now, if you—"

I took a step down the right hallway. Their expressions dropped.

"Thank you, but I'm not running away this time," I whispered. "I couldn't stand up to my father, but I have to do this."

"Princess," the man stepped forward, panic lacing his expression. "Do not call a Royale. It's too risky in his current state. Please. It could mean—"

"My death," I finished for him with a sad smile and took another step back. "I know. But I have to. No one else will."

They started after me, hands raised as if they could stop me. But my mind was made up.

Stay fierce.

I turned on my heel and ran in the opposite direction as fast as I could.

It wasn't long until I could hear the music and smell the blood. Anger flared to life in me when I smelled Vesper's. I used it to push away my fear. To fuel me forward.

Pushing through the crowded throne room felt like an out-of-body experience.

People barely looked at me, only moving out of the way when our bodies were almost touching. Moving to the middle of the room, I stared at my brother.

He was enjoying a feeder on the throne. Vesper was kneeling next to him, her wide eyes on me. Tate was next to her, his poor body covered in blood.

"Adrian Castle, I challenge you to a Royale. A fight to the death. You are not worthy of this position. Better yet, you are not worthy of being in this world."

He pushed the feeder off him, but it was too late. I dug my fangs into my wrist, slicing it open, before letting my blood fall to the ground.

It was the way to start the Royale.

"You kill me, and then what? Take the throne?"

I shook my head.

"Like I said, this family shouldn't have existed in the first place. I am killing you and bringing the legacy down with me."

Vesper tried to stand, but Adrian was there, forcing her down with one hand.

He's going to lose his fucking hand just for daring to touch her.

She was panicking, trying to push against his hold, but even a newborn vampire wasn't a match for the power that was coursing through my brother.

"You always have to ruin everyone's plans, don't you?" he hissed.

I now realized how much my brother had changed since the first moment I saw him in the woods. Back then, he looked like a normal vampire, and I could see the resemblance between us and our father. Now? He looked more like a beast. His eyes sharper, double fangs sticking out of his mouth, long-clawed hands. He was turning into something I didn't recognize.

"You think you're so important, and that all your feelings come before everyone else's, hm?" He stood. "You don't even think about what's good for the kingdom. You missed my announcement, but this isn't for me. This is for the world. For vampires. I'm starting a war with all of them."

My heart fell to the floor. My eyes shifted to Vesper, and the dread in them told me everything I needed to know.

"This whole time you've been searching for a purpose after *Daddy* refused to name you heir," I said as I took one step forward. "You want to make yourself important. You want your name to go down in history to make up for the fact that our father didn't love you."

He let out a growl.

"He never loved you either."

I let out a laugh. "Unlike you, I spent my entire life here. Do you think that is new information to me? More importantly, do you think I care?"

People were making way for us, slowly moving to the sides of the throne room so that they weren't impeding the Royale.

I wanted to look at them. Wanted them to see the person that was going to take down this monster. But I didn't dare because he was suddenly in front of me, his hand grabbing my neck.

His grip was so hard and fierce that he easily picked me up off the floor, holding me up. His claws pricked my skin, drawing blood.

I struggled against him, grabbing his wrist to try to push him away, but he just smiled as if he found my struggle amusing.

"I had big plans for you."

"You're not the only one," I spat. "But you will be the last."

I buried my hands in his hair, pulling with all my might, and then used what little leverage I had to ram my knee into his face. He underestimated me, and it was enough to catch him off guard.

In his shock, he let me go, and I used my chance to lunge at him and throw him to the ground, grabbing the crown off his head and stabbing it into his face.

He let out a yell, his hand catching my wrist and prying me away. Pain shot through me, his force almost enough to break my bones. I could feel them threatening to crack beneath his hold.

Something was happening in the bond, a trickle of an idea, just enough to call my attention to...

"Aurelia!"

It was the only warning I had before Vesper threw the Castle family sword at me with an almost incomprehensible speed.

I grabbed it in midair and, without hesitation, brought it down straight into his chest.

My brother's eyes widened. His mouth opened, disgusting, dark blood pouring out of it. I couldn't help but feel it was my mother's and all those other vampires he had stolen from. That was why it smelled so disgusting and looked rotten.

He shocked me by laughing. A full-force, crazed laugh that showed just how far gone he was.

"You really don't get it, do you?" His hand shook as he pulled the sword out of his chest without so much as a flinch, and then he sent me spiraling.

I turned around and got to my feet, trying to get some space between us, but he pierced my dress with the blade, stopping me in my tracks. I was quick enough to rip it and scurried back, missing a blow that would've meant his fist in my face.

I punched him, but he blocked it before it even got close. He was like a machine. Blood was pouring from his face and chest, but there was no stopping him.

"You can't kill me," he growled and grabbed the corset of my dress. "But now, because of your idiotic actions, I have to kill you. Can't say that I'm sorry."

My chest heated. I could smell magic as it shot through the air.

"What the—"

Light burst from underneath my dress, and my brother was sent flying backwards.

The necklace Vesper gave me. The one with the bird feather she used Cedar's magic to create.

It saved me.

I ran forward, grabbing the sword that was embedded into the ground. My brother was already getting up, but Vesper was there, wrapping her arms around him and immobilizing him.

"The heart," she yelled. "Go for the heart!"

But I hesitated. Because she was standing right behind him, and I was afraid that if I plunged it into his chest, she would be the one who would take the brunt of the attack.

That moment of hesitation cost me everything.

He smirked, seeing my dilemma, and pushed Vesper off right before he came at me and knocked the sword away like it was a silly little toy. Then his clawed hand was there, his target right in my chest.

My heart.

He was moving faster than I'd ever seen him, but time still slowed for me.

I'm going to die here.

I knew it was a possibility, but nothing could prepare me for it. Or for the anguish I felt knowing I would leave Vesper and Cedar in this world alone.

What will happen to them?

Will they try to attack him? Will he kill them too?

I looked at Vesper. Realizing her heartbroken gaze would be the last thing I saw only made it that much more unbearable.

The only ones who could do something to stop this were standing around us. The people who looked at me as I stood up to my brother and just watched. The same people who refused to intervene now.

If anyone truly cared about my brother taking the kingdom and ruining it—ruining *everything*—they would do something.

But these people were simply going to let him.

I failed.

In the end, the vampire world had turned its back on me. It was a devastating realization.

There is no one else.

But then the bond flared to life just as a body appeared right in front of me, red hair flashing in my vision.

The blow never came. Hot witch blood sprayed across my face and chest instead.

Everything froze. I wasn't dead. But the person in front of me would be soon.

Cedar.

Adrian's claws tore through her chest, his angry growl filling the air. As quickly as he struck her, he pulled his hand back, leaving a hole there.

I felt her pain as if it were mine. It was like being ripped in half.

I grabbed her as she collapsed on me.

"No, no, Cedar!" My scream was hoarse, my throat thick as the unimaginable started to happen right in front of my eyes.

Cedar, with her lovely green eyes and freckled face, was

looking up at me with a smile. Blood started falling from her lips as Vesper moved to her other side, taking her hand and helping me steady her.

"Hold on," Vesper said, her voice barely audible. "Please. Let me bite you."

"Wait," Cedar said feebly, already fading away. The blood loss was too much. He might have missed her heart, but there was still a wound to the chest that wasn't easy for anyone to recover from. "I need to tell you—"

"Later!"

I grabbed her wrist and bit into it. Vesper did the same, both of us trying to pump as much venom as we could inside her so she could heal. But even as I did, I knew it wouldn't be enough. The blood gushing out was more than any mortal body like hers, witch or not, could handle.

"I love you both," she whispered. "Sorry it took so long for me to say it."

"Shut up! We can talk about it later," Vesper said, pulling her teeth from her wrist.

I was feeling Cedar's death, all of it amplified by the bond.

No. No. No. This can't be happening.

"How cute," Adrian said in a snide tone. "But you're forgetting we are in the middle of a Royale—"

He staggered back as not one, but four arrows hit him in the chest. Recognition hit me because I had seen those exact arrows before. Turning to the opening of the throne room, I saw the hunters storming in, Gabriel at the lead.

Hope ran through me so violently I let out a sob.

They flanked us, their hands grabbing us as they tried to protect us. Adrian ran back, and there was a gasp of terror throughout the crowd, but none of the hunters cared. All of them were focused on the monster in front of us.

Vesper and I clung to Cedar.

But the hunters weren't the only ones who had finally decided to show up.

The windows shattered behind us, and the very chilling things that made up the Underground started to climb in.

Vampires. Witches. Other things I wasn't familiar with, but I could feel their powers. Half of them were in human form, and the other half were...

"Shifters," Cedar breathed out with a pained gasp. I looked at her and tried to put pressure on the wound. The vampire venom was working slowly. *Too fucking slowly.*

"I was warned that there were things in the Underground that shouldn't be shown to the public, but this..."

Some of them were indeed monsters. Large wolf-like animals circled my brother, growling at him, each with a witch or vampire at their side, showcasing just how large they were in comparison. Their teeth were sharp and deadly. Their legs were bent in unnatural directions. And the closer I looked, the less they looked like wolves. Sharp ears, some even bearing horns, and there was one with multiple tongues sticking out of their mouth.

Are these mutations?

As scary as they were, I couldn't find it in me to care. They were here like they said they would be.

"You got the Underground to come?" Adrian laughed, but for the first time, I saw his mask crack. When he looked at the shifters in front of him... he looked scared. "I knew they dumped rejects there, but I never would've thought that they did experiments too."

No one answered his claim, but the shifters stalked him. He jerked back, baring his teeth at them.

"You underestimated us," I growled.

He turned to me, the anger obvious in his face, but it was his fear that was fueling me now. *Finally.*

"I didn't underestimate anything. You're still a stupid little princess who grew up in a spoiled, rotten castle. You had one job, and even then you found a way to fail at it. You're a disgrace to this family and to all vampires. You and your whore of a mo—"

Adrian's face twisted in agony, and dark blood shot out of his mouth. He grabbed his chest and slowly fell to his knees, revealing a still chained-up Tate behind him with not one but two glowing daggers, obviously infused with magic.

He was breathing heavily but standing tall.

"Don't talk about my sister like that."

My heart soared. Tate, the most unlikely savior of them, but one who perfectly fit the requirements of the prophecy. He would be the one to bring Adrian down. He was the one that was going to usher the Castle rule into ruin.

"Finish him!" I yelled, and everyone attacked at once. Gabriel was there to pull Tate away, just as hunters, vampires, and shifters descended on my brother.

It was a disgusting show, but I watched every second as they tore him apart. Only when one of the shifters had eaten his heart and a hunter had smashed his brain was I finally able to look back at my lover, bleeding out in my arms.

She was still there, but just barely.

"Hang on," I told her. "Just a moment longer."

"You did it," she whispered. "Both of you."

Bloodred tears filled my eyes, slowly starting to drip onto her.

The bond was going haywire between us, urging me to help, but I had no idea how. We had pumped her full of venom, but it didn't seem to be working.

Suddenly, there were two witches from the Underground at our side, their hands reaching out to Cedar.

I pulled her closer, and Vesper growled.

"We have magic," one of them whispered, looking us in the eyes as if trying to show us their sincerity. "Let us try to help."

I looked at Vesper, and we came to a silent agreement to let them touch Cedar. Their magic glowed to life underneath their palms and sunk into her.

They looked at her with the utmost concentration, their eyebrows pulled together and sweat shining on their foreheads. I knew what they were going to tell me, though.

They pulled away, their faces grim.

"I'm sorry... It's too late."

"Don't you dare leave us," Vesper whispered, her hands caressing Cedar's face.

I pushed Cedar's hand against my face. "Please. Please stay."

She gave us one small smile. Her final one.

"I wish I could spend forever in your arms. I never felt more at peace than I do now. Knowing both of you will be safe and live happy lives together."

"It's not happy without you," I forced out.

"We'll all be together. Please, Cedar—"

"Meeting you two and loving you has been the best part of my life. Thank you. I'm sorry I..." She let out a cough, blood splattering.

"Don't force yourself," I said, touching her, wanting to fix her. Fix *something*. But I didn't know where to put my hands or what to do.

She was dying right in front of me, and I couldn't save her.

I didn't care that my brother was dead.

I didn't care about the fucking prophecy.

I would throw it all away if it meant having her here for one more day.

"I need to say it. I'm sorry I can't be there to see what your life will look like. But I know you'll be together, so you'll be in good hands."

"We love you," Vesper whispered. "Please don't do this. Please. I'll do anything." Her own bloodred tears were falling from her eyes and onto Cedar.

"I'm sorry I didn't love you enough," I said, regretting all the time I'd spent worrying about revenge and the prophecy instead of loving my people. Loving *them*.

"Your love was so much more than enough. You two were more than I ever dreamed..."

Her eyes widened, and her words slowly trickled off into nothingness.

Then there was nothing.

No light in her eyes. No magic. The only thing left of her was the slowly retreating part of our bond.

Vesper and I crumpled. Her hands reached out to me, mine reached out to her. But it was useless. The pain was too much.

She's gone.

Cedar

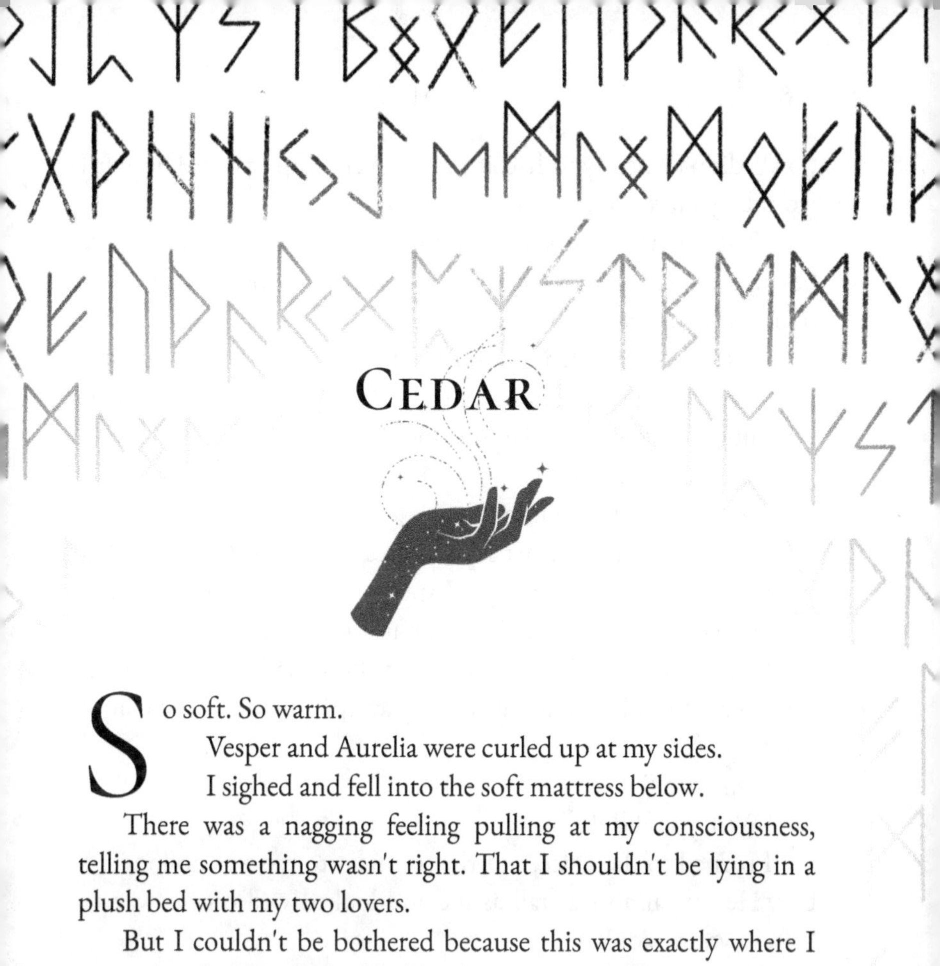

So soft. So warm.

Vesper and Aurelia were curled up at my sides.

I sighed and fell into the soft mattress below.

There was a nagging feeling pulling at my consciousness, telling me something wasn't right. That I shouldn't be lying in a plush bed with my two lovers.

But I couldn't be bothered because this was exactly where I wanted to be. My body felt fine, but my mind felt a weight that kept sinking me into the bed.

I'm so tired.

How long has it been since I felt fully rested?

I tried to think back, but my mind was a jumble, and every time I tried to search my memories, it was like a fog settled over me.

No matter. None of that was important. Especially not when soft kisses were trailed up my shoulder.

I let out a sigh. The bed felt like it was going to suck me down into its soft abyss, but I didn't care.

There's something I need to think about. I need to open my eyes.

But my body would not obey. *Or was it my mind?*

"I didn't know you had it in you. Very impressive. Though I would say martyrdom doesn't really suit you."

That's when my eyes snapped open. Because that voice belonged to someone that definitely should not be in the middle of my cuddle session.

As soon as I opened them, I realized I wasn't in a bed at all. I was back in the throne room. It was filled with vampires, watching the scene unfold in the middle.

The scene where I...

A gasp was torn from my chest.

Aurelia sat there in her ripped dress and blood covering her body, holding me and crying. Vesper was on my other side, her face buried in my chest and her arms around Aurelia.

I was unmistakably dead. My entire body had gone paler than I'd ever seen it. My magic was seeping away from me into the floor below.

"I'm dead."

"Well, you did *die*."

I turned to the voice, but the seer next to me was no longer a boy. He was almost as tall as me and looked well on his way to being a young adult.

"You've gotten taller."

I don't know why that was the first thing out of my mouth, but it was the only thing I could think of. It was also one of the first things I said to Vesper when I saw her again, so maybe this was a full-circle moment.

He let out a laugh.

"The chains kept me in their control. The side effect was losing my ability to age. Thank you for freeing me."

I looked back at my lovers as they cried over my body. My stomach twisted. My gut felt heavy, and my chest started to tighten.

"I can't believe this is it."

"Is it?" he asked, and I turned to him, noticing his raised eyebrow. "I mean, the gods did favor you after all."

I let out a huff.

"If that's what you call it nowadays."

He rammed his elbow into my side.

"They're listening, you know? Don't make them regret what they did."

I knew what he was saying had some merit. I felt them there, and I knew they saved me. But I didn't know how or why.

"It was all in vain," I said with a sigh. "They saved me just so I could die a few hours later."

"Aren't those interesting?" Max suddenly commented, changing the subject, and motioned to the shifters, who still hadn't changed from their beast form.

I let my eyes linger on them.

"I thought they were a rumor. A badly thought-up fairytale," I admitted.

I had heard stories of them, whispered here and there, but nothing credible. I just assumed it was all made up.

"An experiment. Dumped into the Underground by a corrupt ruler. A decade later, that place is filled with them."

"What are they really? Do we consider them witches anymore?"

Max shrugged. "I don't know. I know they started as witches, but now they have turned into something else entirely."

Silence fell between us. I didn't want to look at my dead body anymore. Or watch them cry over me.

"You got really lucky with them. I guess it's good it all worked out in the end."

"Is there a reason why I'm here?" I asked, getting frustrated. "As much as I want to see Aurelia and Vesper, it hurts to see them like this. You being here is telling me this isn't some type of after-life, so... what's happening?"

He sent me a smirk. "Quick one, aren't ya?"

I let out a huff.

"You *were* going to die. You felt it, right? It was warm. Comforting. Just like a lover's embrace. You almost fell into it."

"Until you woke me up."

"You'll thank me in a bit."

He took a step forward, getting closer to my body and my lovers. Unable to stop my curiosity, I followed him.

My eyes started to widen when I realized what he was seeing.

My wound was closing. Vesper and Aurelia were talking, but I couldn't make out what they were saying, all of it melding together into background noise.

"You know, most witches don't make the change," he said. "Their magic fights it off and lets them go back to their gods only to start the cycle again when the time is right. But you're different. Like I said, the gods favored you."

It took me a few seconds to grasp what he meant, but when I did, happiness burst out of my chest.

And then some slight apprehension.

"You were distracting me while the change ran its course."

"Couldn't have you giving up so soon. Their blood was still in you; it just needed some time to start working. Just like when Vesper's human part was starved to death and her vampire part was fed with blood. We have to die in order to be reborn."

"And my magic? Will I get it back one day?"

He shrugged. "I don't know, but is that really what you care about?"

In all honesty, no.

They were.

And I was happy that I would live out my dreams with them.

Magic had once been my life, but it was also the reason why I was stuck in the coven. The reason why I was abused by him.

A part of me that was there my entire life would no longer exist. The Cedar I once was would be gone, but just like Max said, in order to be reborn, I had to die first.

I would gladly take it.

I could feel it working as I stared at myself. My tether to this in-between world we were in was starting to fade.

"Thank you," I told Max. "Because of you, I met them. And because of you, we were able to stay together."

He stood straight and gave me a smile. "You know, I only did it for myself."

It was my turn to smile at him.

"You know I can tell that's a lie. You're a good one, Max. And I hope you can start living the life they stole from you. Morgan is waiting for you. She never gave up hope."

The world around us started to fall away, and just as it was about to fully disappear into darkness, I heard him whisper one last thing.

"Make the most of it. Together."

VESPER

Cedar was dead. There was no bringing her back, no matter how hard we tried.

I couldn't move. I couldn't bring myself to leave her, even as the vampires were gathering around us. Yelling at us.

Neither could Aurelia.

Her fake husband and Atlas were doing the brunt of the work, trying to keep people at bay. We would have to face them sooner or later, but this was not the time. If there would ever be a time for that.

I don't know how long it would take me to recover from this.

How could this happen?

How had we won the battle and still lost in the end? There was no way the world could be this cruel. I would rather have lived the rest of my days in an Adrian-filled misery with them or even died at his hands with them.

In both scenarios, we'd be together.

It wasn't the best, but it was better than this.

My eyes roamed Cedar's body. Logically, I knew that she couldn't have survived something like that, but it didn't feel final. My mind was telling me she was still alive. That at any moment she might sit up, and we would all laugh like this was some stupid joke.

But it isn't.

This was real life, and I had to face it. I had to be strong. Not just for myself but also for…

I couldn't even look at Aurelia for fear that I would break down even further.

The tears running down my face splattered onto Cedar's pale skin. The blood had all but drained out of her, leaving nothing behind to flush her skin.

I'd never felt a pain this strong. It was like someone had ripped my heart out and shredded it to pieces, and I was forced to live through it. I felt her death a hundred times over, but I couldn't turn off the pain.

Turning it off would mean letting her go.

And then I felt it.

A twitch.

I thought it was Aurelia at first, but when she looked at me, I could tell she felt it too.

I wanted to believe it, so I latched onto it. To the hope.

I looked at Cedar, analyzing her face for any sign that she was alive. It was still just as pale, but when I looked down at her chest, the wound was slowly knitting itself back together.

One by one, organs, muscle, skin—all of it had started to grow back, connecting to each other until her chest bore no sign of a wound.

"What's happening?" I forced out, my voice rough from trying to keep my screams locked in me.

"I don't know. She—"

Cedar's eyes snapped open. She was looking up to the ceiling, not noticing us there. Shock, happiness, confusion—I didn't know what to feel first, but I couldn't stifle my gasp.

Because her eyes weren't the same color.

The forest green had been replaced.

With red.

Much like a—

"Vampire?" Aurelia breathed.

"Cedar?" I asked distantly. Her eyes moved to me, and I knew.

I remembered this moment when it happened to me.

One moment I was on the cold ground, shivering, slowly fading. Then, suddenly, I was pulled back, snapped into consciousness and into a body that didn't fully feel like mine.

The first normal reaction was to freak the fuck out. And I had. But Cedar wouldn't be able to, not with the chaos surrounding us.

"Back up!" Aurelia yelled.

Atlas and Caspian echoed her. When people started catching on, a collective gasp ran through the crowd. Somehow, the fact that a witch had turned into a vampire was even more surprising than whatever the experimental shifters we saw were.

"Slowly," I breathed, putting my hand on her chest, the wound now closed.

She watched me, and I saw the ferocity in them. Hunger shot through the bond.

It's still here. She's still a part of this. Of us.

"Breathe in," I said in a whisper.

Aurelia moved closer to me, her hand covering mine.

"And out," Aurelia added.

Cedar's eyes shot to her.

"Thank Krae," Aurelia whispered.

Cedar bolted up, faster than a witch ever could. I braced myself for the attack, but it never came. Instead, she wrapped her arms around us and held us close.

"I almost died," she said, her voice gravelly.

"You did for a second. Or a few minutes," I said with a laugh as I embraced her.

"And don't you ever dare do something stupid like that again," Aurelia told her, her voice thick with tears.

"You're one to talk," I said, pulling away to look at the sobbing princess. "A fucking Royale?"

"And you didn't even think to tell us." Cedar reached out to ruffle Aurelia's hair, but it was too fast, too rough. Aurelia flinched. Cedar's eyes widened, and she looked at her hand. "Sorry!"

I couldn't hold back anymore. I grabbed Cedar's face and kissed her. She kissed me back with a deep hunger, her blood still on her lips.

We were pulled away only for Aurelia to take my place.

Gods. I'd never get tired of seeing them together. They were explosive, even more so now that they were both vampires.

We all are. Forever is looking a hell of a lot better now.

Just as I was about to go in for one with Aurelia, someone cleared their throat behind us. The three of us turned to see Atlas and Caspian looking at us. Atlas was less than pleased, but Caspian had a small smile on his face.

Behind them was a group of people who just watched us blow up Aurelia's marriage.

"I knew they weren't married."

"You know, this is actually common in royal marriages."

"I was always Team Silver-haired, though I can't say I mind watching both of them."

Aurelia stood up to face the crowd. I pulled Cedar up, and while she likely didn't need it, she leaned on me anyway.

"One last thing," she said, her eyes narrowing on a slimy vampire trying to sneak out of the crowd. "*Solei.*"

As soon as her finger was raised to point him out, he started running, but not fast enough. One of the shifters was faster to react, running after him and locking their jaws around his head before shaking him violently.

Another came up to pull on his lower body until they separated it from the head. When they were done, they both looked at Aurelia and lowered their heads. She just smiled.

"Thank you, everyone, for your help," Aurelia said and bowed. Many of the vampires bowed back, and when she stood again, she held her head high. "The Castle family is no more. I apologize for lying to everyone, but I appreciate you all seeing it through. You are free to move out as you wish. I have technically broken the rules of the Royale, so I will accept my exile—"

There was an uproar. Royals were yelling, some for, some against, but the majority wanted the princess to stay right where she was.

Cedar and I smiled at each other as we felt her shock and pride run through the bond.

The people were rallying for her.

"Thank you." She gave them a smile. "But the world doesn't need a Castle rule anymore. As for me..." She reached out to us. "I would like to spend the rest of my days with my loved ones."

There was a noise, and the crowd parted, letting Aurelia's mother through. She was being held up by vampires, her body clearly still weak, but that didn't stop her from beaming at her daughter.

A weight lifted off me as I watched our princess run to her.

Cedar's chuckle was warm in my ear.

"What do you say? Can your blood be the first I drink?"

Her question sent a shiver through me.

"You should get a human's first," I said and nudged her. She sent me a devilish grin.

"And miss out on your intoxicating taste? Plus, I haven't even told you where I want to bite you yet."

Her eyes ran down my body, pulling a smile from me.

She may be a vampire now, but she hasn't changed.

Much to my relief.

And I would give her all the blood in the world if it meant I would have both Cedar and Aurelia by my side.

CEDAR

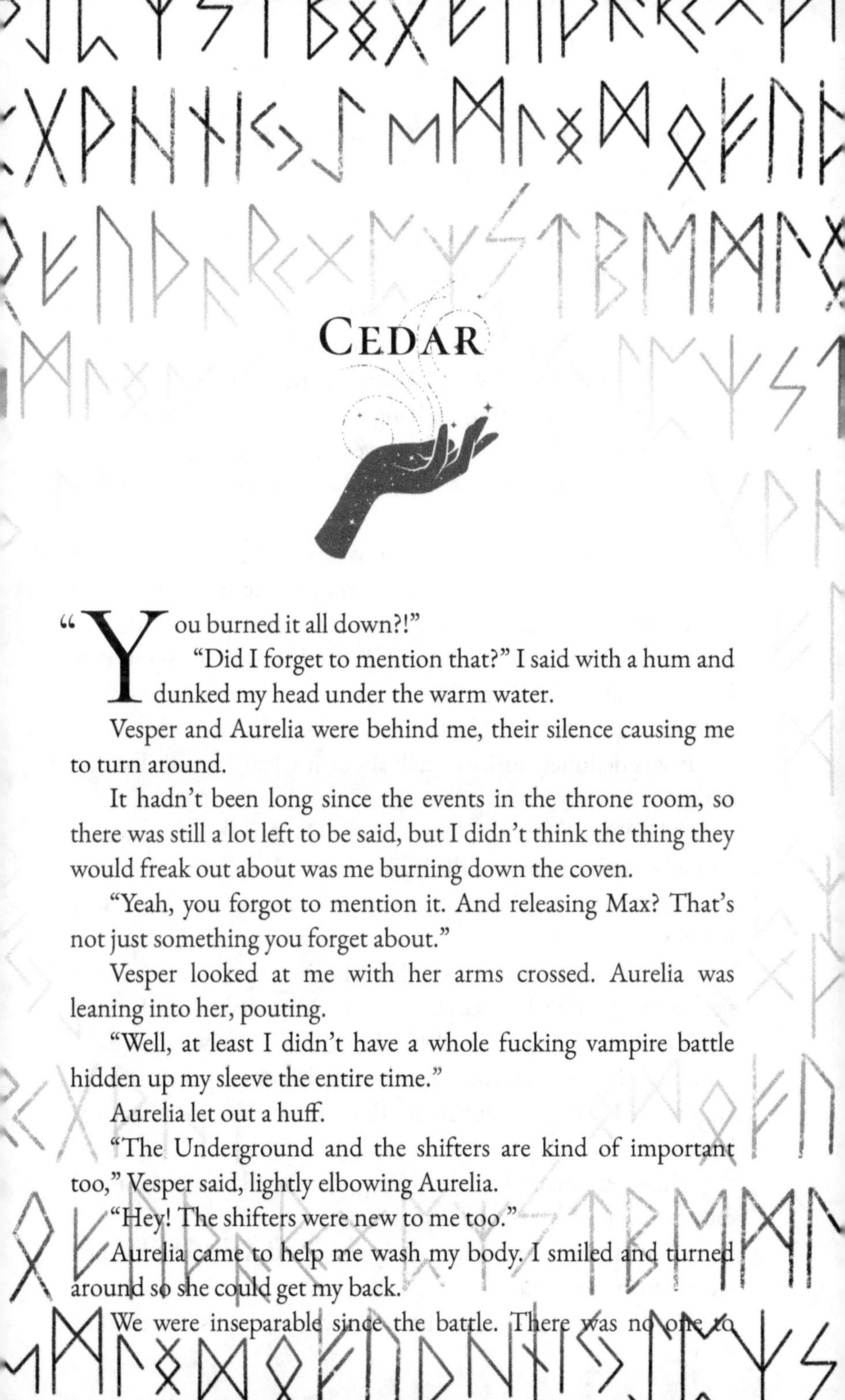

"You burned it all down?!"

"Did I forget to mention that?" I said with a hum and dunked my head under the warm water.

Vesper and Aurelia were behind me, their silence causing me to turn around.

It hadn't been long since the events in the throne room, so there was still a lot left to be said, but I didn't think the thing they would freak out about was me burning down the coven.

"Yeah, you forgot to mention it. And releasing Max? That's not just something you forget about."

Vesper looked at me with her arms crossed. Aurelia was leaning into her, pouting.

"Well, at least I didn't have a whole fucking vampire battle hidden up my sleeve the entire time."

Aurelia let out a huff.

"The Underground and the shifters are kind of important too," Vesper said, lightly elbowing Aurelia.

"Hey! The shifters were new to me too."

Aurelia came to help me wash my body. I smiled and turned around so she could get my back.

We were inseparable since the battle. There was no one to

keep us apart anymore, so nothing would stop us from spending every single moment together.

Including showering.

"You're getting thirsty. Do you want—"

"I'm okay," I said quickly.

Becoming a vampire after a lifetime of being a witch was something that would take some time getting used to. Though with them, and especially with Vesper sharing her newborn experience, I was slowly getting the hang of it.

Speaking of Vesper, her fingers were lightly trailing my back.

"If there are any other secrets, we should share them right here and now."

I knew she was talking about my scars. After I turned into a vampire, they all but disappeared—maybe because I killed the coven leader who gave them to me in the first place—but that didn't mean they were totally gone. With their vampire sight, they had no doubt seen them, but this was the first time they were mentioning them point-blank.

It was definitely easier to talk about it when I wasn't looking at them.

"The White Lotus..." I trailed off. Their fingers were warm, and so were the feelings in the bond.

Right. They won't care about this. Because it's me. And they love me.

"Witch covens like to act like they're superior to hunters because they don't kill people," I said with a shaky breath. "But that's not exactly right. The White Lotus acts like a hunter organization. Each coven has their own special dedicated group, though after what I learned about mine, I'm not sure all others are that brutal."

They were silent, but the feelings coming through the bond didn't change. They weren't judging me.

Vesper's fingers were tracing my scars, and Aurelia had leaned closer, giving me comfort.

"When I went to visit the other coven, I was scared they

would turn me away because of what I had done in service of the White Lotus. But Morgan, the leader, was the one who gave me an orb. The one I used to burn the coven down and rescue the seer."

I finally turned to look at them.

"These scars are from how he punished us."

Their eyes filled with understanding.

"This is a lot," Vesper said. "They may be mostly gone now, but still... He abused you. I wish he were alive again so I could kill him myself."

"You try to scrub these off in the shower sometimes, don't you?" Aurelia asked.

I froze, not really knowing how I felt about being so seen. It was panic-inducing. I didn't know how to admit it, but I knew I had to.

"Yes," I said around the knot in my throat. "I hate them."

"I heard you in the shower a couple of times too," Vesper confessed. "But regardless..." They both hugged me, with Vesper resting her head on my right shoulder and Aurelia placing her cheek against my left arm. "These scars are a part of you. And no one will ever abuse you again. Not even yourself. We love every single part of you."

"We do. Let's be kind to ourselves going forward, yes?" Aurelia added, kissing my upper arm. "Nothing but love here."

Bloodred tears filled my eyes, and I dunked my head in the water to wash them away.

How on this earth did the gods bless me with such perfect partners?

"Okay," I whispered, letting them hold me. "Nothing but love."

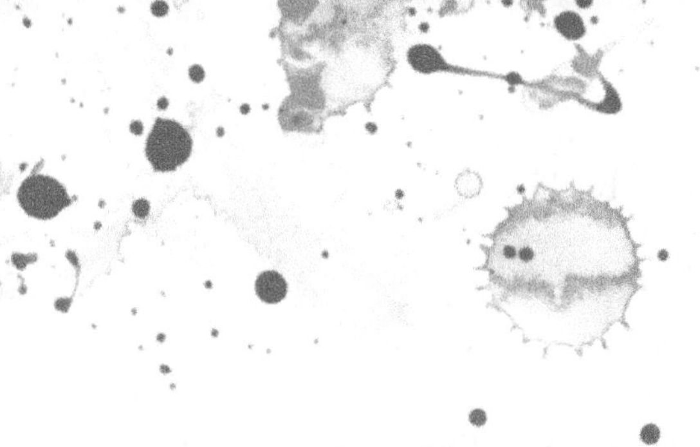

AURELIA

For the first time in centuries, the Castle family held no power.

People weren't flocking to the palace in hopes of joining us, and even though Adrian had declared war on everyone, no one really seemed to take that threat seriously.

Or at least they were smart enough to know I wouldn't be seeing it through.

And that meant that, for the first time in a while, the palace was mostly empty.

Mostly being the keyword.

Because even though we were supposed to be in ruins, this place looked anything but.

"It's a miracle," I said, looking at the garden. The fountain that had once been cracked was now completely redone and flowing with clear water. The weeds and vines that had been growing throughout had been replaced with beautiful flowers of varying colors.

"Just needed some love and care," my mother replied, her head popping up from a giant bush of pink flowers. The hat she was wearing didn't suit a former queen, but she was more than happy to be rid of the title.

She had never smiled so brightly. Her face was smudged with dirt, but it only enhanced her beauty. Her face had gotten plump from finally getting the blood she needed.

"I guess that can be said for a lot of people," I said as I inched closer to her, inhaling her scent.

Even after three months and counting, I couldn't get over the fact that she was here with me. I was afraid to leave her, and she knew it.

"Why are you still here, Aurelia?"

I gave her a mock gasp.

"Are you saying you don't enjoy my company?"

She gave me a look before she let out a chuckle.

"I'm saying that Hunter Girl and Troublemaker are getting antsy. You promised to show them the world, did you not? And here you are, fussing over me."

My heart warmed at the nicknames she had for my lovers.

They had all grown close, something I never imagined possible even when I was a little girl. I never once considered I'd end up with my true loves, let alone that my mother would actually dote on them as much as she did on me.

"I..." I paused, my throat becoming thick with emotion. "I just want to be with you, is that such a crime?"

She gave me a sad smile and scooted closer. When she laid her head on my chest and sighed, I found the knot in my throat getting bigger.

"I love you, Aurelia." She took her glove off and slipped her hand in mine. "I think it's time I apologize to you."

I looked at her in shock.

"Mother, *you* have nothing to apologize for. If anything, I should be the one apologizing because I never knew you were down there."

I looked at our intertwined hands. The guilt sometimes felt like it would eat me alive. She had been down there, suffering, while I was off doing whatever I wanted.

Well, not quite. But still, it paled in comparison to what she went through.

"I had a chance to run away with you," she whispered. "When he was busy dealing with my handmaiden and her pregnancy, I had a chance. I should have taken it. At least then you wouldn't have had to endure all this pain."

"You couldn't have known."

"But I did," she said, finally looking at me. Bloodred tears gathered in her eyes. "I knew he was a monster; I just never thought that he would turn on me like he did. I shouldn't have... I should never have told you to stay fierce. I should have told you to run."

I wrapped my arms around her and pulled her close.

"You and I both know nothing would have taken me away from this place."

She hugged me back.

"Which is exactly why you need to *go.* You can't keep staying here like a princess stuck in her tower waiting to be saved. You've *been* saved. You just refuse to walk through the door."

Her words hit me right in the chest.

It was true. I didn't want to leave. No, it was more accurate to say that I was scared to leave.

I didn't want to leave her in case she wouldn't be here when I got back.

It didn't matter that my lovers were waiting for me. They had been patient and said nothing as they allowed me to spend time with my mother. But this wasn't the life I imagined living once it was all over.

I couldn't stay in the palace ruins for the rest of my life.

All I ever wanted was freedom, but I never really thought about what that freedom would look like. What did I want to do if I wasn't tied down to a title or a palace?

More importantly, *what did that make me?*

If I wasn't the Castle princess, what was I?

"I don't know who I am without this place," I admitted to her, scared to say it any louder than a whisper.

"You're Aurelia. My daughter. Their lover. A headstrong, dependable, passionate woman fate tried to tear down. But you survived. And now you can turn your life into what it always should have been."

I held on to her, clutching her as if it were the last time.

"I'm scared," I whispered.

"I know," she said, her voice quivering. "But you're not alone."

Just as she said that, the sound of footsteps hit our ears. We both turned around to see Vesper and Cedar entering the garden. Vesper was holding a bowl of bright red, sparkling blood candies.

I smiled at them, and they smiled back.

Vesper always offered everything to my mother first, and the candies were no exception.

"You're spoiling me," Mother said as she grabbed a few from the bowl, throwing one into her mouth automatically.

"I can think of no better way to spend my days," Vesper answered as she watched me. "Spoiling my girls."

I rolled my eyes, but I knew they could both feel the warmth through the bond. Cedar came closer, but instead of sitting at my side, she moved behind me, her hands running through my hair.

"Maybe we need a handmaiden," she commented as she gently combed through my hair, breaking up the knots.

I let out a sigh as she began braiding my hair, taken back to another time and another place when she'd done exactly that.

"Hey, that's my job," Vesper said with a fake pout.

Cedar let out a deep chuckle. "Too slow. Even though you did get better at it!"

"If I knew there was a chance vampires would trip over themselves to braid my hair, I would have never cut it," Mother said, unaware of what the moment meant, and took off her hat. Her hair fell down around her face in small waves ending right at her chin.

"Short hair suits you." Vesper gave her a smile and held out the bowl for my mother to grab two more candies.

Cedar finished my braid and gently placed it over my shoulder. I leaned back into her and looked up, meeting her slightly reddening gaze.

She sent me a smile of her own. Relief shot through me for the hundredth time since she woke up as a vampire. It hadn't changed her. She was still the same cocky witch. Her freckles stayed, and when the redness was gone, her forest green eyes came back.

She kept telling me it was the gods. That they had favored her somehow.

Maybe it was true. Or maybe it was fate paying us back for all the shit it put us through.

"What do you say, Princess?" she asked, her tone gentle. "Are we ever going to leave this place?"

I swallowed the knot in my throat and looked over at Vesper and my mother, both waiting for my answer.

My lovers were trying to hold in their feelings so they wouldn't make it to the bond, but I could feel them loud and clear.

"We will be with you the entire way," Vesper said, reaching over to grab my hand.

"And don't worry, we'll come back to visit. This isn't goodbye."

The thought of leaving still felt uncomfortable. Regardless of what happened, this was still my home. This was me.

Maybe it's time to create a new me. I already have a new home in them.

"Just for a few days," I whispered, then my voice came out stronger. "There's a couple of people we should visit, and then we come back."

"Promise me something, my love," my mother said, reaching over to squeeze my thigh. "If there's ever a moment when you want to keep going, just do it, okay? Don't worry about me. I'll be here when you get back."

"Won't you be lonely?"

She opened her mouth to speak but was interrupted by vampires coming around the corner, all of them holding big sacks of soil. A few were holding large planters filled with various different flowers.

"Your Majesty, the shipment just came in!"

I couldn't help but smile at them.

We had told the vampires they could leave, but many of them still stayed on the outskirts of our palace grounds. They showed up for my mother every single day, whether it was to help her with the garden or just to bring things to help redecorate.

"I don't think I can be lonely, even if I tried," she told us with a smile. "Just in time! Place them over there!"

Fate was telling me to leave. *Along with everyone else, apparently.*

Looking at Vesper and Cedar, I stood up, brushing the dirt off my dress.

"Then it's settled. We'll be back in a few days."

My mother pulled me into a tight hug that made my eyes water with blood, and I hugged her back as tightly as I thought she could handle.

"I love you."

"And I love you, my perfect, sweet daughter."

No one ever called me sweet *or* perfect *before.* The thought came unbidden.

As my mother turned away, Vesper lowered her voice so only we could hear.

"Yes, our perfect, sweet princess."

"And our perfect, sweet brat."

CEDAR

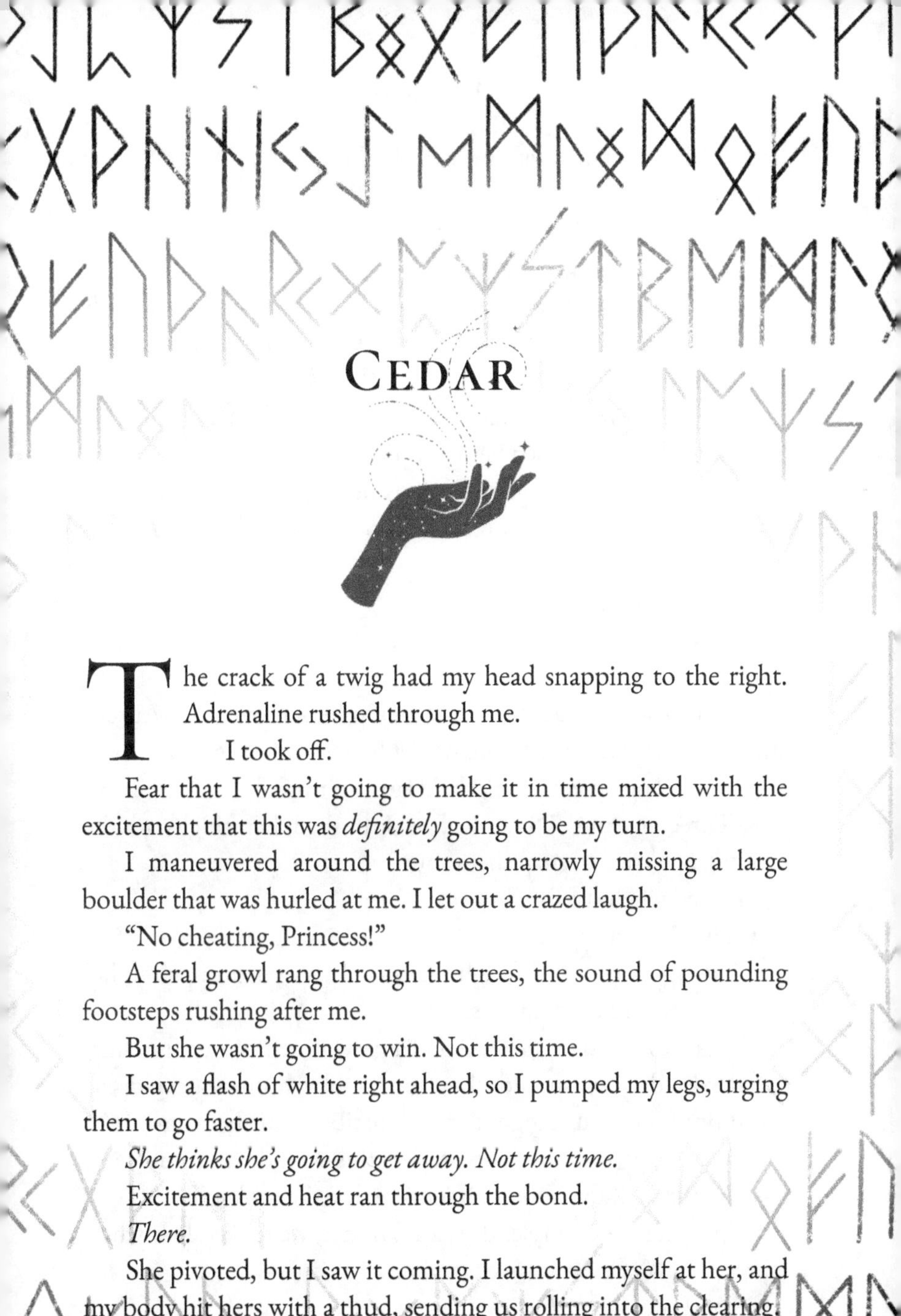

The crack of a twig had my head snapping to the right. Adrenaline rushed through me.

I took off.

Fear that I wasn't going to make it in time mixed with the excitement that this was *definitely* going to be my turn.

I maneuvered around the trees, narrowly missing a large boulder that was hurled at me. I let out a crazed laugh.

"No cheating, Princess!"

A feral growl rang through the trees, the sound of pounding footsteps rushing after me.

But she wasn't going to win. Not this time.

I saw a flash of white right ahead, so I pumped my legs, urging them to go faster.

She thinks she's going to get away. Not this time.

Excitement and heat ran through the bond.

There.

She pivoted, but I saw it coming. I launched myself at her, and my body hit hers with a thud, sending us rolling into the clearing.

I grabbed Vesper just as she tried to escape my grasp.

"Fight me, hunter. *Harder.*"

She was lying on the ground below me, bucking to get me off.

She did her best to push herself off the ground—and even got halfway there.

But then Aurelia was there too.

"Damn it," she growled.

"That's right," I said with a dark chuckle. Heat was already unfurling in my body as I thought exactly of what I wanted to do to our hunter. "My turn."

"No fair," Vesper groaned as Aurelia took my place holding her down and I shimmied her pants down.

I sucked in a sharp gasp of air as her pussy was bared to me. Wet and puffy from the three other rounds, all of which Aurelia had won.

Like I said, my turn.

"Lost your will to fight?" I teased as I ran my fingers up her swollen folds.

Somehow, she was still trying to flip herself over, but Aurelia straddled her at the chest, forcing her hands to the ground.

"How long do you think she'll last this time?"

"Three minutes," I replied as I pushed her thighs to the ground. She tried to snap them shut.

I loved when she fought back.

"Five," Vesper spat.

Anticipation shot through the bond. My eyes dropped to her swollen pussy. I licked my lips.

This was our new game. Aurelia grew bored of our traveling, so she decided we should chase our subby hunter around the forest until one of us caught her and forcibly made her come.

Vesper was the one who started this round, heat and need flashing through the bond moments before she took off.

The rules were simple. If we caught her, we fucked her, wherever and in whatever way we wanted.

And I was *parched.*

I dove right into her cunt, my lips wrapping around her clit while I pushed three fingers inside her, using my vampire strength and speed to fuck her hard and fast.

"Fuck!" she screamed and tried to buck me off.

"Nah, two minutes max," Aurelia said with a chuckle.

I twisted my fingers, then circled them, brushing against the spot that always made her gush around me.

"Delicious," I mumbled, pulling away to look at how well she sucked in my fingers. I licked her with newfound energy, unable to stop myself from cleaning up her wetness.

I had one hand on her thigh so I could feel when it started shaking.

"Let's kick it up a notch," I said and turned to the side, sinking my fangs into her inner thigh. Sweet blood filled my mouth, making my taste buds tingle.

They always said that vampire blood didn't taste as good as human blood, but I didn't believe it. Aurelia's and Vesper's blood were the most delicious.

She arched into Aurelia, who sucked in a breath.

"Come for us, hunter."

"No," Vesper forced out, but we all knew it was useless.

"Fuck, I can't help myself."

I looked up to see Aurelia shoving her hand under her dress. I pounded into Vesper harder, their pleasure mingling together in the bond.

"Sit on her face," I ordered. "Dress off."

Aurelia looked back at me with a smile before doing as I told her, leaving her naked in the middle of the clearing. She climbed onto Vesper's mouth, this time facing me so I could see her as Vesper attacked her cunt.

With Aurelia's knees on either side of her face and her hands on her chest. I could just make out Vesper's mouth as she ate our princess's cunt like it was her job.

Aurelia's eyes rolled back in her head, her lower lip pulled into her mouth.

"Vesper," she moaned and rocked against her mouth. "Fuck, that's it."

I pumped more venom into Vesper before going back and

licking her clit in light strokes. The poor bundle of nerves had already been so used and abused today that just the smallest bit of stimulation had her falling into her first orgasm.

Even as her back bowed and pleasure exploded through the bond, she didn't stop eating her out, and I had a front-row seat to them falling apart.

I am so incredibly lucky.

Sometimes I wasn't sure the gods had done me a favor. Even as they brought me back from the dead, giving me a new chance at life with my lovers, it felt too good to be true.

Is it truly all over?

But the more time I spent with them, spending days in each other's embrace with nothing to do except simply *be*, I started to realize just how blessed I truly was.

"Come for us, Princess."

Her eyes met mine, and she gave me a dangerous grin.

"*No.*"

I kept my fingers inside Vesper, pumping into her lazily as I reached up to grab Aurelia's face.

She tried to kiss me, but I stopped her, moving to her cheek, then her throat. I dragged my fangs across the sensitive column before trailing down her neck and...

Her choked gasp had both Vesper and me shuddering.

I sank my fangs into her breast while my tongue played with her nipple. I pumped venom into her, and I could feel Vesper working her magic through the bond.

"Cheater," she breathed as her orgasm came crashing through her, and I made sure to watch as she fell apart.

And then Vesper slapped Aurelia's thigh three times, and they both turned on me, forcing me to the ground, eager hands tearing at my clothes.

"Who's the cheater now?" I yelled in mock anger, but I couldn't help but laugh right after. That quickly turned into a moan with how fast they were at getting their mouths on me.

I held onto them, and I let go.

Even if it wasn't over, we'd handle whatever came next together.

This life might not be one I planned, but it was one I was given. One I was meant to have.

And it was perfect.

I wasn't alone anymore.

And I never would be again.

VESPER

By week two, I knew we weren't going back to the palace.

At least not for a while.

I wasn't sure if Aurelia knew, but neither Cedar nor I mentioned it.

Time was weird with vampirism. We didn't need to sleep. Didn't need to eat, except for blood. So it was really easy for us to get lost in the days passing and in each other, not really noticing just how long it had been since we left in the first place.

And Aurelia... she was starting to live.

There were no royals to entertain. We bounced from city to city, stopping by the various vampire covens and families as we found them, many of them still treating Aurelia as the princess she had once been, offering us meals and lodging.

They had made their feelings on the now dead Castle king very clear, but now, without the pressure of royal customs, they were much more open and friendly with us.

"What? You didn't know?" Elora said with a scandalous gasp. "Your husband is using the last bit of his inheritance to open a... *sex club.*"

The last bit was spoken in a whisper, likely afraid her own husband would overhear. But he was in the other room, and standing by her side was a tall, stoic guard—a masculine woman, bulky, with a shaved head and tattoos on her face, dressed in an all-black guard uniform.

She was *very* attentive to Elora, and it made me wonder if that was the reason her husband had been treating her so differently.

The first time I'd seen her, she was a shell of a vampire, with her husband keeping blood from her to make her compliant and submissive. But she looked positively lively now.

Aurelia, Cedar, and I were sitting in her parlor, drinking blood and relaxing as they chatted when the topic of Caspian came up.

"*Ex*-husband," Cedar and I said together.

Elora laughed behind her hand, her guard's lips twitching ever so slightly.

"Of course he did," Aurelia replied with a huff and took a sip of her blood.

"The other one just doesn't feel right now." Elora grimaced. "No one really has the energy to play those silly political games anymore."

"It was a stupid idea in the first place. An excuse for unhappy vampires to let loose."

"Is that not what this new one is too?' Cedar asked.

Elora lit up.

"No! It's better! Invite only, and they accept everyone—humans, witches, and vampires alike. I even saw a few of those *shifters* there."

Interest leaked through the bond.

"We may have to pay them a visit," Aurelia said as she stood in a swift motion. "But first, I think we have a few hunters waiting for us, don't we?"

Anxiety ran through my chest as we all stood and started to say our goodbyes. It had been a few months since I'd seen my brothers, and I was both excited and nervous.

Especially since the last time I saw them, they'd been searching for our mother.

Cedar squeezed my arm, and I sent her a smile.

You have them. It will be okay.

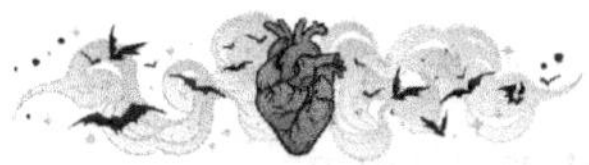

"You're getting taller—*again*," I grumbled as Tate gave me a side hug.

I said nothing as he slipped a small box into my pants.

We met just a few miles away from our next destination, since Gabriel's band of hunters had also been on the move over the last few months. It wasn't easy to plan, but we were finally close enough to meet.

"That's what happens," he said with a smirk. "We humans grow."

"Quarter humans," Aurelia corrected.

Tate rolled his eyes and pulled away. "Think fast."

He grabbed something from his belt and threw it at Aurelia, who caught it with ease. The glint of metal told me what it was.

When she opened her hand to look at it, surprise and something a little heavier settled in the bond.

Cedar looked over her shoulder to see what it was.

"The feather?" Cedar asked. "I thought it exploded."

"You're looking at the hunters' first magical artifact and weapon apprentice," Tate said with a bow.

Pride welled in my chest. I didn't agree with the hunters, but I was happy to see Tate excel in something. I already knew about his work. The thing he slipped into my pocket had been one of the first things he told me he'd work on.

"Thank you." Aurelia fastened the now mostly metal feather to her neck. "I really appreciate this."

He met my eyes and gave me a not-so-subtle wink.

"Anything for my sister."

"Hey! What about me?" Cedar gave him a teasing pout.

"In due time," he said and looked over as Gabriel met us.

"How's life after the fall, Castle? Or are you technically still a Hart?"

She huffed.

"Once a Castle, always a Castle."

He gave her a shit-eating grin.

"So you never changed your name?"

Aurelia let out a playful growl, and Gabriel chuckled before looking at me, turning serious.

"We found her."

My chest constricted.

"Where is she?"

He turned to face the edge of the forest. I hadn't heard my mother come up, but she was there, waiting for us. Seeing her was like a shock to my system. Anger. Pain. Rage. Sadness. I didn't know what to feel.

My lovers came up to my side, both holding onto me.

"You don't have to meet her if you don't want to," Aurelia said.

I gritted my teeth at the look Gabriel gave us.

Do I want to?

"If it makes you feel better, she wants to apologize." Tate moved closer, grabbing my hand and forcing me to look at him. "She would like to hear about what happened."

I looked back at my mother, who was now looking at her feet.

"Okay," I forced out.

Tate gave me a beaming smile.

"Great! We prepared blood, just in case!"

I let myself be pulled into their hunter camp, my mother lingering at the side, waiting for us to get settled.

Gabriel and Tate were talking my ear off about all the places they'd been and what they'd been doing, but I drowned them out. The only thing I could think of was my mother.

"We will wait outside," Cedar said, her hand lingering on my back.

They got me and my mother to sit at a table inside a tent for some semblance of privacy, with blood already ready for me.

When we were finally alone, I spoke.

"Does it hurt?"

She looked up at me.

"What?" she asked, her voice much weaker than I remembered.

We humans age. I became acutely aware of that fact when I saw the wrinkles on my mother's face. Maybe they had always been there, but I was just now noticing them.

"To look at me," I replied, twisting to the side so she could see my slashed-through tattoo. "My scars. How I changed. The realization that you failed your own daughter and put her through hell."

The words spilled out of me like they'd always been there, just waiting for this moment.

"Yes." I was suddenly hit with the smell of salt water as tears gathered in her eyes. "It hurts more than I can ever explain. Vesper, I'm—"

"I don't want your apologies," I spat, my fingers digging into my thigh. "You were complicit in it all. Your *apology* is just to make yourself feel better, and I want nothing to do with it."

She pressed her lips together.

"I'm glad you found somewhere you belong. Where people love and accept you."

"He died because he couldn't bring himself to kill me." She met my gaze. "Father."

Her face tightened.

"I know," she said. "He knew he wouldn't be able to. That was why he sent me away."

I gritted my teeth. I didn't know what to say to her. In all truth, I wanted nothing from her.

"Do you think you deserve the forgiveness my brothers have given you?"

A tear fell.

"No," she whispered.

Good. But a part of me still felt bad for being so harsh to her.

"I am happily going to spend my life with them. I won't think about my past, and especially not about you or what Father did to me."

She nodded. "I accept that. I deserve it."

I wanted to scream at her, but I swallowed it.

"I loved you, and you hurt me."

Her tears were falling freely now. "I regret it all and deserve this."

"And I can't help but still love you, even after it all," I said, blood filling my eyes.

She gave me the most heartbreaking look.

"A child will always love their parents, no matter the horrors they put them through. I just hope one day I can earn a place in your life. I would..." She swallowed a sob. "I would like to see how the three of you end up."

The box felt like it was burning a hole in my pocket. I stood up, unable to stay in the suffocating tent any longer.

"There is nothing more to say." I turned around, heading for the door. "I'm going to say goodbye to Tate and—"

"I'm sorry, Vesper. I love you, and I will spend the rest of my human life trying to show you I mean it."

The image that came to my mind felt like I was being hit in the face with an iron bar.

My mother, old and gray. Me, unchanging.

In a flash, I was by her side, holding her to me in a hug. Hesitantly, she returned it. When she did, she squeezed me as tight as her arms could manage.

"I'll be waiting," she said. "And good luck."

"He told you."

I pulled away as she wiped her tears.

"He showed me. I couldn't be happier for you, Vesper. I mean it."

"Until next time," I said, pausing at the exit. "Maybe if I can find it in me, you'll be invited."

"I'd like that."

I stepped out, my lovers the first thing I saw. Cedar had her arms around Aurelia, holding her close as Tate showed them a sword he made. Gabriel was off to the side, talking to some of the other hunters.

When Cedar and Aurelia looked at me, the weight on my chest lightened. My fingers found the box in my pocket.

Forever. With them.

I couldn't help but smile.

It sounds perfect to me.

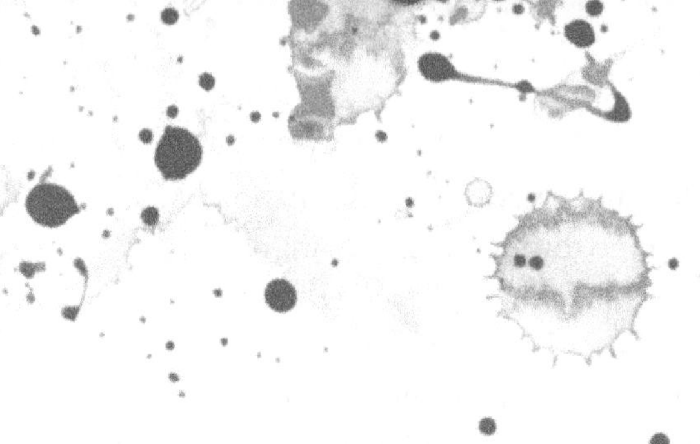

AURELIA

Vesper was hiding something.

It was weird because somehow she had persuaded me to come back to the Castle palace. A place I was convinced I would stay away from for at least another month.

The first few days away from my mother had been hard, but the more Vesper, Cedar, and I explored, the easier it became.

I felt *free.*

Sometimes even a bit bored. But that was life, wasn't it? The boredom I experienced before was due to being literally locked in the palace, but this time it was thanks to peace.

There was no fighting. No running for our lives—unless, of course, Vesper decided she wanted to get fucked. And I was more than okay with that.

Which brought me back to wondering why Vesper would bring us back here. Specifically, to this place, between the large fountain and the millions of colorful flowers my mother had been busy planting.

It was beautiful.

My life before this was filled with black, red, and gold. Limited colors because they matched the Castle family. But now there was pink, green, blue, and every other combination of colors imaginable. It was like walking through a sea of rainbows.

"Why are we back here so soon?" Cedar asked.

"And why are you nervous?" I followed up.

Vesper stood in front of the fountain and faced us.

"There was a specific moment when I knew the course of my life would change. Do you want to know what it was?"

Cedar and I shared a look.

"Enlighten us," I said with a smirk. Cedar wrapped an arm around me and pulled me close.

Vesper motioned to the fountain behind her.

"Once upon a time, there was a spoiled princess who decided the best way to get on her father's nerves was to take a swim."

Amusement tickled the bond. I frowned.

"Spoiled princess," I muttered.

Vesper smiled.

"Spoiled enough that you made me go in there to get you. Do you remember how I did that?"

I pouted, not wanting to respond.

"I said I wouldn't play with you anymore."

"You're such a liar," Cedar said with a huff.

Vesper nodded before continuing. "But for the first time, I knew I couldn't get away from it. From you. From *us*. Fate brought us together, and that night was the first moment that I felt there would be no stopping it." Her eyes shifted to Cedar. "With you, it was the day you brought us back to your cabin. When I started realizing that it was Aurelia and me... but you as well. I yearned for the three of us to be together. So I kept seeking you out."

"While leaving me in the cabin."

"Don't be salty," Cedar whispered. "Our hunter is trying to be sincere."

"Over the last few months, I realized I don't ever want to live without you again. We'll have an eternity together, so I thought it was only right to solidify my intentions with the two of you once and for all."

Vesper dropped to one knee and fished something out of her pocket. My heart dropped.

"Is she...?"

"Oh my gods."

She opened a box, and inside sat three silver rings, all carved with intricate shapes and embedded with rubies.

"Tate helped me make this using my sword and the Castle family sword. They were made with magic that will help us locate each other, in case the bond can't. Because I can't lose you again." She sent us a nervous smile. "Will you please do me the honor of being my eternity?"

We stood there, frozen, not knowing how to react. Cedar was the first one to come to, pushing me forward.

"Do you even have to ask?" I exclaimed and lunged at her.

Cedar was close behind me, grabbing Vesper's hair and forcing their lips together. I kissed up her neck until it was my turn to capture her lips.

Love poured through the bond. She was proposing.

After two engagements and one marriage, this was the first time I had ever been proposed to. And with a ring. By someone I actually love and want.

Is this really my life?

Red tears filled my eyes, and I pulled away, forcing my shaking hand out so Vesper could put my ring on.

Cedar did the same, and when it came to the last ring, Cedar and I put it on Vesper's finger together.

They thrummed with deep magic, tying us together.

"Of course we will," I said. "What do you think we've been doing up until now? Playing around?"

Vesper smiled.

"I hope to *play* with you for the rest of our lives. I just wanted to make it official."

"Good job, my love," Cedar said and placed a lingering kiss on her forehead.

Just as I was about to dive at her again, clapping interrupted us. We turned to look at the entrance of the palace, and my jaw dropped.

My mother was in front, dressed in an extravagant gown, clapping and crying. Behind her was the Castle family. But not just them.

Caspian, Atlas, Elora, Tate, Gabriel, Charlotte, Rose, Dahlia, and almost every other vampire we'd come across in our journey were there, clapping at Vesper's show.

"Let's get the party started!" my mother yelled.

I couldn't help but laugh. Cedar grabbed the two of us in a crushing hug.

"And an engagement party?" I whispered. "You outdid yourself."

Vesper had the gall to look sheepish.

"You two deserve the best, and I want to give it to you."

I sighed and allowed us to be celebrated.

I didn't think of the future or the vampire world or what would happen.

It didn't matter.

I would live and love without fear of consequences. We deserved it.

Love had brought us together. Nothing could tear us apart.

I pulled them into a three-way kiss with a laugh, and welcomed our new eternity.

Together.

AURELIA

Unlike the sex club we'd visited before, the one Caspian opened was much more enticing.

Located in an actual city instead of a random house in the woods, it was like a true club with bouncers at the door and security surrounding the place.

Surprisingly, he used witches for that.

The place itself was dark, with low colorful lights spread out. There was music playing, but not loud enough to hurt vampire ears. Magic lingered, but instead of the Cedar's vine-like magic, it was a low shimmering fog that played at our ankles.

It sent zaps of heat up our legs. The pleasant kind.

There was a large dance floor where vampires, witches, and humans alike were sensually moving together. The main room was relatively tame, acting more as a nightclub as opposed to a hardcore sex club. That was reserved for the adjacent rooms. That's where the debauchery really took place.

My favorite.

Even though I was about to be a happily married woman, it wouldn't hurt to see a little bit of playful vampire action.

Especially when it was between my two lovers.

The room we had picked for tonight was voyeuristic. It was

large, with various seating options, and in the middle you would have your choice of show.

My choice will always be them.

Cedar was standing while Vesper kneeled on an elevated table, leaving her open to be viewed from all directions. She was completely naked and bound by the witch's signature red vines.

Vesper was muzzled, a surprise just for me that turned me on to no end. Sometimes she still acted like a bloodthirsty vampire, and there was something about seeing her tied up that made me hot.

But the real show was Cedar, who was mostly clothed. She wore pants and a button-up, pretty much all the way undone, showing an impressive amount of chest.

Cedar had placed an automatic thrusting vibrator under Vesper. It was harnessed to the table, so she wouldn't be able to move it no matter how much she writhed. Bound, she was forced to endure it.

And I had a perfect view of her wet cunt leaking onto the toy as it fucked her.

I was spread with my legs open, lightly flicking my clit as Cedar ran toys up and down our lover's body.

"What do you think, Princess? Clamps?"

I couldn't help the moan that left my lips.

"Please."

I sank two fingers into me just as Cedar clamped Vesper's nipples.

She let out a growl that quickly turned into pleading moans, grinding against the fake cock pumping in and out of her, desperately chasing release.

"Stop it," I ordered.

Cedar pressed a button, and everything stopped, including me. I let my orgasm fall away just like Vesper's.

"Please," she begged, her eyes wide. She tried to fuck herself on the cock, slamming her hips down, but Cedar was there to hold her in place.

When she grabbed her hips with both hands and forced her to take all of it, Vesper's eyes rolled to the back of her head.

"Now. And keep her there."

Cedar turned on the toy again, one hand leaving Vesper for a second before it was back on her hip, forcing her down.

"Fuck, it's too deep."

We had a safe word, but Vesper rarely called it, and I knew she wasn't about to now.

I plunged my fingers inside me and started fucking myself in tandem.

Cedar leaned close to whisper in Vesper's ear.

"You see what you're doing to our girl?"

Vesper's eyes shot to mine, and I wanted to sweeten the deal, so I pulled the neck of my dress down.

Cedar left Vesper, making sure to add even more vines, so Vesper was stuck there getting fucked while she watched Cedar placing her lips directly on my nipple.

I moaned extra loud, pleasure shooting through the bond as Vesper's orgasm rose sharply.

She tried to fight the bonds, wanting to be part of this. But it was so much sweeter to watch her struggle.

Cedar bit down on my nipple, pulling a strangled yelp from me.

I gave her a look, but she just met me with a smartass smirk before she started kissing down my body, past my stomach to my thighs, and then—

"Oh gods," I moaned as she licked me from entrance to clit.

I was so caught up in the feeling of her tongue that I didn't notice her magic wrapping me and binding me to the chair.

And I was definitely not aware of what she had brought with her until she slipped a vibrator deep into my cunt.

Sneaky witch.

I gasped and tried to sit up, but she was already moving away and back to Vesper.

"Gods, you're so beautiful like this," Cedar said, standing back and looking at her handiwork.

I started realizing just how many eyes were on us. It made everything that much more intense. The pleasure running through the bond. The feeling of the vibrations running through my cunt. The magic as it tied me down to the chair.

Cedar pulled out a bullet vibrator from her stash on the other side of the table and held it against Vesper's pussy. The image of Vesper gushing all over the table was enough to send me spiraling into my first orgasm.

Vesper and I fed into each other, the pleasure so strong it made Cedar moan.

My little mouse writhed against the table, her mouth open, and between the bars of the muzzle, I could make out her fangs. No sound came out as our orgasms took us under.

Wave after wave of pleasure crashed through us, a never-ending cycle as Cedar refused to turn off the toys.

There was a spare chair off to the side. No one would dare sit right next to us.

So Cedar took it and lazily used the same bullet vibrator on herself, letting out a satisfied moan as she watched us pull against our bonds with no success.

"You're going to pay for this," I warned. But I was pretty sure she would welcome the type of punishment I had in mind.

It was too much. Another orgasm was running through me. My head was thrown back, and a gurgled moan forced itself from my chest. It overtook me, the overstimulation becoming painful.

But that was exactly what I wanted.

"Yes, yes, yes," I chanted as another one of Vesper's came through, and I felt it as my own.

"You two are insatiable," Cedar commented, the waves of her orgasm hitting her fast. Our pleasure bounced off each other in the bond.

And then, just when we felt Vesper couldn't take it anymore, Cedar used the same bullet to wring a final one from her.

Mine came with a scream, and then finally I was released from my bondage.

But it wasn't over. Not by a long shot.

Vesper and Cedar were already coming at me, their hands and lips everywhere.

"At this rate, we're never going to leave this place." I panted as Vesper sank her teeth in my thigh and Cedar pulled out the vibrator from my cunt only to press it to my lips.

I opened my mouth and sucked it, cleaning it with my tongue.

"We still have a few hours until the wedding," she said.

Vesper looked up at us, my blood covering her mouth. Her fingers were lazy, stroking my clit.

"A little less than that." I watched her smile. "Though I'm sure we can make our princess come a few more times until then."

"Oh *definitely*," Cedar said and pushed the vibrator back inside me.

I let myself fall into their pleasure, feeling at peace. The whole reason we were here was so they could fuck the nervousness out of me.

There was something about weddings that just put me on edge. No doubt because of my previous experience with them. But I had to say they were doing a pretty good job distracting me.

"No thinking," Vesper growled, fusing her mouth around my clit.

Cedar grabbed my face and forced her lips to mine.

No thinking. Right.

It was so easy with them.

And now, it was our turn for happiness.

Fate had brought them to me. Or maybe it was Krae. Or the witch gods. Or even the human ones.

Whatever it was, I would take it.

Because with each brush of their lips against my skin, they promised me forever.

And who was I to call them liars?

Want to see their WEDDING?!

Read it in WOLF TAKES PRINCESS, a smutty novella following Charlotte and her long lost lover turned shifter Dru.

Charlotte
I lost my one chance at a good marriage.
Regardless, a well-trained princess will never show her true emotions.
I yearned for a love of my own, even if I knew I'd never get it.
But I never thought my prayers would be answered in the form of a wolf shifter.
Or a kidnapping.

Dru
My mind was jumbled.
I had been taken, but I didn't know where to.
They had changed me, but there was one thing the wolf and I started to agree on.
I was going to get my girl.
No matter what I had to do.

And if you want to see their spicy photos...

Check it out here or go to htttps://www.patreon.com/ellemaebooks

The trio is naked and waiting for you...

On patreon!

Get exclusive arcs, spicy art, and more!

Check it out here or go to https://www.patreon.com/ellemaebooks

About the Author

Elle is a native Californian who has lived in Los Angeles for most of her life. From the very start, she has been in love with all things fantasy and reading. As soon as Elle found out that writing books could be a career, she picked up a pen and paper. While the first ones were about scorned love and missed opportunities of lunchtime love, she has grown to love the fantasy genre and looks forward to making a difference in the world with her stories.

Loved this book? Please leave a review!

For more behind the scene content, check out my Patreon or sign up to my newsletter!
https://elegant-mountain-68199.myflodesk.com/y8a9duflae

x.com/mae_books
instagram.com/edenrosebooks
goodreads.com/ellemae